THE EROTIC NOVELS OF ANNE RICE WRITING AS A. N. ROQUELAURE

The Claiming of Sleeping Beauty

•

Beauty's Punishment

•

Beauty's Release

Since 1983, A. N. Roquelaure has envisioned (for the uninhibited reader) a hypnotic and seductive adult fairy tale in the Sleeping Beauty novels. Now, the author of this exquisite erotic trilogy reveals her true identity—beckoning the reader into a sensuous world of forbidden dreams and dark-edged desires . . . a world in which traditional ideas of submission and dominance and gender preference are thrown to the winds . . . a world made irresistibly inviting by the adventurous spirit and imagination of the unrivaled Anne Rice.

an

erotic novel of

discipline,

love and surrender,

for the enjoyment

of men

and women

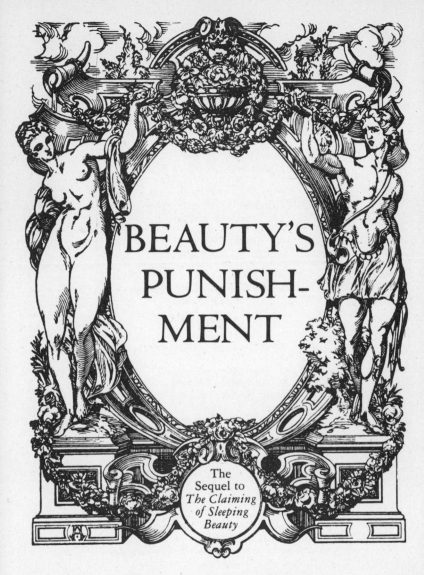

BEAUTY'S PUNISH-MENT

The Sequel to *The Claiming of Sleeping Beauty*

A. N. Roquelaure

Ⓟ

A PLUME BOOK

PLUME
Published by the Penguin Group
Penguin Books USA Inc., 375 Hudson Street,
New York, New York 10014, U.S.A.
Penguin Books Ltd, 27 Wrights Lane,
London W8 5TZ, England
Penguin Books Australia Ltd, Ringwood,
Victoria, Australia
Penguin Books Canada Ltd, 10 Alcorn Avenue,
Toronto, Ontario, Canada M4V 3B2
Penguin Books (N.Z.) Ltd, 182–190 Wairau Road,
Auckland 10, New Zealand

Penguin Books Ltd, Registered Offices:
Harmondsworth, Middlesex, England

Published by Plume, an imprint of Dutton Signet,
a division of Penguin Books USA Inc. Previously published in a
Dutton edition.

First Plume Printing, November, 1990

13 15 17 16 14 12

Roquelaure, A.N.
Beauty's punishment.
Sequel to: The claiming of Sleeping Beauty
I. Title.
PS3568.O696B4 1984   813'.54   83-20587
ISBN: 0-452-26662-9

Printed in the United States of America

Designed by Nancy Etheredge

PUBLISHER'S NOTE
This is a work of fiction. Names, characters, places, and incidents
either are the product of the author's imagination or are used
fictitiously, and any resemblance to actual persons, living or
dead, events, or locales is entirely coincidental.

CONTENTS

CONTENTS

CONTENTS

CONTENTS

THE
STORY
THUS
FAR

Aᴀ HER century-long slumber, the Sleeping Beauty opened her eyes at the kiss of the Prince, to find her garments stripped away and her heart as well as her body under the rule of her deliverer. At once, Beauty was claimed as the Prince's naked pleasure slave to be taken to his Kingdom.

With the grateful consent of her parents, and dazed with desire for the Prince, Beauty was then brought to the Court of Queen Eleanor, the Prince's mother, to serve as one of hundreds of naked Princes and Princesses, all playthings of the Court until such time as they should be rewarded and sent home to their Kingdoms.

Dazzled by the rigors of the Training Hall, the Hall of Punishments, the ordeal of the Bridle Path, and her own mounting passion to please, Beauty remained the undisputed favorite of the Prince and the delight of her sometime Mistress, the lovely young Lady Juliana.

Yet she could not ignore her secret and forbidden infatuation with the Queen's exquisite slave, Prince Alexi, and finally the disobedient slave, Prince Tristan.

After glimpsing Prince Tristan among the disgraced of the castle, Beauty, in a moment of seemingly inexplicable rebellion, brings upon herself the very same punishment destined for Tristan: to be sent away from the voluptuous Court to the degradation of harsh labor in the nearby village.

As our story continues, Beauty has just been placed in the cart with Prince Tristan and the other disgraced slaves to be taken down the long road to the auction block in the village marketplace.

BEAUTY'S
PUNISHMENT

THE PUNISHED

THE MORNING star was just fading in the violet sky as the huge wooden cart, crowded with naked slaves, moved slowly over the castle drawbridge. The white draft horses plodded steadily towards the winding road, and the soldiers drove their mounts close to the high wooden wheels, the better to catch with their thudding straps the naked legs and buttocks of the wailing slave Princes and Princesses.

Frantically, the group huddled together on the rough boards, their hands bound to the backs of their necks, their mouths gagged and stretched by little leather bits, plump breasts and reddened buttocks shivering.

Some, in desperation, glanced back at the high towers of the darkened castle. But no one was awake, it seemed, to hear their cries. And a thousand obedient slaves slept within, on the silken beds of the Slaves' Hall or in their Masters' and Mistresses' sumptuous chambers, unconcerned for those incorrigible ones who were borne away now in the wobbling, high-railed cart, towards the village auction.

The Commander of the Patrol smiled to himself as he saw Princess Beauty, the Crown Prince's dearest slave, press towards the tall, heavily muscled figure of Prince Tristan. She had been the last to be loaded into the cart, and what a lovely slave she was, he mused, her long, straight, golden hair hanging loose down her back, her little mouth straining to kiss Tristan in spite of the leather bit that gagged her. And how could the disobedient Tristan, with his hands bound to his neck as securely as those of any other punished slave, solace her now, the Commander wondered?

He debated with himself: Should he stop this illicit intimacy? It would be simple enough to pull Beauty out of the group and spread her legs as he bent her over the railing of the cart, spanking with his belt her plump disobedient little sex for its impudence. Maybe Tristan and Beauty, both, should be set down on the road and whipped behind the cart to teach them a good lesson.

But in truth the Commander felt just a little bit sorry for the condemned slaves, spoilt as they were, even the willful Beauty and Tristan. By noon they would all have been sold from the block, and during the long summer months of village service they would learn plenty.

The Commander rode alongside the cart now, catching another succulent little Princess with his belt, punishing the rosy pubic lips that peeped through a nest of glossy black curls, and he plied the strap all the harder when a long-limbed Prince sought gallantly to shield her.

Nobility even in adversity, the Commander laughed

to himself, and gave the Prince exactly what he deserved with the strap, all the more amused when he glimpsed the Prince's hard and writhing organ.

Well-trained, the lot, he had to admit, the lovely Princesses with their nipples erect and faces flushed, the Princes trying to conceal their swelling cocks. And as sorry as the Commander felt for them, he couldn't help but think of the glee of the villagers.

All year the villagers saved their money for this day, when only a few coins would purchase, for the whole summer long, a pampered slave who had been chosen for the Court, trained and groomed for the Court, and must now obey the lowliest kitchen maid or stable boy who bid high enough at the auction.

And what an enticing group they were this time, their rounded limbs still fragrant with costly perfume, pubic hair still combed and oiled, as if they went to be presented to the Queen herself and not a thousand leering and eager villagers. Cobblers, Innkeepers, merchants awaited them, determined to exact hard labor for their money as well as pretty looks and abject humility.

The cart jostled the crying slaves, tumbled them together. The distant castle was now no more than a great gray shadow against the lightening sky, its vast pleasure gardens concealed by the high walls that surrounded it.

And the Commander smiled as he rode nearer to the thicket of lovely shaped calves and high-arched feet in the cart, seeing a half dozen splendid unfortunates pressed to the very front rail with no hope at all of escaping the soldiers' straps as the others crowded against them. All they could do was squirm under the playful assault, baring hips and backsides and bellies again to the sting of the belts as they bowed their tear-stained faces.

It was a luscious sight indeed, rendered all the more interesting, perhaps, by the fact that they didn't really know what lay in store for them. No matter how much Court slaves were warned about the village, they were never really prepared for the shocks that awaited them. If they had really known, they would never, never have risked the Queen's displeasure.

And the Commander couldn't help but think ahead to the end of summer when, thoroughly chastened, these same wailing and struggling young men and women would be brought back with heads bowed and tongues silent in utter submission. What a privilege it would be then to whip them one by one to press their lips to the Queen's slipper!

So let them wail now, the Commander mused. Let them twist and turn as the sun rose over the rolling green hills and the cart lumbered ever faster down the long road to the village. And let the pretty little Beauty and the majestic young Tristan cleave to each other in the very middle of the press. They would soon learn what they had brought upon themselves.

He might even stay for the auction this time, the Commander thought, or at least just long enough to see Beauty and Tristan separated and hoisted one after the other to that block as they deserved, and sold off to their new owners.

BEAUTY
AND
TRISTAN

"Bᴜᴛ, ʙᴇᴀᴜᴛʏ, why did you do it?" Prince Tristan whispered. "Why did you disobey deliberately? Did you want to be sent to the village?"

All around them in the rolling cart the Princes and Princesses whimpered and bawled hopelessly.

But Tristan had worked loose the cruel little leather bit that had gagged him, and let it drop to the floor. And Beauty at once did the same, freeing herself of the mean device with the aid of her tongue and spitting it away from her with delicious defiance.

After all, they were condemned slaves, were they not, so what did it matter? They had been given by their parents as naked tributes to the Queen, told to obey during their years of service. But they had failed. They were now condemned to hard labor and cruel use by the common people.

"Why, Beauty?" Tristan pressed. But no sooner did he ask the question again than he covered Beauty's open mouth with his own so that Beauty could only receive the kiss, standing on tiptoe, Tristan's organ lifting her moist sex which hungered for him desperately. If only their hands were not bound, if only she could embrace him!

Suddenly Beauty's feet no longer touched the floor of the cart, and she tumbled forward against Tristan's chest, riding him, the throbbing inside her so violent that it obliterated the cries and loud wallops of the mounted soldiers' leather straps, and Beauty felt her breath sucked up and out of her.

For eternity she seemed to float, unanchored to the real world of the immense creaking wooden cart with its high wheels, the taunting guards, the paling sky arching high over the soft dark hills and the dim prospect of the village lying under a blue mist far below them. There was no rising sun, no clop of the horses hooves, no soft limbs of other struggling slaves mashed against her sore buttocks. There was only this organ splitting her, lifting her, and then driving her remorselessly to a silent yet deafening explosion of pleasure. Her back arched, her legs out straight, her nipples throbbing against Tristan's warm flesh, her mouth filled with Tristan's tongue at the same instant.

And dimly through the ecstasy, she felt Tristan's hips go into their final irresistible rhythm. She could not bear any more, yet the pleasure was fragmented, multiplied, washing through her over and over. In some realm beyond thought, she felt she was not human. The pleasure dissolved the humanity she had known. And she was not Princess Beauty, brought as a slave to serve in the Prince's castle. Yet most certainly she was, because this excruciating pleasure had been learned there.

She knew only the soft wet pulse of her sex and the organ lifting her and holding her. And Tristan's kisses growing more tender, more sweet, more lingering. A weeping slave pressed against her back, hot flesh against her own, and another warm body crushed against her right side, a great sweep of silky hair brushing her naked shoulder.

"But why, Beauty?" Tristan whispered again, his lips still touching hers. "You must have done it deliberately, run from the Crown Prince. You were too admired, too accomplished." His deep almost-violet-blue eyes were thoughtful, meditative, reluctant to reveal him completely.

His face was a little larger than that of most men, the bones strong, perfectly symmetrical, yet the features were almost delicate, and the voice was low and more commanding than the voices of those who had been Beauty's Masters. But there was nothing but intimacy in the voice, and that, and Tristan's long eyelashes, gold in the light of the sun, gave him a touch of enchantment. He spoke to Beauty as though they had been slave companions forever.

"I don't know why I did it," Beauty whispered in answer. "I can't explain, but yes, it must have been deliberate." She kissed his chest, quickly finding the nipples and kissing them both and then sucking them hard one after the other so that she felt his organ thump against her again, though he begged her softly for mercy.

Of course, the punishments of the castle had been voluptuous; it had been exciting to be the playthings of a rich Court, to be the object of relentless attention. Yes, it had been infatuating and confusing, the exquisitely tooled leather paddles and straps and the welts they caused, the exacting discipline that had so often left her crying and breathless. And the warm perfumed baths afterwards, the

massages with fragrant oils, the hours of half-sleep in
which she dared not contemplate the tasks and trials that
awaited her.

Yes, it had been heady and seductive and even terrifying.

And surely she had loved the tall, black-haired Crown
Prince with his mysterious unnamed dissatisfactions, and
the lovely sweet Lady Juliana with her pretty blond braids,
both of whom had been such talented tormentors.

So why had Beauty thrown it all away? Why, when
she had seen Tristan in the stockade with its crowd of
disobedient Princes and Princesses, all condemned to be
auctioned in the village, had she deliberately disobeyed
in order to be sent to the village with them?

She could still remember Lady Juliana's brief de-
scription of the fate awaiting them:

"It is wretched service. The auction itself takes place
as soon as they arrive and you can well suppose that even
the beggars and the common louts about town are there
to witness it. Why, the whole village declares a holiday."

And then that strange remark from Beauty's Master,
the Crown Prince, who never dreamed at that moment
that Beauty would soon disgrace herself: "Ah, but for all
its roughness and cruelty," he had said, "it is *sublime punishment.*"

Was it those words that had undone her?

Did she long to be hurled downward, away from the
high Court of ornate and clever rituals imposed upon her,
into some wilderness of disregard where the humiliations
and spanking blows would come just as hard and just as
fast but with a greater, more savage abandon?

Of course, there would be the same limits. Not even
in the village could a slave's flesh be broken; never could
a slave be burned or truly harmed. No, her punishments
would all *enhance.* And she knew by now just how much
could be accomplished with the innocent-looking black
leather strap and deceptively decorated leather paddle.

But in the village she would be no Princess. Tristan

would be no Prince. And the crude men and women who worked them and punished them would know that with every gratuitous blow they were doing the Queen's bidding.

Suddenly Beauty couldn't think. Yes, it had been deliberate, but had she made some dreadful error?

"And you, Tristan," she said suddenly, trying to conceal the quavering of her voice. "Was it not deliberate with you, too? Didn't you deliberately provoke your Master?"

"Yes, Beauty, but there's a long story behind it," Tristan said. And Beauty could see the apprehension in his eyes, the dread he couldn't admit either. "I served Lord Stefan, as you know, but what you don't know is that a year ago in another land, as equals, Lord Stefan and I were lovers." The large violet-blue eyes became a little more penetrable, the lips a little warmer as they smiled almost sadly.

Beauty gasped to hear this.

The sun was fully risen now, and the cart had taken a sharp turn in the road and the descent was slower over uneven terrain, the slaves pitched more roughly than ever against one another.

"You can imagine our surprise," Tristan said, "when we discovered ourselves Master and slave at the castle, and when the Queen, seeing the blush on Lord Stefan's face, immediately gave me over to him with the sharp instructions that he train me himself to be perfect."

"Unbearable," Beauty said. "To have known him before, to have walked with him, spoken with him. How could you submit?"

All her Masters and Mistresses had been strangers to her, defined perfectly in the instant she realized her helplessness and vulnerability. She had known the color and texture of their magnificent slippers and boots, the sharp tones of their voices, before she had known their names or their faces.

But Tristan gave the same mysterious smile. "O, I

think it was far worse for Stefan than for me," he whispered in her ear. "You see, we had met before at a great tournament, struggling against each other, and in every feat I'd bested him. When we hunted together, I had been the better shot and the better horseman. He had admired me and looked up to me, and I had loved him for it because I knew the extent of his pride and the love that equaled it. When we coupled, I was the leader.

"But we had to return to our Kingdoms. We had to return to the duties that awaited us. Three stolen nights of love we had, maybe more, in which he yielded as a boy might to a man. Then letters that at last became too painful to write. Then war. Silence. Stefan's Kingdom allied with that of the Queen. And later, her armies at our gates, and this strange meeting in the Queen's castle: I on my knees waiting to be given to a worthy Master, and Stefan, the Queen's young kinsman, sitting silently at her right at the banquet table." Tristan smiled again. "No, it was worse for him. I blush with shame to admit it, but my heart leapt when I saw him. And it is I who, out of spite, have triumphed by abandoning him."

"Yes," Beauty understood this because she knew she had done it to the Crown Prince and Lady Juliana. "But the village, weren't you afraid?" Again there came the quavering in her voice. How far were they from the village, even as they spoke of it? "Or was it simply the only way?" she asked softly.

"I don't know. There must have been more to it than that," Tristan whispered, but then he stopped as though bewildered. "But if you must know," he confessed, "I am terrified." Yet he said it so calmly, his voice so full of quiet assurance that Beauty couldn't believe it.

The groaning cart had made another turn. The guards had ridden ahead to hear some orders from their Commander. The slaves whispered among themselves, all too obedient and fearful still to discard the little leather bits in their mouth, yet able to consult frantically on what lay ahead as the cart rocked on slowly.

"Beauty," Tristan said, "we'll be separated when we reach the village, and no one knows what may happen to us. Be good, obey; it can't ultimately—" And again he stopped, unsure. "It can't ultimately be worse than the castle."

And now Beauty thought she heard the barest tinge of real trepidation in his voice, but his face was almost hard when she looked up at him, only the beautiful eyes softening it just a little. She could see the slightest golden stubble of beard on his chin, and she wanted to kiss it.

"Will you watch for me after we're separated, try to find me, if only to say a few words to me?" Beauty said. "O, just to know you are there . . . but I don't think I will be good. I don't see why I should be good any longer. We're bad slaves, Tristan. Why should we obey now?"

"What do you mean?" he asked. "You make me afraid for you."

From far away, there came the faint roar of voices, the sound of a large crowd carrying sluggishly over the low hills, the dim vibration of a village fair, of hundreds talking, shouting, milling.

Beauty pressed close to Tristan's chest. She felt a stab of excitement between her legs, her heart knocking. Tristan's organ was hard again, but it was not inside of her, and it was an agony again that her hands were bound so she couldn't touch it.

Her question seemed meaningless suddenly, yet she repeated it, the distant noise growing louder. "Why must we obey if we are already punished?"

Tristan too heard the distant swelling sounds. The cart was picking up speed.

"We were told at the castle that we must obey," Beauty said, "our parents had willed it when they sent us to the Queen and the Prince as Tributes. But now we're bad slaves . . ."

"Our punishment will only be worse if we disobey," Tristan said, but there was something strange in his eyes that betrayed his voice. He sounded false, as if repeat-

something he thought he should say for her good.

"We must wait and see what happens to us," he said. "Remember, Beauty, in the end they will win over us."

"But how, Tristan?" she asked. "You mean you condemned yourself to this, and yet you will obey?" She felt again the thrill she'd known when she left the Prince and Lady Juliana weeping behind her at the castle. "I am such a bad girl," she thought. Yet . . .

"Beauty, their wishes will prevail. Remember, a willful, disobedient slave will amuse them just as much. Why struggle?" Tristan said.

"Why struggle to obey?" Beauty said.

"Do you have the strength to be terribly bad all the time?" he asked. His voice was low, urgent, his breath warm against her neck as he kissed her again. Beauty tried to shut out the sound of the crowd; it was a horrid sound, like that of a great beast coming out of its lair; she knew she was trembling.

"Beauty, I don't know what I've done," Tristan said. Anxiously he glanced in the direction of that awesome, menacing noise: shouts, cheers, the mayhem of a fair day. "Even at the castle," he said, the violet-blue eyes fired now with something that might have been fear in a strong Prince who could not show it. "Even at the castle, I found it was easier to run when they told us to run, to kneel when they told us to kneel, and there was a triumph of sorts in doing it perfectly."

"Then why are we here, Tristan?" she asked, standing on tiptoe to kiss his lips. "Why are we both such bad slaves?" And though she tried to sound rebellious and brave, she pressed herself against Tristan all the more desperately.

THE
AUCTION
IN THE
MARKET-
PLACE

THE CART had come to a
stop, and Beauty could see through the tangle of white
arms and tousled hair the walls of the village below, with
the gates open and a motley crowd swelling out onto the
green.

But slaves were being quickly unloaded from the
cart, forced with the smack of the belt to crowd together
on the grass. And Beauty was immediately separated from
Tristan, who was pulled roughly away from her for no
apparent reason other than the whim of a guard.

The leather bits were being pulled out of the mouths
of the others. "Silence!" came the loud voice of the Com-

mander. "There is no speech for slaves in the village! Any who speak shall be gagged again more cruelly than they have ever been before!"

He rode his horse round the little herd, driving it tightly together, and gave the order that the slaves' hands should be unbound and woe to any slave who removed his or her hands from the back of the neck.

"The village has no need of your impudent voices!" he went on. "You are beasts of burden now, whether that burden be labor or pleasure! And you shall keep your hands to the back of your necks or be yoked and driven before a plow through the fields!"

Beauty was trembling violently. She couldn't see Tristan as she was forced forward. All around her were long windblown tresses, bowed heads, and tears. It seemed the slaves cried more softly without their gags, struggling to keep their lips closed, and the voices of the guards were miserably sharp!

"Move! Head up straight!" came the gruff, impatient commands. Beauty felt chills rising on her arms and legs at the sound of those angry voices. Tristan was behind her somewhere, but if only he would come close.

And why had they been put out here so far from the village? And why was the cart being turned around?

Suddenly she knew. They were to be driven on foot, like a gaggle of geese to market. And almost as quickly as the thought came to her, the mounted guards swooped down on the little group and started them forward with a rain of blows.

"This is too bitter," Beauty thought. She was trembling as she started to run, the smack of the paddle as always catching her when she did not expect it and sending her flying forward over the soft, newly turned earth of the road.

"At a trot, with heads up!" the guard shouted, "and knees up as well!" And Beauty saw the horses' hooves pounding beside her, just as she'd seen them before on the Bridle Path at the castle, and felt the same wild trepidation as the paddle cracked her thighs and even her calves. Her breasts ached as she ran, and a dull warm pain coursed through her sore legs.

She couldn't see the crowd clearly, but she knew they were there, hundreds of villagers, perhaps even thousands, flooding out of the gates to meet the slaves. "And we're to be driven right through them; it's too awful," she thought, and suddenly the resolves she had made in the cart, to disobey, to rebel, left her. She was too purely afraid. And she was running as fast as she could down the road towards the village, the paddle finding her no matter how she hurried, until she realized she had pressed through the first rank of slaves and was now running with them, no one before her anymore to shield her from the sight of the enormous crowd.

Banners flew from the battlements. Arms waved and cheers rose as the slaves drew closer, and through the excitement there came the sounds of derision, and Beauty's heart thudded as she tried not to see too clearly what lay ahead, though she could not turn away.

"No protection, nowhere to hide," she thought, "and where is Tristan? Why can't I fall back into the flock?" But when she tried, the paddle smacked her soundly again, and the guard shouted to her to go forward! And blows were rained on those around her, causing the little red-haired Princess on her right to break into helpless tears. "O, what's to happen to us? Why did we disobey?!" the little Princess wailed through her sobs, but the dark-haired Prince on the other side of Beauty threw her a warning glance: "Quiet or it will be worse!"

Beauty couldn't help but think of her long march to the Prince's Kingdom, how he had led her through the villages where she had been honored and admired as his chosen slave. Nothing like that was happening now.

The crowd had broken loose and was spreading out on either side of them as they neared the gates. Beauty could see the women in their fancy white aprons and wooden shoes, and the men in their rawhide boots and leather jerkins, robust faces everywhere alight with obvious pleasure, which made Beauty gasp and drop her eyes to the path before her.

They were passing through the gates. A trumpet was being sounded. And hands reached out from everywhere to touch them, pushing them, pulling at their hair. Beauty felt fingers brush roughly across her face; her thighs were slapped. She let out a desperate scream, struggling to escape the hands that shoved her violently forward, while all around came the loud, deep, mocking laughter, shouts and exclamations, random cries.

Tears were flowing down Beauty's face and she hadn't even realized it. Her breasts throbbed with the same violent pulse she felt in her temples. Around her she saw the tall, narrow half-timbered houses of the village opening broadly to surround a huge marketplace. A high wooden platform with a gibbet upon it loomed over all. And hundreds crowded the overhanging windows and balconies, waving white handkerchiefs, cheering, while countless others choked the narrow lanes that led into the square, struggling to get close to the miserable slaves.

They were being forced into a pen behind the platform. Beauty saw a flight of rickety wooden steps leading to the boards above and a length of leather chain dangling above the distant gibbet. A man stood to one side of the gibbet with arms folded, waiting, while another sounded the trumpet again as the gates of the pen were shut. The crowd surrounded them, and there was no more than a thin strip of fencing to protect them. Hands reached for them again as they huddled together. Beauty's buttocks were pinched, her long hair lifted.

She struggled towards the center, desperately looking for Tristan. She glimpsed him only for a moment as he was pulled roughly to the bottom of the steps.

"No, I must be sold with him," she thought and pushed violently forward, but one of the guards shoved her back into the little cluster while the crowd hooted and howled and laughed.

The red-haired Princess who had cried on the road was now inconsolable, and Beauty pressed close to her, trying to comfort her as much as to hide. The Princess had lovely high breasts with very large pink nipples, and her red hair spilled down in rivulets over her tear-stained face. The crowd was cheering and shouting again now that the herald had finished. "Don't be afraid," Beauty whispered. "Remember, it will be very much like the castle finally. We will be punished, made to obey."

"No, it won't be!" the Princess whispered, trying not to move her lips visibly as she spoke. "And I thought I was such a rebel. I thought I was so stubborn."

The trumpet gave a third full-throated blast, a high echoing series of notes. And in the immediate silence that fell over the marketplace, a voice rang out:

"The Spring Auction will now commence!"

A roar rose from all around them, a near-deafening chorus, its loudness shocking Beauty so that she couldn't feel herself breathe. The sight of her own quivering breasts stunned her, and in one sweeping glance she saw hundreds of eyes passing over her, examining her, measuring her naked endowments, a hundred whispering lips and smiles.

Meantime the Princes were being tormented by the guards, their cocks lightly whipped with the leather belts, hands plumping their pendulous balls as they were made to "Come to attention!" and punished with severe cracks of the paddle to the buttocks if they did not. Tristan's back was to Beauty. She could see the hard perfect muscles of his legs and buttocks quivering as the guard teased him, stroking him roughly between the legs. She was miserably sorry now for their stolen lovemaking. If he could not come to attention, she would be to blame.

But the booming voice had sounded again:

"All those of the village know the rules of the auction. These disobedient slaves offered by our gracious Majesty for hard labor are to be sold to the highest bidder for the period of no less than three months' service as their new Lords and Masters shall see fit. Mute menials these incorrigibles are to remain, and they are to be brought to the Place of Public Punishment as often as their Masters and Mistresses will allow, there to suffer for the amusement of the crowd as much as for their own improvement."

The guard had moved away from Tristan, giving him an almost-playful blow with the paddle and smiling as he whispered something in Tristan's ear.

"You are solemnly charged to work these slaves," the voice of the herald on the platform continued, "to discipline them, to tolerate no disobedience from them, and never an impudent word. And any Master or Mistress might sell his slave within this village at any time for any sum as he should choose."

The red-haired Princess pressed her naked breasts against Beauty and Beauty leaned forward to kiss her neck. Beauty felt the tight wiry hair of the girl's pubis against her leg, its moisture and its heat. "Don't cry," she whispered.

"When we go back, I will be perfect, perfect!" the Princess confided, and broke into fresh sobs again.

"But what made you disobey?" Beauty quickly whispered in her ear.

"I don't know," the girl wailed, opening her blue eyes wide. "I wanted to see what would happen!" and she started to cry piteously again.

"Be it understood that each time you punish one of these unworthy slaves," the herald continued, "you do the bidding of her Royal Majesty. It is with her hand that you strike the blow, with her lips you scold. All slaves once a week are to be sent to the central grooming hall. Slaves are to be properly fed. Slaves are to be given time to sleep. Slaves should at all times exhibit evidence of sound whipping. Insolence or rebellion should be thoroughly put down."

The trumpet blasted again. White handkerchiefs waved, and all around hundreds upon hundreds clapped their hands. The red-haired Princess screamed as a young man, leaning over the fence of the pen, caught her by the thigh and pulled her towards him.

The guard stopped him with a good-natured reprimand but not before he had slipped his hand under the Princess's wet sex.

But Tristan was being driven up to the wooden platform. He held his head high, hands clasped to the neck as before, his whole attitude one of dignity despite the paddle soundly playing on his narrow tight buttocks as he climbed the wooden steps.

For the first time Beauty saw beneath the high gibbet and its dangling leather links a low round turntable onto which a tall gaunt man in a bright jerkin of green velvet forced Tristan. He kicked Tristan's legs wide apart as if the Prince could not be addressed even with the simplest command.

"He's being handled like an animal," Beauty thought, watching.

Standing back the tall auctioneer worked the turntable with a foot pedal so that Tristan was turned quickly round and round.

Beauty got no more than a glimpse of his scarlet face and golden hair, blue eyes almost closed. Sweat gleamed on his hard chest and belly, his cock enormous and thick as the guards had wanted it, his legs trembling slightly with the strain of being so widely spread apart.

Desire curled inside of Beauty, and even as she pitied him, she felt her organs swelling and pulsing again, and at the same time the terrible fear, "I can't be made to stand up there alone before everyone. I can't be sold off like this! I can't!"

But how many times at the castle had she said these words. A loud burst of laughter from a nearby balcony caught her off-guard. Everywhere there were loud conversations, arguments, as the turntable went round again and then again, the blond curls slipping off the nape of Tristan's neck to make him appear the more naked and vulnerable.

"Exceptionally strong Prince," cried the auctioneer, his voice even louder, deeper than that of the herald, cutting through the roar of conversation, "long-limbed, yet sturdy of build. Fit for household labor certainly, field labor most definitely, stable labor without question."

Beauty winced.

The auctioneer had in his hand a paddle of the long narrow flexible leather kind that is more a stiff strap almost than a paddle, and with this he slapped Tristan's cock as Tristan faced the pen of slaves again, announcing to one and all:

"Strong, attentive organ, capable of great service, great endurance," and volleys of laughter rose everywhere from the square.

The auctioneer reached out and, taking Tristan by the hair, bent him from the waist suddenly, giving the turntable another whirl while Tristan remained bent over.

"Excellent buttocks," came the deep booming voice, and then the inevitable smacks of the paddle, leaving their red blotches on Tristan's skin. "Resilient, soft!" cried the auctioneer, prodding the flesh with his fingers. Then his hand went to Tristan's face, lifting it, "and demure, quiet of temperament, eager to be obedient! And well he should be!" Another crack of the paddle and laughter all around.

"What is he thinking," Beauty thought. "I can't endure it!"

The auctioneer had caught Tristan by the head again, and Beauty saw the man lifting a black leather phallus, which hung from the belt of his green velvet jerkin by a chain. Before she even realized what he meant to do, he had thrust the leather into Tristan's anus, bringing more cheers and screams from all quarters of the marketplace, while Tristan bowed from the waist as before, his face still.

"Need I say more?" cried the auctioneer, "or shall the bids begin!"

At once they started, bids shouted from everywhere, each topped as soon as it was heard, a woman on a nearby balcony—a shopkeeper's wife, surely, in her rich velvet bodice and white linen blouse—rising to her feet to call her bid over the heads of the others.

"And they are all so very rich," Beauty thought, "the weavers and dyers and silversmiths for the Queen herself, and so any of them has the money to buy us." Even a crude-looking woman with thick red hands and a soiled apron called out her bid from the door of the butcher's shop, but she was quickly out of the game.

The little turntable went round and round slowly, the auctioneer finally coaxing the crowd as the bidding grew higher. With a slender leather-covered rod that he drew from a scabbard like a sword, he pushed the flesh of Tristan's buttocks this way and that, stroking at his anus, as Tristan stood quiet and humble, only the furious blush of his face giving his misery away.

But a voice rose suddenly from far back in the square, topping all the bids by a broad margin, and Beauty heard a murmur rush through the crowd. She stood on tiptoe trying to see what was happening. A man had stepped forward before the platform and, through the scaffolding beneath it, she could just see him. He was a white-haired man, though he was not old enough for such white hair, and it sat upon him with unusual loveliness framing a square and rather pacific face.

"So the Queen's Chronicler wants this sturdy young mount," cried the auctioneer. "Is there no one to outbid him? Do I hear more for this gorgeous prince? Come on, surely . . ."

Another bid, but at once the Chronicler topped it, his voice so soft it was a wonder Beauty heard, and this time his bid was so high that clearly he meant to shut off all opposition.

"Sold," the auctioneer cried out finally, "to Nicolas, the Queen's Chronicler and Chief Historian of the Queen's village! For the grand sum of twenty-five gold pieces."

And as Beauty watched through her tears, Tristan was roughly pulled from the platform, rushed down the stairs, and driven towards the white-haired man who stood composed with his arms folded, the dark gray of his exquisitely cut jerkin making him look the Prince himself as he silently inspected his purchase. With a snap of his fingers he ordered Tristan to precede him at a trot out of the square.

The crowd opened reluctantly to let the Prince pass, pushing at him and scolding him. But Beauty had only a glimpse of this before she realized with a scream that she was herself being dragged out of the gaggle of crying slaves towards the steps.

BEAUTY ON THE BLOCK

"No, it can't be happening!" she thought, and she felt her legs give out from under her as the paddle smacked her. And the tears blinded her as she was almost carried to the platform and the turntable and set down. It did not matter that she had not walked in obedience.

She was there! And before her the crowd stretched in all directions, grinning faces and waving hands, short girls and boys leaping up the better to see, and those on balconies rising to get a more careful look.

Beauty felt she would collapse, yet she was standing, and when the soft rawhide boot of the auctioneer kicked her legs apart, she struggled to keep her balance, her breasts shivering with her muffled sobs.

"Lovely little Princess!" he was calling out, the turntable whirling suddenly, so that she almost fell forward. She saw behind her hundreds and hundreds crowded back to the village gates, more balconies and windows, soldiers lounging along the battlements above. "Hair like spun gold and ripe little breasts!"

The auctioneer's arm wound round her, squeezing her bosom hard, pinching her nipples. She let out a scream behind her closed lips, yet felt the immediate surge between her legs. But if he should take her by the hair as he had done Tristan . . .

And even as she thought it, she felt herself forced to bow from the waist in the same fashion, her breasts seeming to swell with their own weight as they dangled beneath her. And the paddle found her buttocks again, to the screaming delight of the crowd. Claps, laughs, shouts, as the auctioneer lifted her face with the stiff black leather, though he kept her bent over, spinning the turntable faster. "Lovely endowments, fit surely for the finest household, who would waste this pretty morsel in the fields?"

"Sell her into the fields!" someone shouted. And there were more cheers and laughter. And when the paddle smacked her again, Beauty gave out a humiliating wail.

The auctioneer clamped his hand over her mouth and he forced her up with her chin in the air, letting her go to stand with her back arched. "I will collapse, I will faint," Beauty thought, her heart pounding in her breast, but she was standing there, enduring it, even as she felt the sudden tickle of the leather-covered rod between her pubic lips. "O, not that, he cannot . . ." she thought, but already her wet sex was swelling, hungering for the rough stroking of the rod. She squirmed away from it.

The crowd roared.

And she realized she was twisting her hips in horrid

vulgar fashion to escape the sharp prodding examination.

There was more clapping and shouting as the auctioneer forced the rod deep into her hot wet pubis, calling out all the while, "Dainty, elegant little girl, fit for the finest lady's maid or gentleman's diversion!" Beauty knew her face was scarlet. Never at the castle had she known such exposure. And as her legs gave out from under her again, she felt the auctioneer's sure hand lifting her wrists above her head until she dangled above the platform, and the leather paddle slapped at her helpless calves and the soles of her feet.

Without meaning to, Beauty kicked helplessly. She lost all control.

Screaming behind her clenched teeth, she struggled madly as she hung in the man's grip. A strange, desperate abandon came over her as the paddle licked at her sex, slapping it and stroking it, and the screams and roars deafened her. She did not know whether she was longing for the torment or wildly trying to shut it out.

Her own frantic breaths and sobs filled her ears, and she knew suddenly that she was giving the onlookers precisely the kind of show they adored. They were getting much more from her than they had from Tristan, and she did not know whether or not she cared. Tristan was gone. She was forsaken.

The paddle punished her, stinging her and driving her hips out in a wild arc, only to stroke her wet pubic hair again, inundating her with waves of pleasure as well as pain.

In pure defiance, she swung her body with all her force, almost pulling loose from the auctioneer, who gave a loud astonished laugh. The crowd was shrieking as he sought to steady her, his tight fingers biting into her wrists as he hoisted her higher, and out of the corner of her eye Beauty saw two crudely dressed varlets rushing towards the platform.

At once they bound her wrists to the leather chain

that hung from the gibbet above her head. Now she dangled free, the auctioneer's paddle turning her with his blows as she sobbed and tried to hide her face in her upstretched arm.

"We haven't all day to amuse ourselves with the little Princess," the auctioneer cried, though the crowd urged him on with shouts of "Spank her," "Punish her."

"Calling for a firm hand and severe discipline for this lovely lady, what am I bid?" He twisted Beauty, smacking the soles of her naked feet with the paddle, pushing her head through her arms so that she could not conceal her face.

"Lovely breasts, tender arms, delectable buttocks, and a sweet little pleasure cleft fit for the gods!"

But the bids were already flying, topped so quickly he did not have to repeat them, and through her swimming eyes Beauty saw the hundreds of faces gazing up at her, the young men crowded to the very edge of the platform, a pair of young women whispering and pointing, and beyond an old woman leaning on a cane as she studied Beauty, raising a withered finger now to offer a bid.

Again the sense of abandon came over her, the defiance, and she kicked and wailed behind her closed lips, wondering that she didn't shout aloud. Was it more humiliating to admit that she could speak? Would her face have been more scarlet had she been made to demonstrate that she was a thinking, feeling creature, and not some dumb slave?

Her sobs were her only answer to herself, her legs pulled wide apart now as the bidding continued, the auctioneer spreading her buttocks with the leather rod as he had done to Tristan, stroking her anus so that she squealed and clenched her teeth, and twisted, even trying to kick him if she could.

But he was now confirming the highest bid, and then another, and trying to coax more out of the crowd until she heard him announce in that same deep voice:

"Sold to the Innkeeper, Mistress Jennifer Lockley of the Sign of the Lion, for the grand sum of twenty-seven pieces of gold, this spirited and amusing little Princess, surely to be whipped for her bread and butter as much as anything else!"

LESSONS
FROM
MISTRESS
LOCKLEY

THE CROWD applauded as Beauty was unchained and rushed down the steps, her hands clasped behind her back so that her breasts jutted forward. She was not surprised to feel a strip of leather being forced into her mouth. It was buckled tight to the back of her head and her wrists were buckled to it, which also did not surprise her after the struggle she had made.

"So let them do it!" she thought desperately. And when two long reins were brought round from this same buckle on the back of her head and given to the tall black-haired woman standing before the platform, Beauty thought, "Very clever. She will pull me along after her as if I were a little beast."

The woman was studying her as the Chronicler had studied Tristan, her face vaguely triangular and almost beautiful, her black hair free down her back save for one thin braid over her forehead which seemed a decorative way to keep the full dark tresses out of her face. She wore a gorgeous red velvet bodice and skirt with a puff-sleeved linen blouse.

"Rich Innkeeper," Beauty thought. The tall woman pulled the reins hard, almost jerking Beauty off her feet, and then she slung the reins over her shoulder, dragging Beauty into a fast and unwilling trot behind her.

The villagers pushed in on Beauty, shoving her, prodding her, smacking her sore buttocks and telling her what a bad girl she was, and asking her how she liked that slap, and saying how they'd like to have an hour alone with her to make her behave. But she had her eyes on the woman, and she was trembling all over, her mind curiously empty, as if she weren't thinking at all.

Yet she was thinking. She was thinking, as she had before, "Why shouldn't I be as bad as I like?" But she burst into fresh tears suddenly, and why, she didn't know. The woman was walking so fast that Beauty had to trot, whether she wanted to or not, obeying, whether she meant to or not, and the fresh tears stung her eyes and made the colors of the square flow into one hot shifting cloud.

They entered a little street, rushing past stragglers who barely glanced to the side as they moved in the marketplace. And very quickly Beauty was trotting over the cobblestones of a silent and empty little lane that twisted and turned under the dark half-timbered houses with their diamond-paned windows and brightly painted shutters and doors.

Shingles everywhere announced the trades of the village; here hung the boot of the shoemaker and there the leather glove of the glove maker, and the crude painting of a gold cup to mark the dealer in silver and gold plate.

A strange quiet fell over Beauty, in which all the little aches of her body burned brighter. She felt her head pulled forward hard by the leather reins that brushed her cheeks. She breathed anxiously against the strip of leather that gagged her, and for one moment something about the entire scene surprised her, the winding lane, the deserted little shops, the tall woman in the red velvet bodice and broad red skirt walking in front of her, her long black hair curling loosely down her narrow back. It seemed to have happened before, all of it, or rather to be quite the ordinary thing.

Of course it couldn't have happened. But Beauty felt as if she belonged here in some odd way, and the searing terror of the marketplace was drained away. She was naked, yes, and her thighs burned with welts as did her buttocks—she dared not even think of how she looked—and her breasts as always sent that full throb through her, and there was as ever that terrible secret pulsing between her legs. Yes, her sex, teased so cruelly by the strokes of that smooth paddle, was maddening her still.

But these things were almost sweet now. Even the slap of her bare feet on the sun-warmed cobblestones was almost good. And she felt vaguely curious about the tall woman. And she wondered what she, Beauty, would do next.

She had never really wondered that at the castle. She had been afraid of what she would be made to do. But she was not sure now that she should be made to do anything. She didn't know.

And again there was that feeling of utter normality in the fact that she was a naked, bound slave, a punished slave, being jerked cruelly through this lane. It crossed her mind that this tall woman knew precisely how to handle her, rushing her along like this, past all chance of rebellion. And that fascinated her.

She let her gaze drift up the walls, and she realized that there were people in the windows here and there watching her. Ahead she saw a woman with her arms folded before her as she looked down. And across the way farther on was a young man sitting on the window-sill who smiled at her and blew her a little kiss, and then there appeared in the lane a coarsely dressed man with bowed legs who took off his hat to "Mistress Lockley" and bowed as he went past. His eyes barely touched on Beauty, but he gave her buttocks a pat as she went by.

That odd feeling of the regularity of it began to confuse Beauty. At the same time she luxuriated in it, as she was brought swiftly into another very large cobble-stoned square, this one with a public well in the center, surrounded on all sides by the signs of various Inns.

There was the Sign of the Bear and the Sign of the Anchor, and the Sign of the Crossed Swords, but by far the most magnificent was the gilded Sign of the Lion, hanging high over a vast carriageway and under three stories of deeply cut leaded windows. But the most star-tling detail of all was the body of a naked Princess swaying beneath the sign, bound with her ankles and her wrists together on a leather chain, so that she hung like ripe fruit from the shingle, her naked red sex painfully ex-posed.

It was exactly the way that Princes and Princesses had been tethered in the Punishment Hall at the castle, a position Beauty had never suffered and that she dreaded most of all. The Princess's face was fixed between her legs only inches above her swollen and mercilessly re-vealed sex, and her eyes were almost closed. When she saw Mistress Lockley she moaned and wriggled on the chain, straining forward in supplication, just as the pun-ished Princes and Princesses had done in the Hall of Punishments.

Beauty's heart stopped when she saw the girl. But she was pulled right past her, quite unable to turn her head for a better view of the unfortunate, and trotted into the main room of the Inn.

Despite the warmth of the day the enormous room was cool, and a little cooking fire blazed on the giant hearth under a steaming iron kettle. There were dozens of smoothly polished tables and benches spread out over the vast tiled floor. Giant kegs lined the walls. There was a long shelf at one end coming out from the hearth and, on the far wall opposite, what appeared to be a crude little stage.

A long rectangular counter extended towards the door from the hearth, and behind it stood a man with a flagon in his hand and his elbow resting on the wood as if ready to serve ale to any who asked for it. He lifted his shaggy head and caught Beauty with small deep-set dark eyes, and smiling said, "Quite well you've done, I see," to Mistress Lockley.

Beauty's eyes took a moment to get used to the shadows, and when they did she realized there were many other naked slaves in the room. One naked Prince with beautiful black hair was on his knees in the far corner scrubbing the floor with a heavy brush that he held by its wooden handle with his teeth. A dark blond Princess was set to the same task just inside the doorway. Another young woman, her brown hair coiled on top of her head, polished a bench on her knees, mercifully allowed to use her hands to do it. Two others, a Prince and Princess, their hair free, knelt at the far edge of the hearth in the blaze of sunlight from the back door, polishing pewter plates vigorously.

None of these slaves even dared to glance at Beauty. Their whole attitude was one of obedience, and as the little Princess with the scrub brush hurried on to wash the floor very near Beauty's feet, Beauty saw her legs and buttocks had recently been punished.

"But who are these slaves?" Beauty thought. She was almost sure that she and Tristan had been among the first load to be sentenced to hard labor. Were these the incorrigibles who behaved so badly they had been consigned for a year to the village?

"Get the wooden paddle," said Mistress Lockley to the man at the bar. She pulled Beauty forward and quickly threw her over the counter.

Beauty gave a groan before she could stop herself, feeling her legs dangling off the floor. She had not made up her mind whether she should obey when she felt the woman unfastening the gag and the buckle, and then slapping her hands to the back of her neck.

But the woman's other hand had passed between Beauty's legs and the searching fingers found her wet sex and swelling lips and even the burning kernel of the clitoris that caused Beauty to clench her teeth against a pitious moan.

The woman's hand left her in torment.

Beauty breathed freely for an instant, and then she felt the smooth surface of the wooden paddle being pressed softly to her buttocks, and the welts seemed to burn anew.

Red with shame over the little examination, Beauty tensed, waiting for the inevitable spanking, but it didn't come. Mistress Lockley twisted her face so that Beauty could see to the left through the open door.

"Do you see that pretty Princess hanging from the sign?" The Mistress asked. And grasping Beauty's hair she pushed and pulled her head into a nod. Beauty understood that she mustn't speak, and she decided for the moment to obey. She nodded of her own accord. The Princess's body turned a little this way and that on the chain. Beauty could not remember if her unfortunate sex had been wet or shy beneath its inadequate veil of pubic hair.

"Do you want to hang there instead of her?" asked Mistress Lockley. Her voice was flat and severe and cold. "Do you want to hang there hour after hour day after day with that hungry little mouth of yours starved and gaping for all the world to see?"

Quite truthfully Beauty shook her head no.

"Then you'll stop the insolence and rebelliousness you showed on the auction block, and you'll obey every command given you, and you'll kiss your Master's and Mistresses's feet, and you'll whimper in gratitude for your supper when you get it and lick the plate clean!"

She forced Beauty's head into a nod again, and Beauty felt the oddest sensation of excitement. She nodded once more, of her own accord. Her sex pulsed against the wood of the bar.

The woman's hand moved under her and gathered her breasts together, holding them like two soft peaches plucked off a tree. Beauty's nipples burned.

"We understand each other, don't we?" she said.

And Beauty, after a strange moment of hesitation, nodded.

"Now understand this," said the woman in the same no-nonsense voice, "I'm going to spank you till you're raw. And there won't be any rich Lords and Ladies to delight in it, nor any soldiers or other gentlemen to enjoy it, just you and I preparing for the Inn to open for the day and doing what must be done. And I'm doing it for one reason only and that is so you'll be so sore that the touch of my fingernail will make you squeal and scurry to obey my commands. You'll stay raw like that every day this summer that you're my slave, and you'll scamper to kiss my slippers after I spank you, because if you don't you'll dangle from that sign. Hour by hour day after day you'll dangle there, let down only to sleep and eat with your legs bound apart, and your hands bound behind your back and your buttocks spanked just as it's going to be spanked now. And put back to hang there again where the village toughs can laugh at you, and laugh at that hungry little sex. Do you understand?"

The woman waited, her hands still cradling Beauty's breasts, her other hand on Beauty's hair.

Very slowly, Beauty nodded.

"Very good," said the woman softly. She turned Beauty and stretched her out on the length of the counter with her head towards the door. She scooped up Beauty's chin so that Beauty was looking straight through the open door and at the poor dangling Princess, and then the wooden paddle lay against her buttocks again, pressing gently on her welts and making her buttocks feel enormous and hot.

Beauty lay still. She was almost basking in the odd calm she had felt in the cobblestoned lane, but coupled with it was the mounting excitement between her legs. It was as if the excitement cleared everything—even fear and trepidation—out of its path. Or rather the woman's voice cleared these things away. "I might disobey if I wanted to," Beauty thought, in that same strange calm. Her sex was unbelievably swollen and wet.

"Now listen further," Mistress Lockley went on. "When this paddle comes down, you're going to move for me, Princess. You're going to twist and you're going to groan. You're not going to struggle to get away from me. You wouldn't do that. And you're not going to take your hands from the back of your neck. And you're not going to open your mouth either. But you're going to twist and groan. You're going to bounce under my paddle, in fact. Because with every blow you are going to show me how you feel it, and how you appreciate it, and how grateful you are for the punishment you're receiving, and how much you know it's what you deserve. And if that is not exactly what happens, you will be dangling from the sign by the time the auction stops and the crowds come and the soldiers are ready for their first flagon of ale."

Beauty was amazed.

Never at the castle had anyone spoken to her quite like this, quite this coldly and simply, and yet it seemed to have behind it some awesome practicality that almost made Beauty smile. Of course it was exactly what this woman should do, she reflected. Why not? If Beauty were running the Inn and had paid twenty-seven pieces of gold for a rebellious little slave, she might do the same thing.

And of course she'd demand the slave twist and groan to display her understanding that she was being humbled, to exercise the slave's spirit thoroughly rather than simply flail away.

The odd sense of normality came back to Beauty.

She understood this cool shadowy Inn with the sunlight splashing on the cobblestones outside the door, and she understood full well the strange voice that spoke to her with such an air of aloof command. The sugar-coated language of the castle was cloying by comparison, and, yes, Beauty reasoned, for the moment anyway, she would obey, and she would twist and groan.

After all, it was going to hurt, wasn't it? Abruptly she found out.

The paddle slammed her, bringing forth effortlessly the first loud moan. It was a large thin wooden paddle with an unnervingly crisp sound when it smacked again, and in the hail of blows that stung her sore buttocks, Beauty found herself without a conscious decision suddenly writhing and crying, the tears springing freshly to her eyes. The paddle seemed to be making her twist and turn, tossing her about on the rude bar, slamming her buttocks and making them rise again. She felt the counter creak under her as her hips rose and fell. She felt her nipples rub against the wood. Yet she kept her tear-filled eyes on the open doorway, and lost as she was in the sound spanking of the paddle and the loud cries muffled by her sealed lips, she could not help but try to picture herself, wondering if Mistress Lockley were pleased with it, whether it was enough.

Beauty heard her own full-throated moaning in her ears. She felt her tears sliding down her cheeks, to the wood. Her chin hurt as she rocked under the paddle, and she felt her long hair fall down around her shoulders, sheltering her face.

The paddle was really hurting now, hurting her unbearably, and she was rising high off the board as if asking with her whole body, "Isn't it enough, Mistress, isn't it enough?" Never in all her trials at the castle had she so profuse a display of misery.

The paddle stopped. A soft torrent of sobs filled the sudden silence, and humbly, Beauty squirmed against the counter as if imploring Mistress Lockley. Something brushed her sore buttocks very lightly, and behind her clenched teeth Beauty let out a little cry.

"Very good," came the voice. "Now get up on your feet and stand before me with your legs spread apart. Now!"

Beauty rushed to comply. She slipped down off the counter and stood with her legs as wide apart as she could spread them, her whole body shuddering with her sniffles and sobs.

Without looking up, she could see the dim figure of Mistress Lockley with her arms folded, the white of her puff sleeves very bright in the shadows, the big oval wooden paddle in her hands.

"Get down on your knees!" came the sharp command with a snap of the fingers. "And with those hands behind your neck, you put your chin on that floor and crawl to that far wall and back again, fast!"

Beauty scurried to obey. It was miserable trying to crawl in this manner, with her elbows and chin on the floor, and she couldn't bear the thought of how awkward and miserable she looked, but she reached the wall and hurried back to Mistress Lockley's boots at once. On a wild impulse she kissed the boots. The throb between her legs intensified as if a fist had been pressed against her sex and Beauty almost gasped. If she could only press her legs closer together . . . but Mistress Lockley would see and never forgive.

"Kneel up," Mistress Lockley ordered, and grabbing hold of Beauty's hair, she wrapped it in a circle on the back of Beauty's head. With pins from her pockets, she fastened it.

Then she snapped her fingers: "Prince Roger," she said, "bring that bucket and scrub brush here."

The black-haired Prince obeyed at once, moving with a quiet elegance, though he was on his hands and knees, and Beauty saw that his buttocks were raw and red as though he too had known the discipline of the wooden paddle not too long ago. He kissed the Mistress's boots, his dark eyes quite open and direct, and retreated through the back door to the yard at her gesture. The black hair was thick around the little pink mouth of his anus, his small buttocks rather exquisitely round for those of a man.

"Now you're to take that brush in your teeth and you're to scrub the floor with it, starting here and back to there," said Mistress Lockley coolly. "You are to get it good and clean. And you're to keep your legs wide apart when you do it. If I see those legs together, if I see you rubbing that hungry little mouth against the floor or touching it, you're to dangle, is that understood?"

Beauty kissed the Mistress's boots again immediately.

"Very good," said the Mistress. "The soldiers tonight will pay high for that tight little sex. They'll feed it well enough. For now, you'll hunger in obedience and humility, and you'll do as I say."

Beauty went to work at once with the brush, scrubbing hard at the tile floor with a back-and-forth motion of her head. Her sex ached almost as much as her buttocks, but as she worked the ache grew fainter and fainter, and Beauty's head was strangely clear.

What would happen, she wondered, if the soldiers adored her, paid plenty for her, fed her little sex to overflowing so to speak, and *then* Beauty were disobedient? Could Mistress Lockley afford to hang her outside?

"I'm turning into such a bad little girl!" she thought.

But the strange part of it was that her heart beat fast at the thought of Mistress Lockley. She *liked* her coldness and her sharpness in a way she had never liked her fawning Mistress of the castle, Lady Juliana. And she couldn't help but wonder, was there just a smidgen of pleasure in it for

Mistress Lockley, all that paddling? After all, Mistress Lockley did it so well.

She was scrubbing away as she thought, trying to make the brown tiles of the floor as shiny and clean as she could, when she suddenly realized that a shadow had fallen over her from the open door. And she heard Mistress Lockley's voice say softly,

"Ah, Captain."

Beauty raised her eyes cautiously but boldly nevertheless, fully aware it might be impudence to do. And she saw a blond-haired man standing above her. His leather boots went up well over his knees, and a jeweled dagger was buckled to his thick leather belt as well as broadsword and a long leather paddle. He seemed bigger to her all over than the men she had known in this Kingdom, yet he was slender of build except for his massive shoulders. His yellow hair hung luxuriously long down his neck, curling thickly at the ends, and his brilliant green eyes were crinkled with laugh lines as he looked down at her.

She felt a stab of dismay, though she didn't know why, a sudden melting of the coldness and toughness that affected her. And with calculated indifference she went back to her scrubbing.

But the man came round in front of her.

"I didn't expect you so soon," Mistress Lockley said. "Tonight I thought surely you'd bring the whole garrison."

"Most definitely, Mistress," he said. His voice was almost lustrous. Beauty felt a peculiar tightness in her throat and scrubbed on, trying to ignore the softly wrinkled calfskin boots in front of her.

"I saw this little partridge auctioned off," said the Captain. And Beauty flushed as the man made an obvious circle around her. "Quite the little rebel," he said. "I was surprised you paid so much for her."

"I have a way with rebels, Captain," said Mistress Lockley in her iron-cold voice without either pride or humor. "And she's an exceptionally succulent little partridge. I thought you might enjoy her tonight."

"Scrub her and send her up to my room now," said the Captain. "I don't think I want to wait until this evening."

Beauty turned her head, deliberately shooting a harsh glance at the Captain. Brazenly handsome he seemed, with a blond stubble of beard on his chin as if his face had been brushed with gold dust. And the sun had left its mark on him, deeply tanning his skin so that his golden eyebrows and his white teeth seemed all the brighter. He had his gloved hand on his hip, and as Mistress Lockley told her frostily to drop her eyes, he only smiled at Beauty's insolence.

PRINCE ROGER'S STRANGE LITTLE STORY

Beauty was lifted to her feet roughly by Mistress Lockley, who, twisting Beauty's wrists behind her back, forced her out the back door into a large grassy yard of heavy-limbed fruit trees.

In an open shed on smooth wooden shelves half a dozen naked slaves slept as deeply and easily, it seemed, as they had in the more sumptuous Slaves' Hall in the castle. But a crude woman with her sleeves rolled up had another slave standing in a hogshead of soapy water, the slave's hands tethered to an overhanging tree branch. The slave was being scrubbed by the woman as coarsely as if he were salted meat for supper.

Almost before she knew what was happening, Beauty had been forced to stand in such a tub, the soapy water swirling about her knees, and as her hands were tied to the branch of the fig tree above, she heard Mistress Lockley call for Prince Roger.

At once the Prince appeared, upright this time, with the scrubbing brush in his hand, and he went to work on Beauty immediately, covering her with the warm water and scrubbing at her elbows and her knees, and then at her head, as he turned her this way and that very rapidly.

It was all necessity here, and there was no luxury to it. Beauty winced as the brush scrubbed between her legs, and she moaned when the harsh bristles ground at her welts and bruises.

Mistress Lockley was gone. The heavy woman had spanked the poor whimpering scrubbed slave back to bed and disappeared herself into the Inn. And the yard, save for the sleeping ones, was empty.

"Will you answer me if I speak?" Beauty whispered. The Prince's dark skin was waxy smooth against her own as he tilted her head back and poured the pitcher of warm water over her hair. He had cheerful eyes now that they were alone.

"Yes, but be very careful! We'll be sent off for Public Punishment if we're caught. And I loathe amusing the common louts of the town at the Public Turntable."

"But why are you here?" Beauty said. "I thought I came with the first slaves to be sent down from the castle."

"I've been in the village for years," he said. "I scarcely remember the castle. I was sentenced for sneaking off with a Princess. We hid for two full days before they found us!" he smiled. "But I'll never be summoned back."

Beauty was shocked. She remembered her stolen night near the Queen's very bedchamber with Prince Alexi.

"And what happened to her?" Beauty asked.

"O, she was in the village for a while and then she went back to the castle. She became a great favorite of the Queen. And when it was time for her to be sent home, she remained to live here as a Lady."

"You can't be speaking the truth!" Beauty said in amazement.

"O, yes. She became one of the Court. She even rode down to see me in her new finery and asked if I should like to come back and be her slave. The Queen would allow it, she said, because she promised to punish me quite hard and drive me relentlessly. She'd be the wickedest Mistress a slave ever had, she said. I was quite stunned, as you can well imagine. Last time I'd seen her, she was naked, turned over her Master's knee. And now she rode a white horse and wore a gorgeous gown of black velvet trimmed in gold and her hair was braided with gold, and she was ready to have me packed naked over her saddle. I broke and ran away from her, and she had the Captain of the Guard bring me back and she paddled me over her horse right out in the square before a crowd of the villagers. She enjoyed herself immensely."

"How could she do such a thing?" Beauty was outraged. "Did you say she wore her hair in braids?"

"Yes," he said. "I hear she never wears it free. It reminds her too much of when she was a slave."

"She's not Lady Juliana!"

"Yes, that's exactly who she is. How did you know?"

"She was my tormentor at the castle, my Mistress as surely as the Crown Prince was my Master," Beauty said. How well she could see Lady Juliana's lovely face, and those thick braids. How often had Beauty run from her paddle along the Bridle Path? "O, how dreadful of her!" she said. "But what happened after that? How did you manage to escape her?"

"I told you I broke and ran from her, and the Captain of the Guard had to bring me back. It was clear I was not ready to return to the castle." He laughed. "She begged and pleaded for me, I'm told. And promised to tame me herself with no help from anyone."

"Monster!" Beauty said.

The Prince dried her arms and her face. "Step out of the tub," he said, "and be quiet. I think Mistress Lockley is in the kitchen." Then he added in a whisper, "Mistress Lockley wouldn't let me go. But Juliana isn't the first slave to remain and become a terror. Maybe someday you'll face the choice and suddenly have the paddle in your hands, and all those naked bottoms at your mercy. Think of it," he said, his dark face crinkling with a good-natured laugh.

"Never!" Beauty gasped.

"Well, we must hurry. The Captain's waiting."

The image of Lady Juliana naked with Roger flared bright in Beauty's mind. How she would love just once to turn Lady Juliana over her knee! She felt a hard stirring between her legs. But what was she thinking? The mere mention of the Captain caused in her an immediate weakness. She had no paddle in her hands and no one at her mercy. She was a bad, naked slave, about to be sent to a hardened soldier with an obvious taste for rebels. And envisioning that sun-browned handsome face and the deep gleaming eyes, she thought, "If I'm such a bad girl, then I shall act like one."

THE
CAPTAIN
OF THE
GUARD

Mistress Lockley had come out of the door. She untied Beauty's hands and dried her hair roughly. Then she pinioned Beauty's wrists behind her back and forced her into the Inn and up a narrow curved wooden stair behind the giant fireplace. Beauty could feel the warmth of the chimney through the wall, but she was marched upstairs so fast she scarcely felt anything.

Mistress Lockley opened a small heavy oak door and forced Beauty down on her knees in the room, pitching her forward so that she had to put out her hands to catch herself.

"There she is, my handsome Captain," she said.

Beauty heard the door close behind her. She knelt, still uncertain of what she meant to do, her heart racing as she saw the familiar calfskin boots and the glow of the little fire on the hearth, and the large wooden paneled bed under the sloped ceiling. The Captain sat in a heavy armchair beside a long dark wood table.

But as she waited, he gave no orders.

Rather, she felt his hand gathering the length of her hair and lifting her by it, so that she had to crawl forward a little and then kneel up in front of him. She stared at him with astonished eyes, seeing again that brazenly handsome face and luxuriant blond hair of which he was surely vain, and the green eyes deep set in the sunbrowned skin meeting her stare with the same intensity.

A terrible weakness came over her. Something within her softened completely and the softness seemed to grow, infecting all of her heart and spirit. Quickly she shut it off. But some understanding was just coming to her. . . .

The Captain lifted her to her feet, her hair wound around his left hand. Towering over her, he kicked her legs wide apart.

"You will show yourself to me," he said with the barest trace of a smile, and before she could think of what to do, he let her hair go and she was standing free and a wave of humiliation passed over her.

He sank down in the chair again quite confident of her obedience. And her heart thudded so loudly she wondered if he could hear it.

"Put your hands between your legs, and part your private lips. I wish to see your endowments."

A scarlet blush burned her face. She stared at him and didn't move. Now her heart was racing.

And in an instant he had risen, imprisoned her wrists, lifting her and seating her hard upon the wooden table. He bent her back, her wrists pushed against her spine, and forced her legs wide apart with his knee as he looked down at her.

(46)

She didn't flinch or look away, but gazed right into his face as she felt his gloved fingers doing what he had commanded her to do, spreading the lips of her vagina wide, and now he looked down at it.

She struggled, twisted, tried desperately to free herself, the fingers prying her wide apart, pinching hard at her clitoris. She felt the color scalding her face, and she rocked her hips in open rebellion. But under the rough leather casing of his gloves, her clitoris hardened, grew large, bursting over his thumb and forefinger.

She was gasping, and she had turned her face away, and when she heard him unfastening his breeches and felt the hard tip of his cock against her thigh, she moaned and lifted her hips in offering.

At once the cock was driving inside of her. It filled her so completely that she felt the hot, wet pubic hair of the Captain sealing her closed and felt his hands under her sore buttocks as he lifted her.

He carried her away from the table as her arms wound around his neck and her legs about his waist, and with his hands he worked her back and forth on his thrusting cock, lifting her as she almost cried out and then forcing her down on the full length of the organ. Harder and harder he worked her, and she did not even realize that he was cradling her head in his right hand or that he had turned her face up or that he had forced his tongue into her mouth. She felt only the jarring explosions of pleasure washing through her loins and then her mouth clamped shut on his and her body was taut and weightless, being lifted and brought down, lifted and brought down, until with a loud cry, an indecent cry, she felt the final shattering orgasm.

On and on it went, his mouth sucking the cry out of her, not letting her go, and just when she thought with agony it will come to an end, he drove his own climax into her. She heard him groan deep in his throat. His hips froze and then rode her in a frenzy of quick, jerking movements.

The room was suddenly quiet. He stood cradling her, the organ in her giving occasional little spasms that made her whimper softly.

Then she felt herself emptied. She tried to protest in some silent way, but he was still kissing her.

She had been stood on the floor again, and her hands laid on the back of her neck, and legs forced apart by the gentle nudge of his boots, and for all her sweet exhaustion, she remained standing. She stared forward seeing nothing but a blur of light.

"Now, we will have the little demonstration as I requested it," he said kissing her upturned mouth again, opening it and running his tongue inside her lip. She looked into his eyes. There was nothing but these eyes looking at her. "Captain," she thought the word. Then she saw the tangle of blond hair over the sunbrowned forehead with its deep lines. But he had drawn back, leaving her standing there.

"You will put your hands between your legs," he said softly, settling again in his oaken armchair, his breeches neatly fastened, "and will show me your private parts immediately."

She shuddered. She looked down. Her body felt hot, drained, and that weakness had now infected her every muscle. To her own amazement, she dropped her hands between her legs and she felt the wet slippery lips, still burning, pulsing from his thrusts. With her fingertip she touched the vagina.

"Open it and reveal it to me," he said, resting back in the chair, with his elbow on the arm, his hand curled under his chin. "That's it, wider. Wider!"

She stretched her little nether mouth, not believing that she, the bad girl, was doing it. A soft, lazy sensation of pleasure, an echo of the ecstasy of the embrace, further softened her and quieted her. But the lips were so wide apart they were almost aching.

"And the clitoris," he said, "lift it."

It burned against her finger as she obeyed.

"Move your finger to the side so that I can see," he said.

And quickly, as gracefully as she could, she did.

"Now stretch the little mouth wide again and thrust your hips forward."

She obeyed, but with the movement of her hips there came another wave of pleasure. She could feel the blush in her face and in her throat and her breasts. She heard herself moaning. Her hips rose higher, moved ever more forward. She could see the nipples of her breasts contracted to tiny bits of hard pink stone. She heard her own moan become louder and supplicating.

It would begin any moment, the desire that was so sweetly waning. Even now she could feel the lips thickening against her fingers and the clitoris beating hard like a little heart and the pink flesh around her nipples tingling.

She could hardly stand the desire, and then she felt the Captain's hand on her neck. He had swung her forward and around and into his lap, with her head back over the crook of his right arm, his left hand forcing her right leg widely apart from the left, and she felt the smooth calfskin jerkin against her naked side, the leather of the high boots under her thighs, and she saw his face above her. His eyes were boring into her. He kissed her slowly, and she felt her hips lift. She shuddered.

He held something dazzling and beautiful in the light before her, and she blinked to see it. It was the handle of his dagger, thick, encrusted with gold and emeralds and rubies.

It disappeared and quite suddenly she felt the cold metal against her wet vagina. "Ooooooh, yes . . ." she moaned and felt the handle slide in, a thousand times harder and crueler than the largest organ, it seemed, as it lifted her, crushing against her smoldering clitoris.

She almost screamed with desire, her head falling back, her eyes blind except for the Captain's eyes looking down at her. Her hips undulated wildly against his lap, the dagger handle going back and forth, back and forth, until she could not endure it and the ecstasy came again paralyzing her and silencing her open mouth, the vision of the Captain vanishing in a moment of total deliverance.

When she came back to herself, there was still the wild tremor in her hips, the vagina giving quiet gasps, but Beauty was sitting up, and the Captain was holding her face in his hand, and he was kissing her eyelids.

"You're my slave," he said.

She nodded.

"When I come to the Inn, you belong to me. From wherever you are, you come to me and you kiss my boots," he said.

She nodded.

He lifted her to her feet, and before she quite understood what was happening, she had been forced out of the little room again, her wrists behind her back, and she was being marched down the little winding stairs as she had come up.

Her head was spinning. He would leave her now, and she couldn't bear the thought of it. "O, no, no, please don't leave," she thought desperately. He gave her buttocks warm spanks with his large, soft leather-gloved hand and forced her into the cool darkness of the Inn again where six or seven men were already drinking.

Beauty caught the laughter, the talk, the sound somewhere of the paddle coming down and some poor slave groaning and sobbing.

But she was being forced into the open square before the Inn.

"Fold your arms behind your back," said the Captain. "You're to march before me with your knees high and you are to look straight ahead."

THE PLACE
OF
PUBLIC
PUNISH-
MENT

THE SUNLIGHT was too bright for a moment. But Beauty was busy folding her arms and marching, lifting her legs as high as she could, and finally the square became visible as they entered it. She saw its shifting crowds of idlers and gossips, several youths sitting on the broad stone rim of the well, horses tethered at the gates of the Inns, and then other naked slaves here and there, some on their knees, some marching as she was.

The Captain turned her with another one of those large soft spanks, squeezing her right buttock a little as he did it.

Half in a dream it seemed, Beauty found herself in a broad street, full of shops much like the lane down which she had come, but this street was crowded and everyone was busy, purchasing, bargaining, arguing.

That terrible feeling of regularity came back to her, that all of this had happened before, or at least that it was so familiar that it might have. A naked slave on her hands and knees cleaning a shop window looked ordinary enough, and to see another with a basket strapped to his back, marching as Beauty was being marched, before a woman who drove him with a stick—yes, that too looked regular. Even the slaves, bound naked on the walls, their legs apart, their faces in half-sleep, seemed just the ordinary thing, and why shouldn't the young village men taunt them as they passed, slapping an erect cock here, pinching a poor shy nether mouth there? Yes, ordinary.

Even the awkward thrust of her breasts, her arms folded behind her to force her breasts out, all of that seemed quite sensible and a proper way to march, Beauty thought. And when she felt another warm spank she marched more briskly and tried to lift her knees more gracefully.

They were coming to the other end of the village now, the open marketplace, and all around the empty auction platform she saw hundreds milling. Delicious aromas rose from the little cookshops, and she could even smell the wine that the young men bought by the cup at the open stands, and she saw the fabrics blowing in long streams from the fabric shop, and heaps of baskets and rope for sale, and everywhere naked slaves at a thousand tasks.

In an alleyway, a slave on his knees swept vigorously with a small broom. Two others on all fours bore baskets full of fruit on their backs as they hurried at a fast trot through a doorway. Against a wall, a slender Princess hung upside down, her pubic hair gleaming in the sun, her face red and flushed with tears, her feet neatly tethered to the wall above with wide tightly laced anklets.

But they had come into another square opening off the first, and this was a strange unpaved place where the earth was soft and freshly turned as it had been on the Bridle Path at the castle. Beauty had been allowed to stop, and the Captain stood beside her with his thumbs hooked in his belt, watching everything.

Beauty saw another high turntable, like that at the auction, and on it, a bound slave was being fiercely paddled by a man who worked the turntable round and round with a pedal as the auctioneer had done, whipping hard at the naked buttocks each time it spun to the proper position. The poor victim was a gorgeously muscled Prince, with his hands bound tight on his back and his chin mounted up on a short rough column of wood so that all could see his face as he was punished. "How can he keep his eyes open?" Beauty thought. "How can he bear to look at them?" The crowd around the platform squawked and screamed as stridently as they had done at the earlier bidding.

And when the paddler raised his leather weapon now to signal the punishment was at an end, the poor Prince, his body convulsing, his face twisted and wet, was pelted with soft bits of fruit and refuse.

Like the other square it had the atmosphere of a fair, with the same cookshops and wine vendors. From high windows hundreds watched, their arms folded on sills and balcony edges.

But the turntable paddling was not the only form of punishment. A high wooden pole stood far to the right, with many long leather ribbons streaming down from an iron ring at the top of it. At the end of each black ribbon was a slave tethered by a leather collar that forced the head high, and all marched slowly but with prancing steps in a circle around the pole, to the constant blows of four paddle-wielding attendants stationed at four points of the circle like the four points of a compass. A round track was worn in the dust from the naked feet. Some hands were bound behind the back; others were clasped there freely.

A straggle of village men and women watched the circular march, commenting here and there, and Beauty looked on in dazed silence as one of the slaves, a young Princess with large floppy brown curls, was untethered and given back to a waiting Master, who whipped at the slave's ankles with a straw broom as he drove her forward.

"There," said the Captain, and Beauty marched obediently beside him towards the high Maypole with its turning bands of leather.

"Tether her," he said to the guard, who quickly pulled Beauty over and buckled the leather collar around her neck so her chin was forced up over the edge of it.

In a blur, Beauty saw the Captain watching. Two village women were near him and talking to him, and she saw him say something rather matter-of-factly.

The long band of leather running down from the top of the pole was heavy and carried along in a circle on the iron ring by the momentum of the others, and it almost pulled Beauty forward by the collar. She marched a little faster so that it would not, but it tugged her back, until she finally fell into the right step, and felt the first loud spanking blow from one of the four guards who rather casually waited to punish her. There were so many slaves trotting in the circle now that the guards were always swinging their bright ovals of black leather, Beauty realized, though she was blessed with a few slow seconds between blows, the dust and the sunlight stinging her eyes as she watched the tousled hair of the slave ahead of her.

"Public Punishment." She remembered the words of the auctioneer telling all Masters and Mistresses to prescribe it whenever they felt it necessary. And she knew that the Captain would never think, like her well-mannered, silver-tongued Masters and Mistresses at the castle, to give her a reason for it. But what did it matter? That he wanted her punished because he was bored or curious, that was reason enough, and each time she made the full circle she saw him clearly for a few moments, his arms at his sides, his legs firmly apart, his green eyes fixed on her. What were all the reasons but foolishness, she mused. And as she braced herself for another smart blow—losing her footing and her grace for an instant in the powdery dust as the paddle swept her hips forward—she felt an odd contentment, unlike anything she'd known at the castle.

There was no tension in her. The familiar ache in her vagina, the lust for the Captain's cock, the paddle's crack, these things were there as she marched, the leather collar bouncing cruelly against her uplifted chin, the balls of her feet smacking the packed earth, but still it was not that terrible quavering dread she had known before.

But her reverie was broken by a loud cry from the crowd near her. Over the heads of those who leered at her and the other marching slaves, she saw that the poor punished Prince was being taken down from the turntable where he had remained for so long an object of public derision. And now another slave, a Princess with yellow hair like her own, was forced into place, back arching down, buttocks high, chin mounted.

Coming round the dusty little circle again, Beauty saw that the Princess was squirming as her hands were tied behind her back, and the chin rest was being cranked up by an iron bolt so that she couldn't turn her head. Her knees were bound to the turntable and she kicked her feet furiously. The crowd was as thrilled as it had been by Beauty's display on the auction block. And it showed its pleasure with much cheering.

But Beauty's eye caught the Prince who had been taken down and she saw him rushed to a nearby pillory. There were several pillories, in fact, in a row in their own little clearing. And there the Prince was bent over from the waist, his legs as always kicked apart, his face and hands clamped in place, the board coming down with a loud splat to hold him looking forward and quite unable to hide his face, or for that matter to do anything.

The crowd closed in around the helpless figure. As Beauty came round again, groaning suddenly at an unusually hard crack of the paddle, she saw the other slaves, Princesses all, pilloried in the same way, tormented by the crowds, who felt of them, stroked them, pinched them as they chose, though one villager was giving one of the Princesses a drink of water.

The Princess had to lap it, of course, and Beauty saw the pink dart of her tongue into the shallow cup, but still it seemed a mercy.

The Princess on the turntable meantime was kicking and bouncing and giving the most marvelous show, her eyes shut, her mouth a grimace, and the crowd was chanting the number of each blow aloud in a rhythm that sounded oddly frightening.

But Beauty's time of trial at the Maypole was coming to an end. Very quickly and deftly, she was released from the collar and taken panting from the circle. Her buttocks smarted and seemed to swell as if waiting for the next spank, which never came. Her arms ached as they lay doubled behind her back, but she stood waiting.

The Captain's large hand turned her around and he seemed to tower over her, gilded with sunlight, his hair sparkling around the dark shadow of his face as he bent to kiss her. He cradled her head in his hands and drew on her lips, opening them, stabbing his tongue into her, and then letting her go.

Beauty sighed to fell his lips withdrawn, the kiss rooting deep into her loins. Her nipples rubbed against the thick lacing on his jerkin, and the cold buckle of his belt burned her. She saw his dark face crease with a slow smile and his knee pressed against her hurting sex, teasing its hunger. Her weakness seemed complete suddenly and to have nothing to do with the tremors in her legs or her exhaustion.

"March," he said. And turning her around he sent

her with a soft squeeze of her sore buttock towards the far side of the square.

They drew near to the pilloried slaves, who writhed and twisted under the taunts and slaps of the idle crowd milling about them. And behind, Beauty saw closely for the first time a long row of brilliantly colored tents set back beneath a line of trees, each tent with its canopied entrance open. A young man handsomely dressed stood at each tent and though Beauty could glimpse nothing in the shadowy interiors, she heard the voices of the men one by one tempting the crowd:

"Beautiful Prince inside, Sir, only ten pence." Or "Lovely little Princess, Sir, your pleasure for fifteen pence." And more invitations like these. "Can't afford your own slave; enjoy the best for only ten pence." "Pretty Prince needing punishment, Madam. Do the Queen's bidding for fifteen pence." And Beauty realized that men and women were going and coming from the tents, one by one, and sometimes together.

"And so even the commonest of the villagers," Beauty thought, "can enjoy the same pleasure." And ahead at the end of the row of tents, she saw a whole gathering of dusty and naked slaves, their heads down, their hands tethered to the tree branch above behind a man who called out to one and all: "Hire by the hour or the day these lovelies for the lowliest service." On a trestle table at his side was an assortment of straps and paddles.

She marched on, absorbing these little spectacles almost as if the sights and the sounds were stroking her, the Captain's large firm hand now and again punishing her softly.

When at last they reached the Inn, and Beauty stood in the little bedchamber again, her legs wide, her hands behind her neck, she thought drowsily, "You are my Lord and Master."

It seemed in some other incarnation she had lived all her life in the village, had served a soldier, and the mingling of noises coming from the square outside was a comforting music.

She was the Captain's slave, yes, utterly his, to run through the public streets, to punish, to subjugate totally.

And when he tumbled her on the bed, spanked her breasts, and took her hard again, she turned her head this way and that, whispering, "Master, and then Master."

Somewhere in the back of her mind she knew it was forbidden to speak, but this seemed no more than a moan or a scream. Her mouth was open and she was sobbing as she came, her arms rising and encircling the Captain's neck. His eyes flickered, then blazed through the gloom. And there came his final thrusts, driving her over the brink into delirium.

For a long time she lay still, her head cradled in the pillow. She felt the long leather ribbon of the Maypole prodding her to trot as if she were still lost in the Place of Public Punishment.

It seemed her breasts would burst as they throbbed from the recent slaps. But she realized the Captain had taken off all his clothes and was slipping into the bad naked beside her.

His warm hand lay on her drenched sex, his fingers parting the lips ever so gently. She drew close to his naked limbs, his powerful arms and legs covered with soft curly golden down, his smooth clean chest pressed against her arm and her hip. His roughly shaven chin grazed her cheek. Then his lips kissed her.

She closed her eyes against the deepening afternoon light from the little window. The dim noises of the village, thin voices from the street, the dull bursts of laughter from the Inn below, all merged into a low hum that lulled her. The light grew bright before it began to fade. The little fire leapt on the hearth, and the Captain covered Beauty with his limbs and breathed in deep sleep against her.

TRISTAN IN
THE HOUSE
OF
NICOLAS,
THE QUEEN'S
CHRONICLER

Tristan:

I N A near daze, I thought of
Beauty's words, even as the auctioneer called for the bids,
my eyes half closed, the screaming crowd a swirling current around me. Why should we obey? If we were bad,
if we had been sentenced to this penitential place, why
must we comply with anything?

Her questions echoed through the cries and jeers,
the great inarticulate din that was the crowd's true voice,
purely brutal, endlessly renewing its own vigor. I clung
to the silver memory of her exquisite little oval face, eyes
flashing with irrepressible independence, as all the while
I was poked, slapped, turned round, examined.

Maybe I took refuge in the strange inner dialogue, because it was too excruciating to bear the blazing actuality of the auction. I was on the block, just as they had threatened I would be. And the bids were rising from everywhere.

It seemed I saw everything and nothing, and in a dim moment of excruciating remorse, I pitied the foolish slave whom I had been, dreaming in the castle gardens of disobedience and the village.

"Sold to Nicolas, the Queen's Chronicler."

Then I was being roughly shuffled down the steps, and the man who had bought me stood before me. He seemed a silent flame in the midst of the press, the rough hands slapping at my erect cock, pinching me, tugging at locks of my hair. Wrapped in a perfect stillness all his own, he lifted my chin, and our eyes met, and with an exquisite shock, I thought, yes, this is my Master!

Exquisite.

If not the man himself, robust enough for all his slender height, then the manner of it.

Beauty's question thudded in my ears. I think I closed my eyes for a moment.

I was being pushed and shoved through the crowd, told by a hundred taskmasters to march, to lift my knees, lift my chin, to keep that cock erect, while the auctioneer's loud bark called the next slave behind me to the platform. The roaring din enveloped me.

I had only glimpsed my Master, but in the glimpse all the details of his being were fixed perfectly. Taller than I by only an inch, he had a square but lean face and a wealth of white hair curling thickly well above his shoulders. He was much too young for the white hair, almost boyish despite his great height and the pure ice of his gaze, his blue eyes full of darkness at the very centers. He seemed much too finely dressed for the village, but there were others like him on the balconies over the square, watching from high-backed chairs set in the open windows. Well-to-do shopkeepers and their wives, surely, but they had called him Nicolas, the Queen's Chronicler.

He had long hands, beautiful hands that had almost languidly gestured for me to precede him.

At last I reached the end of the square, felt the last rough slaps and pinches. I found myself marching with low panting breaths in an empty street walled on either side with little taverns and stalls and bolted doorways. Everyone was at the auction, I saw with relief. And it was quiet here.

Nothing but the sound of my feet on the stones and the crisp click of my Master's boots behind me. He was very close. So close I almost felt him brush against my buttocks. And then with a shock I felt the wallop of a stout strap and his voice very low near my ear: "Pick up those knees, and hold your head high and back." At once I straightened, alarmed that I had let myself lose any measure of dignity. My cock stiffened, despite the fatigue in my calves. I pictured him again, so puzzling, that smooth young face, and the shining white hair, and the finely stitched velvet tunic.

The street twisted, narrowed, grew a little darker as the high-peaked roofs jutted overhead, and I flushed to see a young man and woman coming towards us, all crisp in clean starched clothes, their eyes dusting me carefully. I could hear my labored breath echoing up the walls. An old man on a stool at a doorway glanced up.

The belt walloped me again just as the couple drew alongside and I heard the man laugh to himself and murmur, "Beautiful, strong slave, Sir."

But why did I try to march fast, to keep my head up? Why was I caught again in the same anxiety? Beauty had looked so rebellious when she asked her questions. I thought of her hot sex clamping so boldly to my cock. That, and the sound of my Master's voice again urging me on, maddened me.

"Stop," he said suddenly and jerked my arm around so I faced him. Again I saw those large shadowy blue eyes with the black centers, and the fine long mouth without a single line of mockery or hardness. Several shadowy shapes appeared ahead of us, and I felt a dreadful sinking feeling as I saw them pause to watch us.

"You have never been taught to march, have you?" he said, and he forced my chin so high I groaned and had to exert all my will not to struggle just a little. I didn't dare to answer. "Well, you will learn to march for me," he said and forced me down on my knees in the street before him. He took my face in both hands, though he still held the belt in his right, and tilted it up.

I felt powerless and full of shame gazing up at him. I could hear the sound of young men nearby murmuring and laughing to themselves. He forced me forward until I felt the bulge of his cock in his breeches, and my mouth opened and I pressed my kisses to it fervently. It came alive under my lips. And I felt my own hips move, though I tried to still them. I was trembling all over. His cock pulsed like a beating heart against the silk. The three observers were drawing closer.

Why do we obey? Is it not easier to obey? The questions tormented me.

"Now, up, and move fast when I tell you. And lift those knees," he said, and I turned and rose, the belt cracking against my thighs. The three young men moved aside as I started off, but I could feel their attention; common youths they were, in coarse clothing. The belt caught me with fast thudding wallops. A disobedient Prince cast down lower than the village louts, one to be enjoyed as well as punished.

I was drenched in heat and confusion, yet I put all my strength into doing as I was told, the strap licking my calves and the backs of my knees, before it lashed hard against the undercurve of my buttocks.

What had I said to Beauty, that I had not come to the village to resist? But what was my meaning? It *was* easier to obey. I knew already the anguish that I had displeased and might be corrected again in front of these common boys; I might hear that iron voice again and this time in anger.

What would have soothed me, a kind word of approval? I had had so many from Lord Stefan, my Master at the castle, and yet I had deliberately provoked him, disobeyed him. In the early hours of the morning, I had risen and boldly walked out of Lord Stefan's chamber, breaking and running to the far reaches of the garden where the pages saw me. I'd led them a merry chase through the thick trees and shrubbery. And when I was caught, I fought and kicked, until, gagged and bound, I was put before the Queen and a grieving and disappointed Stefan.

I had deliberately cast myself down. Yet in the midst of this terrifying place with its brutal, jeering throngs, I was struggling to stay ahead of the strap for another Master. My hair was in my eyes. My eyes swam with tears that had not yet started to flow. The twisting lane with its endless shingles and glistening windows dimmed in front of me.

"Stop," my Master said, and gratefully I obeyed, feeling his fingers curled around my arm with a strange tenderness. There was the sound behind me of several pairs of feet and a little eruption of masculine laughter. So the miserable youths had followed!

I heard my Master say, "Why do you watch with such interest?" He was talking to them. "Don't you want to see the auction?"

"O, there's plenty more to see, Sir," said one of the young men. "We were just admiring that one, Sir, the legs and the cock on that one."

"Are you buying today?" asked the Master.

"We haven't the money to buy, Sir."

"We'll have to wait for the tents," said a second voice.

"Well, come here," my Master said. To my horror, he went on, "You may have a look at him before I take him inside; he is a beauty." I was petrified as he turned me around and made me face the trio. I was glad to keep my eyes down, to see nothing but their dull yellow raw-hide boots and worn gray breeches. They gathered close.

"You may touch him if you like," said the Master, and lifting my face again, he said to me, "Reach up and hold tight to the iron bracket on the wall above you."

I felt the bracket jutting out from the wall before I actually saw it, and it was just high enough that I had to stand on tiptoe to grasp it, with some four feet of space behind me.

The Master stood back and folded his arms, the belt gleaming as it hung at his side, and I saw the hands of the young men closing in, feeling the inevitable squeeze to my flaming buttocks before the hands lifted my balls and pressed them lightly. The loose flesh came alive with sensation, tingling, quivering. I squirmed, almost unable to stand still, and smarted at the immediate laughter. One of the young men spanked my cock so that it bobbed sharply. "Look at that thing, hard as a stone!" he said and spanked it again this way and that as another man weighed the balls, juggling them slightly.

I struggled to swallow the huge lump in my throat and stop shaking. I felt drained of all reason. In the castle there had been those lavish rooms devoted exclusively to pleasure, slaves decorated as exquisitely as sculptures. Of course I'd been handled. I'd been handled in the camp months before by the soldiers who brought me to the castle. But this was a common cobblestoned street like the streets of a hundred towns I had known, and I was not the Prince riding through on my handsome mount, but a helpless naked slave examined by three youths right before shops and lodging places.

The little group shifted back and forth, one of the men pushing at my buttocks and asking if he might see my anus.

"Of course," said the Master.

I felt all the strength go out of me. At once my

buttocks were pried apart as they had been on the auction block and I felt a hard thumb pushed in me. I tried to stifle a grunting cry and almost let go of the bracket.

"Give him the belt if you like," said the Master, and I saw it held out in his hand just before I was twisted to the side, and then it struck at my buttocks viciously. Two of the youths still toyed with my cock and balls, tugging at the hair and skin of my scrotum and cradling it roughly. But I was shaken by each stripe of pain across my backside. I couldn't help but moan aloud again, as the stinging strap came harder from the youth than it had from my Master, and when the prying fingers touched the tip of my cock, I strained back desperately trying to control it. What would it mean if I were to come in the hands of these loutish youths? I couldn't bear the thought of it. And yet my cock was deep red and iron hard from its torment.

"How's that for a whipping?" said the one behind me, reaching around and jerking my chin towards him. "As good as your Master?"

"That's enough sport," said the Master. He stepped forward, taking the leather strap, and received their grateful thanks with a polite nod as I stood trembling.

It had only begun. What was to follow? And what had happened to Beauty?

Others were passing in the street. It seemed I heard a faint distant roar as from a crowd. There was a thin unmistakable blast of a trumpet. My Master was studying me, but I looked down feeling the passion in spasms in my cock, my buttocks tightening and relaxing involuntarily.

My Master's hand rose to my face. He ran his fingers down my cheek and lifted several locks of my hair. I could see the dusty sunlight striking the big brass buckle of his belt and the ring on his left hand with which he held the stout strap beside him. The touch of his fingers was silky and I felt my cock rising with a shameful, uncontrollable jerking motion.

"Into the house, on your hands and knees," he said softly. And he pushed open the door to my left. "You will always enter that way without being told." And I found myself moving silently across a finely polished floor through small crowded rooms, a diminutive mansion it seemed, a rich town house to be exact, with an immaculate little stairs and crossed swords above the little fireplace.

It was dim, but very quickly I saw rich paintings on the walls of Lords and Ladies at their courtly amusements, with their hundreds of naked slaves forced to a thousand tasks and positions. We passed a small, heavily carved armoire. And high-backed chairs. And the hallway became narrow and close around me.

I felt enormous and vulgar here, more animal than human, crawling painfully through this little world of townsman's wealth, not a Prince surely, but a rude domesticated beast. With a silent burst of alarm, I glimpsed my reflection in a fine mirror.

"To the back, through that door," my Master commanded, and I entered a rear alcove where a well-done-up little village woman, a maid obviously, moved aside with her broom in hand as I passed her.

I knew my face was disfigured with my struggle. And it struck me suddenly what the terror of the village really was.

It was that we were true slaves here. Not playthings in a palace of pleasure, such as the slaves in the paintings on the walls, but real naked slaves in a real town, and we would suffer at every turn from common men at their leisure or tasks, and I felt my agitation increase along with the sound of my labored breathing.

But we had entered another chamber.

I moved across the soft carpet of this new room in the burnished light of oil lamps, and was told to remain still, which I did, without even trying to compose my limbs for fear of disapproval.

At first all I saw were books, shining in the glow of the lamps. Walls of books, it seemed, all bound in fine morocco and decorated in gold, a King's ransom in books surely. And the oil lamps stood on stands here and there and on a great oaken writing table that was covered with loose sheets of parchment. Feather quills stood together in a brass stand. There were pots of ink. And then high above the shelves the glimmer of more paintings.

Then out of the corner of my eye I saw a bed in the corner.

But the most surprising thing in this room, other than the incalculable wealth in books, was the vague figure of a woman materializing slowly in my vision. She was writing at the table.

I have not known many women to read and write, only a few great Ladies. Many Princes and Princesses at the castle could not even read the punishment placards fixed to their necks when they were disobedient. But this Lady was writing quite fast, and when she looked up she caught my glance before I looked down subserviently. Then she rose from the table, and I saw her skirts come round before me. She seemed small all over with tiny wrists and long graceful hands like the Master. I didn't dare to look up, but I had seen that her hair was dark brown and that it was parted in the middle and fell down her back in ripples. She wore a dress of deep burgundy, rich, like that of the man, but she also wore an apron of dark blue, and there were ink stains on her fingers that made her look interesting.

I was afraid of her. Afraid of her and the man standing silently behind me, and of the small silent room and my own nakedness.

"Let me look at him," she said, and her voice, like that of my Master, was finely turned and faintly resonant. She put her hands under my chin and urged me to kneel up. And with her thumb she stroked my wet cheek, causing me to blush all the harder. I looked down, naturally, but I had seen her high jutting breasts and slender throat, and a face like the man's, not physically so, but just as serene and impenetrable.

I slipped my hands behind my neck and hoped desperately that she would not torment my cock, but she bid me stand up and her eyes were fixed on it.

"Spread your legs; you know better than to stand like that," she said sternly but slowly. "No, very wide," she said, "until you feel it in those exquisite thigh muscles. That's better. That's how you'll always stand for me, with your legs widespread, almost at a squat but not quite. And I will not tell you again. Slaves in the village are not coddled with constant orders. You will be strapped on the Public Turntable for any failing."

These words sent a shudder through me, with an odd sense of fatality. Her pale hands seemed almost to glow in the light of the lamps as they moved towards my cock. And then she squeezed the tip, bringing out of it a drop of clear fluid. I gasped, feeling the orgasm ready to explode inside, to roll up through my organ and out of it. But mercifully she let it go and lifted my balls now as the youths had done.

Her little hands felt of them, massaging them gently, moving them back and forth in their sheathing, and the flicker of the oil lamps seemed to expand and to dim my vision.

"Flawless," she said to my Master. "Beautiful."

"Yes, I rather thought so myself," said the Master. "Easily the pick of the herd. And the cost was not so terribly great, as he was the first one auctioned. I think had he been last it would be have been double. Observe the legs, the strength in them, and these shoulders."

She lifted both her hands and smoothed back my hair. "I could hear the crowd from here," she said. "They were in a fury. Have you thoroughly examined him?"

I tried to still my panic. After all I had been six months in the castle. Why was it so terrifying, this little room, these two cold townspeople?

"No, and that should be done now. His anus should be measured," said the Master.

I wondered if they could perceive the effect the words had on me. I wished I'd taken Beauty a half dozen times in the cart so that at least my cock would be better under my control, but the thought of that only further inflamed me.

Frozen in this shameful stance, legs sprawled, I watched, powerless, the Master going to one of the shelves and reaching up for a morocco-covered case, which he set on the table.

I was turned by the woman so that I faced the table. She brought down my hands and placed them on the edge of it so that I was bending over from the waist, and I struggled to spread my legs as wide as I could so that she wouldn't have to correct me.

"And his buttocks are hardly reddened, that's good," she said. I felt her fingers toying with the welts and sore places. Little riots of pain broke out in the flesh, like lights in my mind, and right before my eyes I saw the leather case opened and two large leather-covered phalluses taken out of it. One was the size of a man's cock, I would say, and the other somewhat larger. And the large phallus was decorated at the base with a long bushy shock of black hair, a horsetail. Each was fitted with a ring, a sort of handle.

I tried to brace myself. But my mind rebelled as I stared at that thick, glossy hair. I could not be made to wear such a thing, a thing to make me look even more lowly than a slave, a thing to make me look like an animal!

The woman's hand opened a red glass jar on the desk, the light seeming to strike it for the first time as I noticed it. And her long fingers gathered up a large dab of cream and disappeared behind me.

I felt the coldness of it against my anus, and knew the appalling helplessness I always experienced when my anus was touched, opened. Gently but quickly, she spread the moisture, smoothing it well into the crack, and then into my anus itself as I tried to be silent. I felt the Master's cold eyes; I felt the Mistress's skirts against me.

The smaller of the two phalluses was lifted from the desk, and slipped sharply and firmly into me. I shuddered, tensed. "Shhhh . . . don't be stiff," she said. "Push out with your hips, yes, and open to me. Yes, that's much better. Don't tell me you were never measured or mounted on a phallus at the castle."

My tears came in a flood. Violent tremors went through my legs and I felt the phallus sliding in, impossibly large and hard, my anus contracting in spasms. It was as if there had been no other time, yet every other time had been as debilitating, as mortifying as this one.

"He's almost virginal," she said, "a mere child. Feel this." And with her left hand she lifted my chest up until I was standing again, my hands behind my neck, legs throbbing, the phallus thrust up and into me, her hand securing it.

My Master came round behind me, and I felt the phallus rocked back and forth. I felt it shift in me even as he obviously let it go. I felt stuffed and impaled. And my anus, a quivering heated mouth around it.

"And why all those lovely tears?" The Mistress drew near to my face, her left hand lifting it higher. "Haven't you ever been fitted before?" she asked. "You're going to have a great many of them ordered for you now this very day with a great many different decorations and harnesses. It's very seldom that we'll leave your anus unplugged. Now keep those legs wide." To my Master she said, "Nicolas, give me the other one."

With a sudden muffled cry I protested as best I could. I couldn't bear to look at that thick mass of black horsetail, and yet I stared full at it as it was lifted. But she only laughed softly and stroked my face again, "There, there," she said sincerely. And the smaller phallus was slid out with lightning quickness, leaving my anus to grasp with an odd sensation that sent shivers through me.

She was applying more of the chilling cream, rubbing it in deeper this time, her fingers prying me open, while with the left hand she kept my face high, the room nothing but light and color in my vision. I couldn't see my Master. He was behind me. And then I felt the larger phallus breaking me open wide, and I groaned. But again, she said:

"Push your hips back, open. Open . . ."

I wanted to cry out, "I cannot," but I felt it worked slowly back and forth, stretching me, and finally sliding in so that my anus felt enormous, throbbing around this immense object, which seemed three times what I had seen with my own eyes in the case before me.

But there was no sharp pain—only the intensification of feeling opened and rendered defenseless. And the coarse, tickling hair against my buttocks, being lifted and dropped, it seemed, the stroking almost maddeningly tender. I couldn't bear to picture it. She held the hook, it seemed, and she moved the giant shaft, pushing upwards so that I stood on tiptoe as best I could and she said, "Yes, excellent."

There it was, the soft words of approval, and I felt a lump in my throat break, felt the warmth in my face and in my chest expanding. My buttocks swelled. I felt shoved forward by the thing, though I stood still, and the soft tingling touch of the hair was all the more mortifying.

"Both sizes," she said. "We will use the smaller ones most often for regular wear and the larger when it seems necessary."

"Quite good," said the Master. "I'll send for them this afternoon." But she did not remove the larger instrument. She was looking at my face most carefully and I could see the light flickering in her eye, and a swallowed sob caught in my throat silently.

"Now it's time for us to ride out to the farm," said my Master, and the words seemed for my benefit. "I've already ordered the coach to be brought around with a harness free for this one. Leave the large phallus in for now, it will be good for our young Prince to be broken properly to harness."

But I was only given a second or two to think what all this meant. At once, the Master had his firm hand on the ring of the phallus and was pushing me forward with the command, "March." The hair stroked and tickled the backs of my knees. And the phallus seemed to shift in me as if it had life of its own, poking and prodding me forward.

A
SPLENDID
EQUIPAGE

Tristan:

N o," I THOUGHT, "I can't
be driven outdoors, not disfigured with this bestial decoration. Please . . ." And yet I was hurried through a rear
corridor and out a back door into a broad paved road
enclosed on the other side by the high stone ramparts of
the village.

This was a much bigger thoroughfare than the one
through which we had come. It was bordered with tall
trees, and I could see guards high above walking in lei-
surely fashion along the battlements. And immediately
before me I saw the shocking sight of coaches and market
carts rattling past, pulled by slaves instead of horses. As

many as eight and ten slaves were harnessed to the large coaches, and here and there a small chariot rolled by pulled only by a couple of pairs, and there were even small market carts without drivers being pulled by lone slaves, the Masters on foot beside them.

But before I could overcome my shock, or perceive how the slaves were turned out, I saw the Master's leather coach before me, and five slaves, the four in pairs, all laced into boots and well harnessed with bits jerking back their heads, and their naked buttocks decorated with horsetails. The coach itself was open with two velvet upholstered seats, and the Master handed the Mistress up to take her place as a smartly dressed youth pushed me forward to complete the third and last pair nearest to the vehicle.

"No, please," I thought as I had a thousand times at the castle, "no, I beg you . . ." But no real belief in resistance galvanized me. I was in the power of these villagers, who placed the long thick bit firmly back in my mouth and the reins over my shoulders. The thick phallus ground into me as it was shifted up, and I felt a finely made harness coming down over my shoulders with thin straps that went down to a band around my hips, which was buckled at once very securely to the ring of the phallus. I couldn't now push the thing out. In fact, it was rammed hard into me and bound to me, and I felt a firm tugging that almost pulled me off my feet as a pair of reins was obviously fixed to this hook and given to those behind me, who could now control both the bit and the phallus as they drove me.

As I looked ahead I saw that all the slaves were so tethered and that all were Princes, the long reins of those in front passing beside my thighs or above my shoulders. Tight leather rings gathered them together neatly just before me and probably right behind me. But I was startled to feel my arms being folded against my back and laced tight with harsh tugs. Rough, gloved hands quickly clamped small black leather weights to the nipples of my chest and gave them little pats to make sure they hung securely. Like leather teardrops they were, with no other purpose, it seemed, than to make the unspeakable degradation of the equipage all the more piercing.

And with the same silent quickness, my feet were being laced into thick boots with horseshoes on them, like the boots used at the castle for the devastating runs on the Bridle Path. The leather felt cold against my calves, and the horseshoes felt heavier.

But no wild run on that path, driven by the paddle of a mounted rider, had been as degrading as being tethered with these other human ponies. Even as I grasped that it had been completely done—I was now outfitted exactly like the others and all those I saw clopping past on the busy road—my head was jerked up, and I felt two sharp pulls of the reins, which started the whole team moving.

Out of the corner of my eye I saw the slave next to me lifting his knees in the usual high march, and I did the same, the harness tugging on the shaft in my anus as the Master called out, "Faster, Tristan, better than that. Remember how I taught you to march." And a thick strap licked down with a loud popping noise at the welts on my thighs and buttocks as, in a blur, I ran with the others.

We couldn't have been traveling very fast, but it seemed we were racing. Ahead of me I could see the limitless blue sky, the ramparts, and the high-seated drivers and occupants of passing carriages. And again there was that horrid sense of actuality, that we were true naked slaves here, not royal playthings. We were the groaning underbelly of a place so vast and vital and overwhelming it made the castle seem a monstrous confection.

Before me the Princes strained under their harnesses almost as if outdoing one another for speed, reddened buttocks jogging the long sleek horsetails back and forth, muscles standing out in their strong calves above the tight leather of the boots, horseshoes ringing on the cobblestones. I groaned as the reins jerked my head higher and the strap walloped the backs of my knees, and the tears flowed more freely than ever down my face so that it was almost a mercy to have the bit to cry against. The weights tugged at my nipples, knocked against my chest, sending ripples of sensation through me. I felt my nakedness perhaps as I'd never felt it before, as though the harnesses and reins and the horsetail only further revealed me.

The reins were given three jerks. The team slowed to a rhythmic trot as if it knew these commands. And winded and wet with tears, I fell into it gratefully. The strap licked at the Prince beside me now, and I saw him arch his back and lift his knees even higher.

And over the jumble of sounds, the clops of the shoes, the groans and outright cries of the other ponies, I could hear the thin rise and fall of the sound of the Master and Mistress talking together. The words weren't clear, only the unmistakable sound of a conversation.

"Head up, Tristan!" the Master said sharply, and there came that cruel jerk of the bit along with another through the ring in my anus, lifting me right off my feet for a moment, so I cried loudly behind the gag and ran fast when I was let down, the phallus seeming to enlarge inside me as if my body existed for no other purpose than to embrace it.

I sobbed against the gag, trying to catch my breath the better to measure it and weather the pace of the team. And there came the rise and fall of conversation again, and I felt utterly forsaken.

Not even the whippings in the soldiers' camp when I had tried to escape on the journey to the castle had violated me and debased me as this punishment. And the glimpse of those on the battlements above, leaning idly against the stone or pointing now and then to the passing coaches, only made my soul feel all the more frail. Something in me was being absolutely annihilated.

We rounded a turn, the road widening, the rush of horseshoes and rolling wheels growing louder. The phallus seemed to drive me, lift me, propel me forward, the long popping strap lapping my calves almost playfully. I seemed to have caught my breath, to have gotten a merciful second wind, and the tears streaming down my face felt cold in the breeze instead of scalding hot.

We were moving through the high gates, out of the village by another way than that through which I had entered with the other slaves that morning.

And I saw about me the open farmland, dotted with thatched cottages and little orchards, and the road beneath became freshly turned earth, softer under my feet. But a new sense of dread came over me. A warm sensation crawled over my naked balls, elongating and toughening my never-flagging organ.

I saw naked slaves tethered to plows or working on their hands and knees in the wheat. And the feeling of being utterly bereft intensified.

Other human ponies, rushing towards us and past us, evoked greater and greater trepidation in me. I looked like they did. I was merely one of them.

Now we were turning into a small road, trotting briskly towards a large half-timbered manor house with several chimneys rising from its high-pitched slate roof, and the strap was only flicking me now and then, stinging me and making my muscles jump.

With a fierce pull on the reins we were brought to a stop, my head snapped back as I cried out, the sound completely distorted by the thick bit, and I stood with the others panting and shivering as the dust of the road settled.

THE FARM
AND
THE
STABLE

Tristan:

At once several naked male slaves advanced towards us. I could hear the coach creaking as the Master and Mistress were helped down. And these slaves, all very darkly browned by the sun, their shaggy hair sun-bleached and gleaming, commenced to unharness us, slipping the immense phallus out of my buttocks and leaving it tethered to the equipage. I let go of the cruel bit with a gasp. I felt emptied like a sack, light and without will.

And as two roughly dressed youths appeared, both with long flat wooden sticks in their hands, I followed the other ponies along a narrow path to a low building that was obviously a stable.

At once we were bent at the waist over a huge wooden beam, our cocks pressed down by the wood, and made to grasp with our teeth leather rings that hung from another such rough bar before us. I had to strain to catch the thing in my teeth, the beam against my belly biting into the flesh, and once I did, my feet almost left the ground. My arms were still laced behind my back so I couldn't have caught myself. But I didn't fall. I held fast to the soft leather of the ring like the others. And when I felt the splash of warm water all over my aching backside and legs, I was grateful for it.

Nothing had ever felt so delicious, I thought. That is, until I was dried all over and the oil was rubbed into my muscles. This was ecstasy, even as I stretched my neck so torturously. And it did not matter much that the shaggy-haired sunbrowned slaves were so rough and quick, their fingers pressing forcefully at the welts and lacerations. I heard grunts and groans all around, as much from pleasure as from the effort of biting the ring. Our shoes were removed, and my burning feet were oiled which made them tingle exquisitely.

Then we were pulled up and led to another beam over which we were made to lean in the same manner, to lap our food from an open trough just as if we were ponies.

Greedily the slaves ate. I struggled to overcome the pure mortification of the image. But my face was pressed into the stew. The taste was rich and good. The tears standing in my eyes again, I lapped as sloppily as the others, one of the groom slaves lifting my hair and stroking it almost lovingly. I realized he was stroking me just as one might a beautiful horse. In fact, he was patting my rump. And the mortification shot through me again, my cock pushing against the beam that held it bent down towards the earth and my balls feeling mercilessly heavy.

When I could eat no more, a bowl of milk was held for me to lap, and pushed into my face again and again as I hurriedly tried to empty it. And by the time I had lapped this up, and had some cool fresh spring water, all the painful fatigue in my legs had melted. What was left was the throb of the welts and that feeling that my buttocks were frightfully enormous and scarlet with lash marks and that my anus gaped for the phallus that had widened it.

But I was merely one of six, arms tightly laced like the others. All the ponies were the same. How could they not be?

My head was lifted, and another soft leather ring with a long leather lead attached was forced into my mouth. I bit down and was pulled up and back away from the trough by it. All the ponies were being pulled up in the same manner, and they ran ahead, struggling after a dark-skinned slave who tugged us by the leads towards the orchard.

We trotted fast, pulled with hard humiliating tugs, groaning and grunting as our feet crushed the grass beneath us. Now our arms were being unbound.

I was taken by the hair, the ring removed from my mouth, and I was pushed down on my hands and knees. The branches of the trees spread out above making a green shade from the sun, and I saw the beautiful burgundy velvet of the Mistress's dress beside me.

She took me by the hair, just as the groom slave had done, and lifted my head so that for one second I looked directly at her. Her small face was very white and her eyes were a deep gray with the same dark center I saw in the Master's eyes, but at once I looked down, my heart thudding in fear of her correction.

"Do you have a soft mouth, Prince?" she asked. I knew I was not to speak, and confused by her question, I shook my head gently. All around me the other ponies were busy at some task, but I could not clearly see what they were doing. The Mistress pushed my face into the grass. I saw before me a ripe green apple. "A soft mouth will take that piece of fruit firmly in its teeth and deposit it there in the basket as the other slaves are doing and never leave the slightest teeth marks on it," she said.

As she let my hair go, I picked up the apple and, frantically searching for the basket, trotted forward to put the apple in it. The other slaves worked fast and I rushed to imitate their speed, seeing not only the Mistress's skirts and boots, but also the Master standing not far away from her. I went desperately at my task, finding another apple, and another and another, and becoming anxious and frenzied when I could find no more.

But quite suddenly another phallus was rammed dry into my anus and I was forced forward with such speed that surely a long rod was driving it. I was rushing after the others deeper into the orchard, the grass prickling my penis and balls, and once again I had an apple in my teeth, and the phallus stabbed me towards the waiting basket. I glimpsed a young man's worn boots behind me. And that gave some relief, that it was not the Master or Mistress.

I tried to find the next apple on my own, hoping the tool would be withdrawn, but I was tumbled forward by it and could not reach the basket quick enough. The phallus drove me this way and that as I piled up the apples, until the basket was quite full and all the slaves in a little flock were sent scampering to another stand of trees; I was the only one driven by a phallus. My face burned at the thought that I alone required it, but no matter how I hurried, it pushed me ruthlessly forward. The grass tortured my penis. It tortured the tender insides of my thighs and even my throat as I scooped up the apples. But nothing could stop me from trying to keep pace.

And when I saw the dim figures of the Master and Mistress quite far away, moving towards the manor house, I felt a flush of gratitude that they wouldn't see my difficulties. And I continued to work frantically.

Finally all the baskets were filled. We searched in

vain for more of the apples. And I was pushed after the little group as we rose to our feet and started to trot again towards the stables, our arms folded behind our backs as if they'd been laced there. I thought the phallus would let me alone then, but it pierced me and drove me still, and I struggled to catch up with the others.

The sight of the stables filled me with dread, though I didn't know why.

We were whipped into a long hay-strewn room, the hay feeling good under my feet, and then the other slaves were gathered up one by one and made to squat beneath a long thick beam some four feet above the ground and at least that many feet from the wall behind it. Each slave had his arms lashed around the beam, elbows pointing sharply forward. And his legs were positioned wide and back at a low squat so that his cock and balls jutted pain-fully. Each head was bowed beneath the beam, hair fallen in reddened faces. I waited, trembling, for the same, re-alizing that this had been done very fast, all five slaves tethered at once, and that I had been spared. The fear in me blazed a little hotter.

But I was forced to my hands and knees again and driven towards the first of the slaves, the one who had led the team, a powerfully built blond-haired slave who twisted and thrust his hips out as I approached, struggling it seemed for some comfort in the miserable squatting position.

At once I realized what I was to do, and absolute perplexity stopped me. I was so starved for the thick glistening cock before my face. But how the sucking of it would torture my own organ! I could only hope for mercy afterwards. But as I opened my mouth, the groom pulled up on the phallus.

"Balls first," he said, "a good tongue bathing!"

The Prince groaned and rolled his hips towards me. I hastened to obey, my buttocks held up by the phallus, my own cock ready to burst. My tongue lapped at the soft, salty skin, lifting the balls and letting them slide out of my mouth, then lapping fast again, trying to cover them, as the taste of the warm flesh and salt intoxicated me. The Prince wriggled and danced as I licked, his extraordinarily muscled legs flexing up and down as much as the space would allow. I mouthed all of the scrotum, sucking on it, nipping at it. And unable to wait any longer for the cock, I drew back and closed my lips on it, plunging to the nest of pubic hair in a fury of sucking. Back and forth I went until I realized that the Prince was driving at his own rhythm. And all I need do was hold my head still, the phallus burning into my anus as the cock slipped in and out of my lips, grazing my teeth, and I grew ever more delirious with the thickness of it, the wetness of it, the smooth tip pumping against the roof of my mouth, my own hips pumping shamelessly now, grinding up and down in the same rhythm. But when it emptied into my throat, there was no relief for my cock dancing in the empty air. I could only swallow the sour, salty fluid hungrily.

At once I was pulled back. A dish of wine was given me to lap. And I was marched to the next waiting Prince, who was already struggling in the inevitable rhythm.

My jaws ached when I finished the row.

My throat ached. And my own cock could not have been any stiffer, any more eager. I was now at the mercy of the groom and desperate for even a sign that I should know some relief from the torture.

He immediately bound me to the beam, my arms thrust over it, my legs in the same awkward, degrading squat. But there was no slave there to satisfy me. And as the groom left us alone in the empty stable, I broke into soft muffled groans, my hips straining forward helplessly.

The stable was quiet now.

The others must have slumbered. The late afternoon sun leaked like a vapor through the open door. I dreamed of relief in all its glorious forms, Lord Stefan lying under me in that land long ago where we had been friends and lovers before either of us had ever come to this strange

Kingdom, Beauty's delicious sex riding my cock, the Master of the Mistress's hand touching me.

But this only made my torment worse.

Then softly I heard the slave next to me. "It's always so," he said sleepily. He stretched his neck, twisting his head so that his loose black hair fell down more freely. I could only see a little of his face. Like all the rest he had an obvious beauty. "One is made to satisfy the others," he said. "And when there is a new slave he is always the one. Other times it's chosen in various ways, but the one chosen must suffer."

"Yes, I see," I said miserably. It seemed he was slumbering again.

"What is our Mistress's name?" I pressed, thinking he might know, since surely this was not his first day.

"Mistress Julia is her name, but she's not my Mistress," he whispered. "Rest now. You need your rest, uncomfortable as it is, believe me."

"My name is Tristan," I said. "How long have you been here?"

"Two years," he said. "My name is Jerard. I tired to run away from the castle and almost reached the border of the next Kingdom. I would have been safe there. But when I was only an hour or less away a band of peasants hunted me down and caught me. They never help an escaping slave. And I had stolen clothes from their cottage. They stripped me fast enough and bound me hand and foot and brought me back, and I was sentenced to three years in the village. The Queen never even looked at me again."

I winced. Three years! And he had served two already!

"ut would you really have been safe if you . . . ?"

"Yes, but the great difficulty is reaching the border."

"And you weren't afraid that your parents . . . ? Didn't they send you to the Queen and tell you to obey?"

"I was too afraid of the Queen," he said. "And I wouldn't have gone home anyway."

"Have you ever tried since?"

"No," he laughed softly under his breath. "I'm one of the best ponies in the village. I was sold right away to the public stables. I'm rented out every day by the rich Masters and Mistresses, though Master Nicolas and Mistress Julia rent me most often. I still hope for clemency from her Majesty, that I'll be allowed back to the castle early, but if not, I won't weep. If I weren't run hard every day I'd probably become anxious. Now and then I feel fretful and I kick or struggle, but a good thrashing quiets me down beautifully. My Master knows just when I need it; even if I've been very good, he knows. I like pulling a handsome coach like your Master's coach. I like the shiny new harnesses and reins, and he swings a hard strap, that one, the Queen's Chronicler. You know he means it. Every now and then he'll stop and rub my hair, or give me a pinch, and I almost come on the spot. He declares his authority over my cock, too, lashing it and then laughing at it. I adore him. Once he had me pull a little basket cart on two wheels all by myself while he walked beside it. I hate the small carts, but with your Master, I tell you I almost lost my mind from pride. It was so lovely."

"Why was it lovely?" I asked, mutely fascinated. I was trying to picture him, his long black hair, the hair of the horsetail, and the slender elegant figure of my Master walking beside him. All that lovely white hair in the sun, my Master's lean thoughtful face, those deep blue eyes.

"I don't know," he said. "I'm not much with words. I'm always proud when I am trotting. But I was all alone with him. We came out of the village for a twilight walk in the country. All the women were out at their gates to bid him good evening. And gentlemen passed, returning from a day of inspection at their farms to their lodgings in the village.

"Every now and then your Master would lift my hair off the back of my neck and smooth it out. He'd tethered the rein good and high so my head was way back, and he gave me many a crack on the calves I didn't need just because he liked it. It was the most exhilarating feeling, trotting on the road, and hearing the crunch of his boots beside me. I didn't care if I ever saw the castle again. Or ever left the Kingdom. He always asks for me, your Master. The other ponies are terrified of him. They come back to the stables with their buttocks raw and they say he whips them twice as much as does anyone else, but I revere him. He does what he does well. And so do I. And so will you now that he's your Master."

I couldn't answer.

He didn't say any more after that. He soon fell asleep, and I squatted very still, my thighs aching, my cock as miserable as before, thinking of his little descriptions. It sent chills through me to listen to what he said, and yet I *understood* what he was saying.

It unnerved me. But I understood it.

When they released us and drove us out to the coach, it was almost dark, and I felt myself fascinated by the harness and the nipple clamps and the reins and the lacings and the phallus as they were all refitted. Of course they hurt and frightened me. But I was thinking of Jerard's words. I could see him harnessed in front of me. I stared at the way he tossed his head, stamped his feet in the boots as if to improve the fit. And I stared forward at nothing with wide, baffled eyes as the phallus was worked well into me and the straps pulled tight, lifting me off the ground, and we were jerked into a fast trot down the road, away from the manor house.

Tears were already spilling down my face as we turned on the road, the dark battlements of the village looming before us. Lights burned in the north and south towers. And it must have been that same time of evening that Jerard had described, as there were few carriages on the road, and women leaned on their gates, waving as we passed. Now and then I saw a lone man walking. I was marching as briskly as I could, my chin painfully high, the heavy, thick phallus seeming to pulse with heat inside me.

I was cracked over and over again with the strap, but not once was I reprimanded. And just before we reached the Master's house, I remembered with a start what Jerard had said about nearly reaching the neighboring Kingdom! Perhaps he was wrong that he would have been received. And what about his father? Mine had said to obey, that the Queen was all powerful and I would be well rewarded for my service, well enhanced in wisdom. I tried to put it out of my mind. I'd never really thought of escape. It was too baffling a thought, too much against the grain of what was already so hard to accommodate.

It was dark when we pulled up to the Master's door. My boots and harnesses were taken off, everything but the phallus, and all the other ponies were whipped away to the public stables, pulling the empty coach after them.

I stood still thinking of Jerard's other words and wondering at the strange, hot shiver that went through me when the Mistress lifted my face and brushed my hair back from it.

"There, there," she said again in that tender voice. She blotted my forehead and my wet cheeks with a smooth handkerchief of white linen. I looked right into her eyes, and she kissed my lips, my cock almost dancing, as the kiss took the breath out of me.

She slipped the phallus out so quickly I was pulled off-balance, glancing back at her in alarm. And then she disappeared into the rich little house, and I stood shaken, gazing up at the high-peaked roof and the fine sprinkling of stars above it, realizing I was alone with the Master, his thick strap in his hand as always.

He turned me around and had me march along the broad paved road back in the direction of the marketplace.

SOLDIERS' NIGHT AT THE INN

FOR HOURS Beauty slept.
And only vaguely was she aware of the Captain jerking the bell rope. He was up and dressed without an order to her. And when she fully opened her eyes, he stood over her in the dim light of a new hearth fire, his belt still unbuckled. In one swift movement he slipped it from around his waist and snapped it beside him. Beauty couldn't read his face. It looked hard and removed and yet there was a little smile on his lips, and her loins immediately acknowledged him. She could feel a deep stirring of passion inside, a soft discharge of fluids.

But before she could break through the languor, he

had pulled her up and deposited her on the floor on her hands and knees, pressing her neck down and forcing her knees wide apart. Beauty's face flamed as the strap walloped her between the legs, stinging her bulging pubis. Again came a hard slap to the lips, and Beauty kissed the boards, wagging her buttocks up and down in submission. The licking of the strap came again, but carefully, almost caressingly punishing the protuburant lips, and Beauty, fresh tears spilling to the floor, gave an openmouthed gasp, lifting her hips higher and higher.

The Captain stepped forward, and with his large naked hand covered Beauty's sore bottom, rotating it slowly.

Beauty's breath caught in her throat. She felt her hips lifted, swung, pushed down, and a little throbbing noise came out of her. She could still remember Prince Alexi at the castle telling her he had been made to swing his hips in this ghastly, ignominious fashion.

The Captain's fingers pressed into Beauty's flesh, squeezing her buttocks together.

"Wag those hips!" came the low command. And the hand thrust Beauty's bottom up so high that her forehead was sealed to the floor, her breasts pulsing against the boards, a throbbing groan choked out of her.

Whatever she had thought and feared so long ago at the castle didn't matter now. She churned her bottom in the air. The hand withdrew. The strap licked up at her sex, and in a violent orgy of movement she wagged and wagged her buttocks as she had been told to do.

Her body loosened, lengthened. If she had ever known any other posture but this she couldn't clearly remember it. "Lord and Master," she sighed, and the strap smacked her little mound, the leather scraping the clitoris as it thickened. Faster and faster Beauty swung her bottom in the circle, and the harder the strap licked her the more the juices in her surged, until she could not hear the sound of the strap against the slick lips, her cries coming from deep in her throat, almost unrecognizable to her.

At last the licking stopped. She saw the Captain's shoes before her and his hand pointing to a small-handled broom beside the fireplace.

"After this day," he said calmly, "I won't tell you this room is to be swept and scrubbed, the bed changed, the fire built up. You will do it every morning when you rise. And you will do it now, this evening, to learn how to do it. After that you'll be scrubbed in the Inn yard to properly serve the garrison."

At once Beauty started to work, on her knees, with swift careful movements. The Captain left the room, and within moments Prince Roger appeared with the dustpan, scrub brush, and bucket. He showed her how she must do these little tasks, how to change the linen, build up the wood on the hearth, clear away the ashes.

And he did not seem surprised that Beauty only nodded and didn't speak to him. It didn't occur to her to speak to him.

The Captain had said "every day." So he meant to keep her! She might be the property of the Sign of the Lion, but she had been chosen by its chief lodger.

She could not do her tasks well enough. She smoothed the bed, polished the table, careful to kneel at all times, and rise only when she must.

And when the door opened again, and Mistress Lockley took her by the hair and she felt the wooden paddle driving her down the steps, she was softened and carried away by thoughts of the Captain.

Within seconds, she'd been stood in the crude wooden hogshead tub. Torches flickered at the Inn door and on the side of the shed. Mistress Lockley scrubbed fast and roughly, flushing out Beauty's sore vagina with wine mixed in water. She creamed Beauty's buttocks.

Not a word was spoken as she bent Beauty this way and that, forcing her legs into a squat, lathering her pubic hair, and roughly drying her.

And all around Beauty saw other slaves being coarsely bathed, and she heard the loud bantering voices of the crude woman in the apron and two other strong-limbed village girls who went at the task, now and then stopping to smack the buttocks of this slave or that for no apparent reason. But all Beauty could think of was that she belonged to the Captain; she was to see the garrison. Surely the Captain would be there. And the volleys of shouts and laughter from the Inn tantalized her.

When Beauty was thoroughly dry, and her hair had been brushed, Mistress Lockley put her foot on the edge of the hogshead and threw Beauty over her knee and swatted at her thighs hard with the wooden paddle several times, and then pushed Beauty down on her hands and knees as Beauty gasped for breath and sought to steady herself.

It was positively odd not to be spoken to, not even sharp impatient commands. Beauty glanced up as Mistress Lockley came around beside her, and for one instant she saw Mistress Lockley's cool smile, before the woman had the chance to remember herself. Quite suddenly Beauty's head was lifted gently by the full weight of her long hair, and Mistress Lockley's face was right above hers.

"And you were going to be my little troublemaker. I was going to cook your little buttocks so much longer than the rest for breakfast."

"Maybe you still should," Beauty whispered without intention or thought. "If that's what you like for breakfast." But she broke into violent trembling as soon as she finished. O, what had she done!

Mistress Lockley's face lit up with the most curious expression. A half-repressed laugh escaped her lips. "I'll see *you* in the morning, my dear, with all the others. When the Captain's gone, and the Inn's nice and quiet, and there's no one here but the other slaves waiting in line as well for their morning whipping. I'll teach you to open that mouth without permission." But this was said with unusual warmth, and the color was high in Mistress Lockley's cheeks. She was so very pretty. "Now trot," she said softly.

The big room of the Inn was already packed with soldiers and other drinking men.

A fire roared on the hearth, mutton turned on the spit. And upright slaves, their heads bowed, scurried on tiptoe to pour wine and ale into dozens of pewter flagons. Everywhere Beauty glanced in the crowd of dark-clad drinkers with their heavy riding boots and swords, she saw the flash of naked bottoms and gleaming pubic hair as slaves set down plates of steaming food, bent over to wipe up spills, crawled on hands and knees to mop up the floor, or scampered to retrieve a coin playfully pitched into the sawdust.

From a dim corner came the thick, resonant strumming of a lute and the beat of a tambourine and a horn playing a slow melody. But riots of laughter drowned the sound. Broken fragments of a chorus rose in a full burst only to die away. And from everywhere came shouts for meat and drink and the call for more pretty slaves to entertain the company.

Beauty didn't know which way to look. Here a robust officer of the guard in his vest of shining mail pulled a very pink and pale-haired Princess off her feet and set her standing on the table. With her hands behind her head she quickly danced and hopped as she was told, her breasts bouncing, her face flushed, her silvery blond hair flying in long perfect corkscrew curls about her shoulders. Her eyes were bright with a mixture of fear and obvious excitement. There another delicate-limbed female slave was being thrown over a crude lap and spanked as her frantic hands went to cover her face before they were pulled aside and playfully held out before her by an amused onlooker.

Between the casks on the walls, more naked slaves stood, their legs apart, their hips thrust out, waiting to be picked, it seemed. And in a corner of the room, a beautiful Prince with full red curls to the shoulders sat with legs apart on the lap of a hulking soldier, their mouths locked in a kiss as the soldier stroked the Prince's upright organ. The red-haired Prince licked at the soldier's coarsely shaven black beard, mouthed his chin, then opened his lips to the kissing again. His eyebrows were knit with the intensity of his passion, though he sat as helplessly and still as if he had been tied there, his bottom riding up with the shift of the soldier's knee, the soldier pinching the Prince's thigh to make him jump, the Prince's left arm hanging loosely over the soldier's neck, right hand buried in the soldier's thick hair with slow, flexing fingers.

A black-haired Princess in the far corner struggled to turn round and round, her hands clasped to her ankles, her legs apart, long hair sweeping the floor as a flagon of ale was poured over her tender private parts and the soldiers bent to lap the liquid playfully from the curling hair of her pubis. Suddenly she was thrown standing on her hands, her feet hoisted high above, as a soldier filled her nether mouth with ale to overflowing.

But Mistress Lockley was pulling Beauty so that she might take a flagon of ale and a pewter plate of steaming food in her hands, and Beauty's face was turned to see the distant figure of the Captain. He sat at a crowded table far across the room, his back to the wall, his leg outstretched on the bench before him, his eyes fixed on Beauty.

Beauty struggled fast on her knees, her torso erect, the food held high until she knelt beside him and reached over the bench to place the food on the table. Leaning on his elbow, he stroked her hair and studied her face as though they were quite alone, the men all around them laughing, talking, singing. The golden dagger gleamed in the candlelight and so did the Captain's golden hair and the bit of shaven hair on his upper lip, and his eyebrows. The uncommon gentleness of his hand, lifting Beauty's hair back over her shoulders and smoothing it, brought chills over Beauty's arms and throat; and between her legs the inescapable spasm.

She made some small undulation with her body, not truly meaning to. And at once his strong right hand clamped on her wrists and he rose from the bench lifting her off the floor and up so she dangled above him.

Caught off-guard, she blanched and then felt the blood flooding to her face, and as she was turned this way and that, she saw the soldiers turning to look at her.

"To my good soldiers, who have served the Queen well," the Captain said, and at once there was loud stomping and clapping. "Who will be the first?" the Captain demanded.

Beauty felt her pubic lips growing thickly together, a spurt of moisture squeezing through the seam, but a silent burst of terror in her soul paralyzed her. "What will happen to me?" she thought as the dark bodies closed in around her. The hulking figure of a burly man rose in front of her. Softly his thumbs sank into the tender flesh of her underarms, as, clutching her tightly, he took her away from the Captain. Her gasps died in her throat.

Other hands guided her legs around the soldier's waist. She felt her head touch the wall behind her and she tucked her hands behind her head to cradle it, all the while staring forward into the soldier's face, as his right hand shot down to open his breeches.

The smell of the stables rose from the man, the smell of ale, and the rich, delicious scent of sun-browned skin and rawhide. His black eyes quivered and closed for an instant as his cock plunged into Beauty, widening the distended lips, as Beauty's hips thudded against the wall in a frantic rhythm.

Yes. Now. Yes. The fear was dissolved in some greater unnameable emotion. The man's thumbs bit into Beauty's underarms as the pounding went on. And all around her in the gloom she saw a score of faces looking on, the noises of the Inn rising and falling in violent splashes.

The cock discharged its hot, swimming fluid inside her and her orgasm radiated through her, blinding her, her mouth open, the cries jerked out of her. Red-faced and naked, she rode out her pleasure right in the midst of this common tavern.

She was lifted again, emptied.

And she felt herself being set down on her knees on the table. Her knees were pulled apart and her hands placed under her breasts.

As the hungry mouth sucked on her nipple, she lifted her breasts, arching her back, her eyes turned shyly away from those who surrounded her. The greedy mouth fed on her right breast now, drawing hard as the tongue stabbed at the tiny stone of the nipple.

Another mouth had taken her other breast. And as she pressed herself against the mouths that suckled her, the pleasure almost too acute, hands spread her legs wider and wider, her sex almost lowered to the table.

For one moment the fear returned, burning white-hot. Hands were all over her; her arms were being held, her hands forced behind her back. She could not free herself from the mouths drawing hard on her breasts. And her face was being tilted up, a dark shadow covering her as she was straddled. The cock pushed into her gaping mouth, her eyes staring up at the hairy belly above her. She sucked the cock with all her power, sucking as hard as the mouths at her breasts, moaning as the fear again evaporated.

Her vagina quivered, fluids coursing down her wide-spread thighs, and violent jolts of pleasure shook her. The cock in her mouth tantalized her but could not satisfy her. She drew the cock deeper and deeper till her throat contracted, the come shooting into her, the mouths pulling gently at her nipples, snapping her nipples, her nether lips closing vainly on the emptiness.

But something touched her pulsing clitoris, scraped it through the thick film of wetness. It plunged through her starved pubic lips. It was the rough, jeweled handle of the dagger again . . . surely it was . . . and it impaled her.

She came in a riot of soft muffled cries, pumping her hips up and up, all sight and sound and scent of the Inn dissolved in her frenzy. The dagger handle held her, the hilt pounding her pubis, not letting the orgasm stop, forcing cry after cry out of her.

Even as she was laid down on her back on the table, it tormented her, making her squirm and twist her hips. In a blur she saw the Captain's face above her. And she writhed like a cat as the dagger handle rocked her up and down, her hips spanking the table.

But she was not allowed to come so soon again.

She was being lifted. And she felt herself laid over a broad barrel. Her back arched over the moist wood, she could smell the ale, and her hair fell down to the floor, the Inn upside down in a riot of color before her. Another cock was going into her mouth while firm hands anchored her thighs to the curve and a cock pushed into her dripping vagina. She had no weight, no equilibrium. She could see nothing but the dark scrotum before her eyes, the unfastened cloth. Her breasts were slapped, sucked, and gathered by strong kneading fingers. Her hands groped for the buttocks of the man who filled her mouth and she clung to him, riding him. But the other cock pummeled her against the barrel, plugged her, grinding her clitoris to a different rhythm. Through all her limbs she felt the searing consummation, as if it did not rise from between her legs, her breasts teeming. All her body had become the orifice, the organ.

She was being carried into the yard, her arms around firm, powerful shoulders.

It was a young brown-haired soldier who carried her, kissing her, petting her. And they were all over the green grass, the men, laughing in the torchlight as they surrounded the slaves in the tubs, their manner easy now that the first hot passions had been satisfied.

They circled Beauty as her feet were lowered into the warm water. They knelt with the full wineskin in their hands and squirted the wine up into her, tickling her, cleansing her. They bathed her with the brush and the cloth, half playing at it, vying to fill her mouth slowly, carefully with the tart, cool wine, to kiss her.

She tried to remember this face, that laugh, the very soft skin of the one with the thickest cock, but it was hopeless.

They laid her down in the grass beneath the fig trees and she was mounted again, her young captor, the brown-haired soldier, feeding dreamily on her mouth, and then driving her in a slower, softer rhythm. She reached back and felt the cool, naked skin of his buttocks and the cloth of his breeches pulled halfway down, and touching the loosened belt, the rumpled cloth, and the half-naked backside, she clamped her vagina tight on his cock so that he gasped aloud like a slave on top of her.

It was hours later.

She sat curled in the Captain's lap, her head against his chest, her arms about his neck, half sleeping. Like a lion he stretched under her, his voice a low rumble from his broad chest, as he spoke to the man opposite. He cradled her head in his left hand, his arm feeling immense, effortlessly powerful.

Only now and then did she open her eyes on the smoky glare of the whole tavern.

Quieter, more orderly than before. The Captain talked on and on. The words "runaway Princess" came clear to her.

"Runaway Princess," Beauty thought drowsily. She couldn't worry about such things. She closed her eyes again, burrowing into the Captain, who tightened his left arm about her.

"How splendid he is," she thought. "How coarsely beautiful." She loved the deep creases of his tanned face, the luster of his eyes. An odd thought came to her. She had no more care what his conversation was about than he had care to talk to her. She smiled to herself. She was his nude and shuddering slave. And he was her coarse and bestial Captain.

But her thoughts drifted to Tristan. She had declared herself such a rebel to Tristan.

What had happened to him with Nicolas the Chronicler? How would she ever find out? Maybe Prince Roger could tell her some news. Perhaps the dense little world of the village had its secret arteries of information. She had to know if Tristan was all right. She wished she could just see him. And dreaming of Tristan, she drifted into sleep again.

GRAND ENTERTAIN-MENT

Tristan:

Without the dread pony harnesses, I felt rudely bare and vulnerable as I marched fast towards the end of the road, expecting any second the tug of the reins as if I still wore them. Many coaches roared by us now, decorated with lanterns, the slaves clopping fast, heads high, just as mine had been. Did I like it better that way? Or this way? I didn't know! I only knew fear and desire, and an absolute awareness that my handsome Master Nicolas, my Master who was stricter than so many others, was walking behind me.

A brilliant light poured into the road ahead. We were coming to the end of the village. But as I marched around the last of the high buildings to my left, I saw, not the marketplace, but some other open place, immensely crowded and full of torchlight and lantern light. I could smell the wine in the air and hear the loud, drunken laughter. Couples danced arm in arm, and winesellers with full wineskins over their shoulders pushed through the crowd offering cups to all comers.

My Master stopped suddenly and gave a coin to one of these and held the cup before me to lap the wine from it. I flushed to the roots of my hair at the kindness of it, drinking the wine greedily but as neatly as I could. My throat had been burning.

And when I looked up I saw clearly that this was some sort of fairgrounds of punishments. Surely it was what the auctioneer had called the Place of Public Punishment.

Slaves were pilloried in a long row to one side, others were tethered in dimly lit tents with the entrances open for villagers to go and come, paying a coin to an attendant. Other tethered slaves ran in a circle around a high May-pole, punished by four paddlers. Here and there a pair of slaves scampered in the dust to retrieve some object tossed before them, while young men and women urged them on, obviously having placed some bet on the hoped-for winner. Against the ramparts far to the right, giant wheels turned slowly, spread-eagle slaves going round and round, their enflamed thighs and buttocks targets for apple cores, peach stones, and even raw eggs from the crowd, while several other slaves hobbled along at a squat behind their Masters, necks tethered by two short leather chains to their widespread knees, their arms stretched out to support long poles with baskets of apples for sale dangling from the ends of them. Two pink, plump-breasted little Princesses, glistening with sweat, rode wooden horses with wild rocking gestures, their vaginas obviously im-paled by wooden cocks. And as I watched astonished, my Master walking me slowly now, his own eyes sweeping the fair, one Princess reached her flushing, red-faced climax for the crowd and was obviously applauded the winner of the contest. The other was paddled, castigated, and scolded by those who had laid down bets on her.

But the grand entertainment was the high turntable where a slave was being thrashed by a long rectangular leather paddle. My heart sank when I saw it. I remembered the Mistress's words, threatening me with the Public Turntable.

And I was being forced steadily towards it. We were pushing right through the sea of howling, whooping spectators that radiated out some fifty feet from the high platform and right towards the slaves who knelt up with their hands behind their necks, much berated by the onlookers, as they waited obviously at the wooden steps to be taken up and paddled.

As I stared in disbelief my Master forced me directly into place at the end of this line. Coins were passed to an attendant. I was pushed to my knees, unable to conceal my fear, the tears stinging my eyes at once, my whole frame shuddering. What had I done? Dozens of round faces turned towards me. I could hear their taunts:

"Oh, is the castle slave too good for the Public Turntable? Look at that cock." "Has that cock been a bad boy?" "What's he being whipped for, Master Nicolas?"

"His good looks," said my Master with a soft touch of dark humor. I looked towards the steps and the high platform in horror. But I could see almost nothing but the lower steps now, as I knelt, the crowd some twenty or thirty deep in all directions. But laughter exploded at my Master's answer, the light of torches glinting on moist cheeks and eyes. The slave in front of me struggled forward as another was rushed up the steps. From somewhere came the loud roll of a drum and renewed screams from the crowd. I twisted around to face my Master frantically. I went down kissing his boots. The crowd pointed and laughed. "Poor desperate Prince," a man taunted. "Do you miss your nice perfumed bath at the castle?" "Did the Queen paddle you over her knee?" "Look at that cock, that cock needs a good Master or Mistress."

I felt a firm hand grasp my hair and raise my head, and I saw through my tears that handsome face above me, smooth and a little hard. The blue eyes narrowed very slowly, their dark centers seeming to expand, as the right hand was raised, the first finger wagging back and forth stiffly, the lips forming the word "no" silently. The breath went out of me. The eyes grew still and stone-cold and the left hand let me go. I turned back in line of my own accord, clamping my hands to the back of my neck, again shuddering and swallowing as the crowd gave exaggerated "ooooh's" and "awwww's" of mock sympathy.

"That's a good boy," shouted a man in my ear, "you don't want to disappoint this crowd, now, do you?" I felt his boot touch my buttocks. "I'm betting ten pence he puts on the best show tonight."

"And who's to judge that?" said another.

"Ten pence he really moves that bottom!"

It seemed an eternity before I saw the next slave go up, and then the next and the next, and finally I was the last one struggling forward in the dust, the sweat pouring down me in rivulets, my knees burning and my head swimming. Even in this moment I believed somehow I had to be rescued. My Master had to be merciful, change his mind, realize I'd done nothing to deserve it. It had to happen because I could not endure it.

The crowd shifted and pressed in. Loud cries rose as the Princess being paddled above squealed and I heard the thunder of her feet on the turntable. I felt the sudden impulse to rise and run, but I did not move, and the noise in the square seemed pumped to greater and greater volume by a roll of drums again. The paddling was over and I was next. Two attendants were rushing me up the steps while with my whole soul I rebelled, and I heard my Master's firm command, "No fetters."

No fetters. So there had been that choice. I almost broke into a wild struggle. O, please for the mercy of fetters. But to my horror I was of my own accord stretching out to place my chin on the high wooden post and spreading my knees, and clasping my hands on my back with the rough hands of the attendants merely guiding me.

Then I was alone. No hands touched me. My knees rested in only the shallowest indentations in the wood. Nothing but the slender post of the chin rest came between me and thousands of pairs of eyes, my chest and belly tightening in rolling spasms.

The turntable was cranked around fast and I saw the huge figure of the shaggy-haired Whipping Master, sleeves rolled above his elbows, the giant paddle in his mammoth right hand as with the left he scooped up from a wooden bucket a great dripping dollop of honey-colored cream. "Ah, let me guess!" he shouted. "It's a fresh little boy from the castle who's never been paddled here before! Soft and pink as a piglet for all his golden hair and sturdy legs. Now are you going to give these good people a fine show, young man?" He spun the turntable again half around and slapped the thick cream to my buttocks, working it in well as the crowd reminded him in loud shouts that he would need plenty. The drums gave their chilling deep-throated roll. I saw the whole square spread out before me, hundreds of eager gaping villagers. And the poor unfortunates circling the Maypole, the pilloried slaves struggling as they were pinched and prodded, slaves hung upside down from an iron carrousel being cranked slowly around just as I was being moved now in a relentless circle.

My buttocks warmed and then seemed to simmer and cook under the thick massaging of cream. I could almost feel it glistening. And I knelt freely, unfettered! My eyes were so dazzled by the torches suddenly that I blinked. "You heard me, young man," came the Whipping Master's booming voice again, and I was back facing him and he was wiping his hand dry on his stained apron. He reached out now and cradled my chin, pinching my cheeks as he wagged my head back and forth. "Now you will give these people a good show!" he said loudly. "You hear me, young man? And do you know why you'll give them a good show? Because I'll thrash your pretty buttocks until you do it!" And the crowd squealed in derisive laughter. "You're going to move that handsome rump, young slave, if you've never moved it before. This is the Public Turntable!" And with a sharp slap of the foot pedal, he gave the turntable another whirl, the long rectangular paddle spanking both my buttocks with a shattering crack, driving me frantically to struggle for balance.

The crowd gave a genial roar as I was whirled around again and the second blow came and then the whirl and another and then another. I clenched my teeth on my cries, the warm pain radiating out from my buttocks through my cock. I heard taunts of "Harder." "Really thrash the slave," and "Work that rump." "Pump that cock." And I realized I was obeying these commands, not deliberately but helplessly, wriggling as I was sent into frantic upheaval by each deafening smack, trying not to slip out of place on the turntable.

I tried to close my eyes, but they opened wide with each blow, and my mouth was wide, my cries erupting uncontrollably. The paddle spanked me to one side and the other, almost toppling me and then righting me, and yet I felt my starved cock jerking forward at each blow, throbbing with desire at each blow, and the pain flashed in my head like a fire exploding.

The myriad tints and shapes of the square were mired together. My body, caught in the whirl of spanking blows, seemed to fly loose from itself. I could no longer struggle for balance, yet the paddle would not let me slide or fall; there had never been any such danger. And I was caught in the speed of the turns, riding the heat and force of the paddle, crying aloud in short wrenching bursts, the crowd clapping and shouting and chanting.

All the images of the day fused in my brain, Jerard's strange speech, the Mistress thrusting the phallus between my spread buttocks—and yet I thought of nothing clearly except the slamming of the paddle and the laughing crowd that seemed to flow out from the turntable forever. "Snap those hips!" cried the Whipping Master, and without thought or will, I obeyed, overcome by the force of the command, by the force of the will of the crowd, snapping wildly and hearing hoarse raucous cheers, the paddle slapping first the left and then the right side of my buttocks and then thundering on my calves and rising to my thighs and my buttocks again.

I was lost as I had never been lost. The shouts and jeers washed me as surely as the light washed me and the pain washed me. I was only my burning welts and swelling flesh and the hard rod of a cock jerking vainly as the multitude screamed, the paddle smacking again and again, my own cries vying with it in volume. Nothing in the castle had so drenched my soul. Nothing had so seared me and emptied me.

I was plunged into the depth of the village, abandoned there. And it was luxurious suddenly, horribly luxurious, that so many should witness this delirium of abasement. If I must lose my pride, my will, my soul, let them revel in it. And it was natural too that hundreds milling in the square should not even notice it.

Yes, I was this thing now, this nude and bulging mass of genitals and sore muscles, the pony who pulled the coach, the sweating, crying object of public ridicule. And they could take pleasure in it or ignore it as they wanted.

The Whipping Master stepped back. He whirled the turntable round and round. My buttocks boiled. My open mouth shuddered, cries choking loose as loudly as ever.

"Get those hands down between your legs and cover your balls!" roared the Whipping Master. And mindlessly, in a last gesture of debasement, I obeyed, hunching, my chin still well propped, to shield my balls as the crowd stamped and laughed all the harder. Suddenly I saw a shower of objects sailing through the air. I was being pelted with half-eaten apples, crusts of bread, the soft crush of raw eggs as the shells exploded against my buttocks and back and shoulders. I felt sharp stings on my cheeks, the soles of my naked feet, my eyes wide as the hail continued. Even my penis was struck, which brought sharp shrieks of laughter.

Now a rain of coins commenced to hit the boards. The Whipping Master shouted "More, you know it was good. More! Buy out the slave's whipping and the Master will bring him back all the sooner!" And I saw a youth rushing around me in an anxious circle gathering up the money. It was being placed in a little sack and bound with cord. And as my head was lifted by the hair, the sack was shoved in my open panting mouth as I grunted in astonishment. Clapping sounded all around, shouts of "Good Boy!" And teasing demands, how had I liked the paddling, would I like another tomorrow night?

I was being yanked up and rushed down the wooden steps, marched out of the brilliant torchlight and away from the turntable. I was thrown forward on my hands and knees and driven through the crowd until I saw my Master's boots and, glancing up, saw his languid figure leaning against the wooden counter of a little wine stall. He gazed down at me without a smile or a word. And taking the little sack out of my mouth, weighed it in his right hand, put it away, and continued to look down at me.

I bowed my head. I laid my head in the dust and felt my hands slide out from under me. I couldn't move, but mercifully there came no order to move. And the din of the square merged into a single sound that was almost like silence.

But I felt my Master's hands, soft hands, the hands of a gentleman, lifting me. I saw a little bath stall before me where a man waited with a brush and scrub bucket. And quite firmly I was led towards it and given over to the man, who, setting down his cup of wine, took a coin gratefully from my Master. Then he reached out and silently forced me down into a squat over the steaming bucket.

At any other moment in the past months, the rough public bathing on the edge of an indifferent crowd would have been unspeakable. Now it was nothing but voluptuous. I was barely conscious as the warm water poured over my smoldering welts; of it sluicing away the sticking egg yolk and dust that clung to it; of my cock and balls being well soaked and much too swiftly oiled to alleviate their grievous hunger.

My anus was thoroughly lubricated and I hardly noticed the fingers driving in and out, and still I seemed to feel the shape of the phallus stretching me. The hair of my head was rubbed dry and combed. My pubic hair was brushed, and even the hair between my seething, quivering buttocks was combed out to right and left, all of this completed so fast that in moments I knelt before my Master again and heard his command to precede him to the road along the ramparts.

NICOLAS'S
BED-
CHAMBER

Tristan:

WHEN WE reached the road, my Master told me to stand up, and told me to "walk." Without hesitation, I kissed both his boots and then rose to face the road and obey him. I put my hands behind my neck, just as I had done when I had been made to march. But quite suddenly, he caught me in his arms and turned me and put my hands down at my sides and kissed me.

For a moment I was so perplexed that I didn't respond, but then I returned the kiss, almost feverishly. My mouth opened to receive his tongue, and I had to move my hips back so that my cock would not rub against him.

My body seemed to lose the very last of its strength, all my remaining vigor collected in my organ. My Master drew back a little and fed on my mouth and I could hear my own loud sighs echoing up the walls. Tentatively I lifted my arms, and he did nothing to prevent it as I embraced him. I felt the smooth velvet of his tunic and the soft silk of his hair. This was almost ecstasy.

My cock twitched, lengthened, and all the soreness in me pulsed with renewed fire. But he let me go, turned me, and put my hands on my neck again. "You may walk slowly," he said. And his lips brushed my cheek, and the mingling of distress and longing in me was so enormous, I was almost in tears again.

Only a few open coaches moved along the drive, pleasure riders it seemed, making a broad circle when they reached the square and turning back to rush past us. I saw slaves in brilliant silver harnesses with heavy silver bells tinkling from their cocks and a rich townswoman in a bright-red velvet hood and cape, snapping a long silver strap at these ponies.

It crossed my mind that my Master should get an equipage like that, and I smiled to myself at the quality of the thought.

But I was still shaken by the kiss, and still thoroughly vanquished by the Public Turntable. As my Master stepped into stride beside me I thought I must be dreaming. I felt the velvet of his sleeve against my back and his hand touching my shoulder. I was so debilitated I had to make myself move forward.

His hand curling around the back of my neck sent a tingling all through me. The knot in my cock ached and tightened, but I luxuriated in these sensations. I half-closed my eyes, seeing the lanterns and torches ahead like little explosions of light. Now we were far from the noise of the public place, and my Master walked so close to me that I felt his tunic against my hip and his hair touching my shoulder. Our shadows leapt out before us for a moment as we passed a torchlit door, and we were almost the same height, one man naked and the other elegantly clothed, carrying a strap in his hand. Then darkness.

We had come to his house, and as he turned the big iron key in the heavy oak door, he said softly, "Down on your knees," and I obeyed, entering the world of the dimly lit polished hallway. I moved beside him until he paused at a door, and I found myself entering a new and strange bedchamber.

Candles were lit. There was a little fire on the grate, perhaps to dry the dampness of the stone walls, and the great hulk of a bed made out of carved oak against the wall, its paneled roof and three sides inlaid with green satin. There were books here, too, old scrolls as well as leather volumes. And a desk with pens, and again the paintings. But it was a larger room than the other, more shadowy yet more comforting.

I did not dare to hope or fear what might happen here. My Master was removing his clothes, and as I watched amazed, he peeled off everything, neatly folding it on the chest at the foot of the bed, and then he turned to face me. His sex was as alive and hard as mine was. It was slightly thicker but no longer and his pubic hair was the same stark white as the hair of his head which looked almost ethereal in the light of the oil lamps.

He turned down the green coverlet of the bed and beckoned for me to come up into it.

I was so stunned I could not move for a moment. I looked at the fine weaving of the linen sheets. For three nights and two days I had been in the crude stockade at the castle. And I had expected to sleep here in some miserable corner on bare boards. But this was the least of it. I could see the light playing on the Master's tightly muscled chest and arms and the cock seeming to grow as I watched it. I glanced up right into his dark blue eyes and came forward to the bed, and climbed upon it, still on my knees, and he knelt on the coverlet facing me. I had my back to the pillows and he slipped his arms around me and kissed me again. And answering the strong bold sucking of his mouth, I couldn't stop the tears from coursing down my cheeks or the sob from sticking in my throat as I tried to conceal it.

He urged me back gently and with his left hand he lifted his balls and his cock. I dropped down and kissed his balls immediately. I ran my tongue over them as I had been taught to do with the ponies in the stable, mouthing them and feeling them tenderly with my teeth, and then I took the cock in my mouth and pulled hard on it, a little startled by its thickness. It was no thicker than the large phallus, I thought. No, just that thick, and the dizzying thought came to me that he had prepared me for himself, and when I thought of him entering me that way himself I became almost uncontrollably excited. I sucked and licked at the cock, tasting it, and thinking this is the Master and not one of the other slaves, this is the man who has all day silently commanded me, subjugating me, defeating me, and I felt my legs slide apart and my belly dip down and my buttocks rise in a spontaneous motion as I sucked, groaning softly.

I almost wept when he lifted my face. He pointed to a small jar on a little shelf in the paneled wall. At once I opened it. The cream in it was thick and pure white. He pointed to his cock and at once I took some of the cream on my fingers. But before I applied it, I kissed the tip and tasted a little trace of moisture. I dabbed my tongue into the tiny hole, gathering all that was there of the clear fluid.

Then I rubbed in the cream well, even creaming the balls and smoothing the thick curly white hair with the cream until it was glistening. The cock was dark red now, and shuddering.

The Master put out his hands to me. Tentatively I dabbed more cream onto his fingers. He gestured for more, and I applied it. "Turn around," he said. I did so, my heart racing. I felt the cream in my anus, rubbed deep and thick, and then his hands wrapped around me, the left scooping my balls up and binding the loose flesh to my cock so that my balls were pushed forward. I gave a short desperate imploring cry as I felt his organ slide into me.

It found no resistance. I was lanced again as surely as I had been by the phallus, and with hard slapping thrusts I felt it jab deeper and deeper. The hand around my cock forced it out straight, and I felt the Master's right hand surrounding the tip, the cream slipping around the tortured flesh and then the hand tightening and riding the cock up and down in rhythm with the thrusts into my backside.

My loud groans echoed through the room. All my pent-up passion jetted out, my hips rocking violently back and forth, the cock splitting me open, and my own organ shot its fluids in wild spurts out of me.

For a moment I saw nothing. I rode the spasms in darkness. I hung helpless on the cock that skewered me. And gradually on the very end of the wave I felt my cock rising again. My Master's greased hands were coaxing it to rise. And it had been tormented too long to be so easily satisfied. Yet the rally was excruciating. I almost whimpered to be released, but my whimpers sounded too much like sighs of pleasure. His hand was working me well, his cock pumping me, and I heard myself giving the same short openmouthed cries I'd given under the Whipping Master's paddle on the turntable. I felt my cock jerking as it had then and saw all those faces around me, and I knew I was alone in the Master's bedchamber and that I was his slave and he wouldn't let me go until he had brought it again thundering out of me.

My cock was remembering nothing. It was driving back and forth through his slick fingers, and his thrusts in my rear grew longer, faster, rougher. I felt myself coming to the pinnacle as his hips slammed against my scalded rear. And as he let out a low shuddering moan, jerking wildly into me, I felt my cock explode again in the tight sheath of his hand, and this time it seemed slower, deeper, more utterly devastating. I collapsed back against him, my head rolling on his shoulder, his cock thumping and twitching inside me.

We did not move for a long moment. Then he lifted me and pushed me towards the pillows. And I lay down and he lay down beside me. His face was turned away and I stared drowsily at his naked shoulder and white hair. I should have slept irresistibly. But I didn't.

I kept thinking I was alone with him in this bedchamber and he had not yet sent me away, and all that had happened to me would not recede. It stayed ever-present in my mind. It made my tongue catch in my mouth as if on the verge of speech. It made my eyes remain open.

A quarter of an hour passed perhaps. The candles gave a lovely dim golden light, and I leaned forward and kissed my Master's shoulder. He did not stop me. I kissed the small of his back and then I kissed his buttocks. Smooth, free of all welts and red marks, virginal, the buttocks of a Master in the village, a Lord or Sovereign at the castle.

I felt him stir under me, but he didn't speak. And I kissed the crack between his buttocks and darted my tongue down to the pink circle of his anus. I felt him quicken slightly. He moved his legs ever so slightly apart, and I pushed the buttocks a little wider. I lapped at the little pink mouth, tasting its strange sourness. I bit at it with my teeth.

My own cock swelled against the sheet. I inched down in the bed and moved gently on top of his legs, crouching over him, and I pressed my cock against his legs as I licked at the little pink mouth and stabbed my tongue into it.

Softly I heard him say, "You may take me if you like."

I felt the same paralyzing astonishment I'd felt when he told me to get into the bed. I kneaded and kissed his silky buttocks and then I shot up, covering him, pressing my mouth to the nape of his neck and sliding my hands under him. I found his cock already stiff and I held it in my left hand as I jutted my own cock into him. It was tight and scratching and unspeakably luscious.

He gave a little wince. But I was still well-greased and it slid back and forth easily. And I clasped both my hands around his cock and pushed up so that he was on his knees just barely, his face still pressed into the pillow. And then I galloped him hard under me, spanking my belly against his soft clean buttocks as I heard him moan, pulling his cock stiffer and stiffer, until when I heard him cry out, I released into him, his semen spilling over my fingers.

This time when I lay back I knew I could sleep. My buttocks simmered under me, and the welts itched on the backs of my knees, but I was contented. I looked up at the green satin canopy over my head, and consciousness slid away from me. I knew he was pulling up the coverlet over us, and that he had put out the candles, and I knew his arm was over my chest, and then I knew nothing, except I was sinking down and down, and the soreness in all my muscles and in my flesh was lovely.

TRISTAN'S
SOUL
FURTHER
REVEALED

Tristan:

I<small>T MUST</small> have been mid-morning when I was awakened and quickly pulled from the bed by one of the servants. Too young to be a Master, surely, the boy seemed to relish the task of feeding me my breakfast in a pan on the kitchen floor.

Then he rushed me out to the road behind the house, where two splendid ponies stood side by side, their reins connected to a single harness some five feet or so behind them that was held by another boy who quickly assisted the first in fitting me into it. My cock was already at attention, though I felt myself freeze inexplicably so that the boys had to handle me roughly.

There was no coach near, except for those that roared past, ponies at full trot, straps cracking. The horseshoes had a crisp, silvery sound, much lighter and faster than real horses, I thought, and my pulse was already racing.

I was positioned alone behind the first two, and straps were quickly wound round my balls and cock, binding the balls up to the cock to pooch forward under it. I couldn't stop myself from squirming as the firm hands made these lacings tight and then laced my arms behind my back, and brought a thick belt around my hips, my cock laced up against it. A phallus was shoved into place in my rear and this too secured by tethers running up to the belt in back, and through my legs to the belt in front, much more snugly, it seemed, than I had been fitted yesterday. But there was no horsetail and I was being given no boots, and when I realized this I was more afraid than I might have been.

I could feel my buttocks closing on the leather tethers that held the phallus, and it made me feel more opened there and naked. The horsetail, after all, had been a sort of cover.

But I felt the first real panic when a harness was fitted over my head and shoulders. The traps were thin, almost delicate and very finely polished, and one ran over the top of my head and down the sides, branching neatly to fit around my ears without covering them, and connecting at the neck with a thick and loose collar. Another thin strap ran down over my nose, bisecting yet a third, which went round my head directly at my mouth, fitting into place a short, immensely thick phallus that was forced through my lips before I could cry in protest. It filled my mouth, though it did not go in very deep, and I bit down on it and licked at the bottom of it almost uncontrollably. I could breathe well enough, but my mouth was stretched painfully wide as was my anus. And the feeling of being stretched and penetrated at both ends gave me a desperate drunken feeling that made me whimper miserably. All this was tightened and adjusted, the collar buckled on the back of my neck and the reins of the ponies in front tethered over my shoulders to that rear buckle. Another set of reins from their well-harnessed hips was bound to the buckle of the belt that circled my belly.

It was a most ingenious harnessing. I would be tugged forward by their marching, and I could not fall even if I lost my balance. And there were two of them to my weight and I could see by the thick muscles of their calves and thighs that they were accomplished ponies.

They tossed their heads as they waited, as though they liked the feel of the leather, and I felt the tears already flowing. Why couldn't I be harnessed as they were to a cart? What was being done to me? They looked sleek and privileged suddenly, with their shining horsetails and high-pitched heads, and I felt bound like a lowly prisoner. My naked feet would pound the road behind the loud metallic ring of their shoed feet. I twisted and pulled, but the straps were tight and the boys, busy with oiling my buttocks, ignored me.

But I was suddenly startled by the Master's voice as he appeared in the corner of my eye with that long leather strap dangling from his waist and asked softly if I was ready. The boys answered yes, one of them giving me a good smack with his open hand, the other pushing the phallus into my wide-open mouth more firmly. I gave a desperate coughing sob and saw the Master step in front of me.

He wore a beautiful doublet of plum velvet with fancy balloon sleeves and looked every inch as fine as the Princes of the castle. And the warmth of our lovemaking last night swept over me and caused me to swallow my cries silently. But desperate unfamiliar sounds came from me.

I tried to restrain myself, but I was already so severely restrained that I seemed to lose all interior command. And pulling against all my bonds at once I realized

I was absolutely helpless. I could not even drop to my feet if I wanted to, and the strong ponies held me effortlessly.

My Master drew close and, turning my head roughly towards him, kissed both my eyelids. The tenderness of his lips, the clean fragrance of his skin and hair, brought back all the closeness of the bedchamber. But he was the Master. He had always been the Master, even when I rode him and made him groan under me. My cock writhed and a fresh volley of groans and cries broke from me.

I saw a long stiff flat thrash in his hand, which he tested now against one of the ponies. Two feet of it was rigid handle tapering out into another two feet of flat slapping leather that stood straight out when it was not being snapped at the pony's buttocks.

In a clear voice, he said: "The usual morning round of the village."

The ponies started off at once, and I stumbled into a march behind them.

My Master was walking beside me. It was just as it had been last night when the two of us had walked down this road, only now I was a prisoner of these monstrous straps, these tightly bound phalluses. And terrified of his correction, I tried to march well as he had taught me.

The pace was not too fast. But the flat snapping switch played with my welts. It stroked and petted the underside of my buttocks. My Master moved on in silence, and the pair ahead turned as if they knew the way, into a broad lane that led to the center of the village. It was the first real look I had had at the village on a regular day, and I was astonished.

White aprons, wooden clogs, rawhide breeches. Rolled sleeves and loud convivial voices. And everywhere there were toiling slaves. I saw naked Princesses scrubbing thresholds and balconies above and washing shop windows. I saw Princes bearing baskets on their backs, hopping ahead of their Mistress's lash as fast as they could, and through an open gateway a gathering of naked, reddened rumps around a great laundry tub.

A harness shop loomed ahead as we turned a bend, with a Princess manacled much as I was manacled and hanging from the shingle over the door, and then came a tavern in which I saw a row of slaves along a ramp waiting to be punished one by one on a little stage for the indifferent amusement of dozens of patrons. There was a phallus shop beside it, and on display in front three Princes squatting with their faces to the wall, their buttocks well outfitted with samples of the merchandise.

And I could be one of these, I thought, squatting in the hot dusty sun as the crowd passed. Was it worse than trotting with anxious breaths, my head and my hips pulled inexoraby forward, my sore flesh reanimated by the long, loud snapping behind me? I couldn't really see my Master. But with every lick, I saw him as he had been last night, and the ease with which he tormented me again astonished me. I had never dreamed it would stop because of our embraces. But for it to be intensified like this . . . I felt suddenly some awesome sense of the depth of submission he wanted from me.

The ponies pressed proudly through the thick crowd, making many a head turn, as villagers milled everywhere with market baskets or slaves at tether. And over and over, the observer glanced from the finely turned-out ponies to the slave behind them. But if I expected scornful looks, I was disappointed. What I saw was simply muted amusement. Everywhere these people looked they saw some delectable bit of naked flesh, punished or positioned or harnessed for their pleasure.

And as we turned corner after corner, rushing through this narrow lane and that, I felt more surely lost than I had been on the turntable.

Each day would have its dreadful course, its obliterating surprises. And though I wept more desperately when I thought of it, and my cock swelled in the lacings, and I marched harder, trying to squirm away from the snapping thrash, it gave a strange luster to my surroundings. I felt the undeniable urge to fall at my Master's feet, to tell him silently that I understood my lot, that I understood it more clearly with every excruciating trial and that I gave thanks from the depths of my being that he had seen fit to break me so thoroughly. Hadn't he used that word yesterday, "breaking" a new slave, said the thick phallus was good for it, and the phallus was splitting me wide again, and another stretched my mouth making my cries hoarse and wildly unmanageable.

Maybe he understood from my cries. If only he would condescend to comfort me with just a little touch of his lips. . . . And I realized almost with a start that never had I felt this softened and subservient in all the rigors of the castle.

We had come to a large square. All around I saw the signs of the Inns, and the carriageways and the high windows. Rich and fancy Inns they were, windows as ornate as those of a manor house. And as I was whipped and pulled in a broad circle around the well, the crowd agreeably letting the ponies through, I saw with a shock the Captain of the Queen's Guard lounging at a doorway.

It was unmistakably the Captain.

I remembered his blond hair and coarsley shaven beard and those brooding green eyes. Quite unforgettable. It was he who had taken me from my native land, captured me when I tried to break and run from the camp, and brought me back, my hands and ankles bound to a pole carried between two of his horsemen. I could still remember that thick cock spiking me and that silent smile as he ordered me whipped through the camp evening after evening until we reached the castle. And that strange inexplicable moment when we parted and both of us looked at each other.

"Good-bye, Tristan," he had said in the most cordial voice, and I had kissed his boot of my own will, my eyes still fixed on his silently.

My cock recognized him, too. And as I was drawn near to him, I was in sudden terror that he would see me.

My disgrace seemed too much to bear. All the strange rules of the Kingdom seemed for the moment immutable and just, and I was bound, penitent, condemned to the village. He would know I had been sent down from the castle to harsher treatment than even he had given me.

But he was watching something through the open door of the Sign of the Lion, and in one glance I saw the little spectacle. A lovely village woman with a pretty red skirt and white ruffled blouse was spanking her slave quite diligently upon a wooden counter, and the lovely face peering out through its tears was that of Beauty. She writhed and struggled under the paddle. But I could see she was unfettered, just as I had been last night on the Public Turntable.

We passed the door. The Captain looked up, and as if in a nightmare I heard my Master halt the ponies. I stood still, my cock straining against the leather. But this was inescapable. My Master and the Captain were greeting each other and exchanging pleasantries. And the Captain was admiring the ponies. Roughly he jerked the horsetail up in the one on the right, lifting and stroking the shining black hair, and then he pinched the red thigh of the slave as the slave tossed his head and sent a shiver through the harnesses. The Captain laughed.

"O, we have a little high spirits here!" he said, and he turned to the pony with both hands, apparently provoked by the gesture. He lifted the slave's chin and then the phallus and gave it several strong rocking upward jerks until the pony kicked and worked his legs friskily. Then came a soft pat on the rump, and the pony settled quietly.

"You know, Nicolas," he said in that familiar deep voice, able to strike fear with one syllable, "I've told her Majesty several times that she should give up her horses for short journeys and rely on slave ponies. We could outfit a great stable for her quickly enough, and I think she would find it delightful. But she sees it as a village occupation and won't really consider it."

"She has very particular taste, Captain," said my Master. "But tell me, have you ever seen this slave before?"

And to my horror he pulled my head back by the straps of the harness.

I could feel the Captain's eyes on me, though I didn't look. I could picture my cruelly stretched mouth, the straps of the harness scoring me.

He drew closer. He stood not three inches from me. And then I heard his low voice deeper still.

"Tristan!" and his large warm hand closed on my penis. He squeezed it hard, pinching the tip shut, and then let it go as sensation knotted at the end of it. He fondled my balls, pinching between his fingernails the covering of skin that was already pulled so tight around them by the lacings.

My face was scarlet. I couldn't meet his gaze, my teeth clamping down on the huge phallus as if I could devour it. I felt my jaws working, my tongue lapping the leather as if I were somehow forced to do it. He stroked my chest, my shoulders.

A flashing image of the camp returned, of being tethered to that great wooden X in a circle of X's and the soldiers standing idle about me, teasing my cock, educating it as I waited hour by hour for the evening whipping. And the Captain's secretive smile as he strode past, his gold cape over one shoulder.

"So that is his name," said my Master, his voice sounding young and more refined than the deep murmur of the Captain. "Tristan." And hearing him speak it further tormented me.

"Of course I know him," said the Captain. His large shadowy figure moved just a little to let a collection of young women pass, who were laughing and talking loudly.

"I brought him to the castle only six months ago. He was one of the wildest, broke and ran through the forest when he was ordered to strip, but I had him beautifully tamed when I put him at her Majesty's feet. He'd become the darling of the two soldiers whose duty it was to whip him daily through the camp. They missed him more than any slave they ever had to discipline."

I shivered silently, swallowing the sound, as the gag, strangely enough, made it all the harder.

"A rather volcanic passion," said that soft rumbling voice. "It wasn't the severity of the whippings that made him eat from my hand; it was the daily ritual."

O, how true, I thought. My face smarted. That fearsome, inevitable sense of nakedness again descended on me. I could still see the freshly turned earth before the tents, feel the straps and hear their steps and their conversation as they moved along with me. "Only one more tent, Tristan." Or that greeting every evening, "Come on, Tristan, time for our little trek through the camp, that's it, that's it, look at this, Gareth, how quickly this young man learns. What did I tell you, Geoffrey, that after three days I wouldn't have to use the manacles?" and their feeding me with their hands after, wiping my mouth almost affectionately and patting me and giving me too much wine to drink, and taking me out after dark into the forest. I remembered their cocks, the argument about who would go first, and whether it was better with the mouth or the anus, and sometimes one of them fore and one of them aft, and the Captain never very far away it seemed, and always smiling. So they had felt affection for me. It had not been my imagination. And neither was the warmth I felt for them. And a slow, undeniable realization was dawning on me.

"But he was one of the finest, most beautifully mannered of all the Princes," the Captain murmured, that voice seeming to come from his chest, not his mouth. I wanted suddenly to turn my head and look at him, see if he was just as handsome now as he had been then. My glimpse before had been too quick. "Given to Lord Stefan as his personal slave," he continued, "with the Queen's blessing. I am suprised to see him here." Anger crept into his voice. "I told the Queen that I myself had broken him."

He lifted my head, pushed it this way and that. I realized with mounting tension that I had been almost silent all this while, struggling not to make a sound in his presence, but I was now about to give way, and at last I couldn't control it. I gave a low moan, but it was better than crying.

"What did you do? Look at me!" he said. "Did you displease the Queen?"

I shook my head no, but I wouldn't look into his eyes, my whole body seeming to swell under the harnessing.

"Was it Stefan you displeased?"

I nodded. I glanced into his eyes and away, unable to stand it. Some strange bond existed between me and this man. And no bond—that was the horror of it—existed between me and Stefan.

"And he'd been your lover before, hadn't he?" the Captain pushed, drawing close to my ear, though I knew my Master could hear him. "Years before he came to live in the Kingdom."

I nodded again.

"And that humiliation was more than you could bear?" he demanded. "You who were taught to part your buttocks for common soldiers?"

"No!" I cried behind the gag, shaking my head violently. My head was pounding. And that slow, inescapable realization that had begun only moments before became clearer and clearer.

Out of sheer frustration, I cried. If only I could explain.

But grasping the little silver buckle of the phallus in my mouth, the Captain pushed my head back.

"Or was it," he said, "that your former lover didn't have the strength to master you?"

I turned my eyes, staring directly at him now, and if one can be said to smile with such a gag in one's mouth,

I smiled. I heard my own sigh come slowly. And then despite his hand on the phallus, I nodded.

His face was clear and beautiful as I remembered. I saw his full and robust figure in the sun as he took the snapping thrash from my Master. And as we looked each other in the eye, he commenced to whip me.

Yes, the realization was complete. I had *wanted* the total degradation of the village. I could not bear Stefan's love, his tentativeness, his inability to govern me. And for his weakness in our predestined bond, I despised him.

Beauty had understood my aims. She had known my soul better than I knew it. This was what I deserved and hungered for because it was as violent as the soldiers' camp, where my dignity, my pride, my self had been so thoroughly plundered.

Punishment—here in this busy, sun-drenched square, even with the little village girls gathering round, and a woman standing in the door of the Inn with her arms folded, and the loud snapping blows of the thrash—punishment was what I deserved, thirsted for, even in terror. And in a moment of utter surrender I spread my legs wide and thrust my head back and rocked my hips in a gesture of total recognition of the whipping.

The Captain gave great swinging sweeps with the flat lash.

My body was alive with the stings and hurts he had inflicted. And surely my Master understood the secret. And there would be no mercy for me as, reading this little dialogue, my Master would take me the full journey no matter how I might later plead with whines and whimpers.

The whipping was over but I did not break my supplicating position. And the Captain gave back the thrash and caressed my face suddenly, impulsively it seemed, kissing my eyelids just as my Master had done. The last knot in me broke. It was agony that I couldn't kiss his feet, his hands, his lips. That I could only incline my tortured body towards him.

He drew back, his arm out to my Master. I saw them embrace rather naturally it seemed, my Master slighter of build, elegant as a fine carved silver knife beside the solidly made Captain.

"It's always so," the Captain said with a slow smile, looking into my Master's cold and clever eyes. "Out of a batch of a hundred timid and anxious little slaves sent down for purification, there are those who have invited the punishment, needing the rigors not to purify their faults but to tame their boundless appetites."

It was so true that I was weeping, struck to the soul by the incentives this would give to all my tormentors.

"But please," I wanted to plead, "we don't know what we do to ourselves. Please have mercy."

"My little girl at the Sign of the Lion, Beauty, is the same," the Captain said. "A naked ravenous soul that foments the passion in me dangerously."

Beauty. And he had been watching her through the Inn door. So he was her Master. I felt a divine ripple of jealousy and solace.

My Master's eyes pierced me. The sobs shook me, the spasms passing through my cock and my sore calves.

But the Captain was at my side. "I'll see you again, my young friend," he breathed against my cheek, his lips tasting my face, it seemed, his tongue licking at my cruelly opened lips. "That is, with your gracious Master's permission."

I was inconsolable as we moved on, my low weeping turning heads as we marched out of the square and through other lanes, and past hundreds of other unfortunates. Had they been revealed as I was revealed, both to themselves and to their Masters and Mistresses?

So sore from the Captain's lashing that the merest flick of the thrash made me jump, I tried in no way to hold back, wailing as the ponies pulled me after them.

We passed through a narrow street where slaves for hire were hung by their hands and feet on the wall, pubes oiled and glistening, prices scratched upon the plaster above them. In a little shop, I saw a naked seamstress pinning up a hem, and in a small open place a band of naked Princes driving a treadmill. Princes and Princesses alike knelt here and there with trays of fresh cakes for sale, no doubt from the Master or Mistress's oven, a little basket hanging from the mouth of the slave to humbly receive the coins of the purchaser.

All the regular life of the village passing as if my misery did not exist, was not so loudly lamented.

A poor Princess chained to a wall whimpered and struggled as three laughing village girls idly stroked and teased her pubis.

And though I saw nowhere the theatrical savagery of the Public Punishment Grounds the night before, it was magnificent, and horrifying, this daily life of the village.

In a doorway, a buxom matron on a stool soundly spanked a naked Prince over her knee with her thick broad hand as she castigated him angrily. And a Princess holding with two hands a water jug on her head waited meekly as her Master implanted between her red pubic lips a good-size phallus with a leash attached, by which he made her smartly follow.

And we were now in quieter streets, streets where men of property and position lodged, and there were shiny doors with brass knockers. And from the high iron brackets above, slaves hung here and there as ornaments. The hush descended and the horseshoes of the ponies sounded louder and sharper up the walls, and I heard my weeping more clearly.

I could not think what the days held in store for me. So solid it all seemed, the population so accustomed to our wails, our servitude nourishing the place as surely as meat and drink, and sunshine.

And through it all, I was to be borne along on a wave of desire and surrender.

We had come round again to my Master's lodgings.

My lodgings. We passed the front door, quite as ornate as any we had seen, and the large costly leaded glass windows. And we went round the corner, through the little lane to the back road along the ramparts.

The straps and phalluses were stripped away in a great rush, the ponies sent off, and I collapsed at my Master's feet, kissing them all over. I kissed the insteps of the smooth morocco boots, the heels, the lacings. My agonized sobs broke louder and louder.

What was I pleading? Yes, make me your abject slave, be merciless. But I am frightened, frightened.

And in a moment of pure madness I wished he would take me again to the place of Public Punishment. I would have rushed with all my strength to the Public Turntable.

But he only turned to go into the house, and I came on hands and knees after him, lapping at his boots, giving darting kisses as he walked, following him down the corridor, until he left me in the small kitchen.

I was bathed, fed by the young male servants. No slaves worked in this house. I alone was kept, it seemed, for torment.

And quietly, without the slightest explanation, I was brought into a small supper room. Quickly I was stood up against the wall and chained with legs and arms in the form of an X and left there.

The room was polished and neat—I could see all of it now—a real rich little village-house room such as I never knew in the castle where I was born and reared, or in the Queen's castle. The low beams of its ceiling were painted and decorated with flowers, and I felt as I had when I first entered this house, huge and shamefully exposed in it, a true slave bound there among the shelves of gleaming pewter and the high-backed oak chairs and clean-swept chimneypiece.

But my feet were flat on the waxed floor, and I could rest my weight on them and rest back against the plaster.

And if only my cock would go to sleep, I thought, I could rest also.

The maids came and went with their brooms and mops, arguing about supper, whether to roast the beef with red wine or white, and whether to put in the onion now or later. They took no note of me except to pat me gently as they passed, dusting about me, fussing, and I smiled, listening to this chatter. But just as I was dozing off, I opened my eyes with a start to see the lovely face and form of my dark-haired Mistress.

She touched my cock, bending it down, and it came to life violently. She had several small black leather weights in her hands with clamps like those I had worn on my nipples yesterday, and as the maids talked on behind a closed door, she applied these clamps to the loose skin of my scrotum. I winced. I couldn't keep still. The weights were just heavy enough to make me painfully aware of every inch of the sensitive flesh and of the slightest shift of my balls—and a thousand such shifts seemed inevitable. She worked thoughtfully, pinching the skin as the Captain had pinched it with his fingernails. When I flinched she took no note of it.

Then she manacled my penis at the base with a heavy weight dangling beneath it, and as my organ bobbed I felt the coldness of the iron weight against my testicles. The touch of these things, their movements, were unendurable reminders of these bulging organs, this degrading exposure.

The little room grew dim and close. Her figure loomed large before me. I clenched my teeth hard not to plead with some mortifying little cry, and then that sense of surrender returned, and I pleaded quietly with low sighs and moans. I had been a fool to think I would be let alone.

"You will wear these," she said, "until your Master sends for you. And if that weight slips from your cock, there will be only one reason for it, that your cock has gone soft and released the manacle. And your cock will be whipped for that, Tristan."

I nodded as she waited, unable to meet her gaze.

"Do you need that whipping now?" she asked.

I knew better than to answer. If I said no, she would laugh and take it as impertinence. If I said yes, I was sure she would be outraged and the whipping must follow.

But she had already lifted a little delicate white strap from beneath her dark blue apron. I gave a series of short sighs. But she whipped my penis this way and that, sending shocks through all my loins, my hips lifting towards her. All the little weights pulled at me, like fingers stretching my skin and tugging on my cock. And the organ itself was purplish red, jetting straight forward.

"That is only a little example," she said. "When on display in this household, you must be turned out properly."

Again I nodded. I bowed my head and felt the hot beads of tears at the corners of my eyes. She lifted a comb to my hair and ran it through carefully and gently, arranging the curls neatly over my ears and drawing them back from my forehead. "I must tell you," she whispered "you are easily the most beautiful Prince in the village. I warn you, young man, you're in good danger of being bought outright. But I don't know what you could do to prevent it. Misbehave and you need the village all the more. Thrash your handsome hips in charming submission and you make yourself just as seductive. Already, there may be no hope for you. Nicolas has wealth enough to purchase you for three years, should he so desire. I'd love to see the muscles in those calves after three years of pulling my coach, or Nicolas's little walks through the village."

I had lifted my head and I was staring down into her blue eyes. Surely she could see I was puzzled. Could we be made to remain here?

"O, he can make a good argument for keeping you," she said. "That you need the discipline of the village, or perhaps even only that he has at last found the slave he desires. He is no Lord, but he is the Queen's Chronicler."

There was a growing warmth in my chest, pulsing like the slow fire in my cock. But Stefan would never . . . But then maybe Nicolas was in higher favor than Stefan!

"He has at last found the slave he desires." The words were crashing in my head.

But she left me to my own whirling, challenging thoughts in the little room and went out in the dim little hallway and up the dark steps, her burgundy skirts bright in the shadows for only a moment.

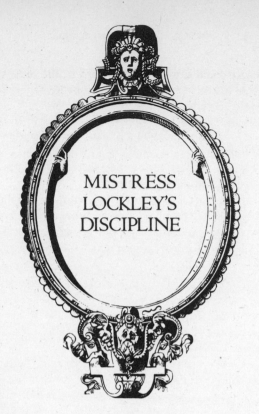

MISTRESS
LOCKLEY'S
DISCIPLINE

Beauty HAD almost completed her morning chores in the Captain's bedchamber when she remembered with a sudden shock her impertinence to Mistress Lockley.

The recollection came to her along with the faint sound of steps advancing towards the door of the Captain's room from the stairway. She was suddenly terrified. O, why had she been so insolent! All her resolve to be a bad, bad little girl abandoned her immediately.

The door opened and the pert figure of Mistress Lockley appeared, all fresh linen and lovely blue ribbons, her blouse brought down so low over her mounded breasts that Beauty could almost see the nipples. The most wicked smile was on Mistress Lockley's exquisite face, and she came right towards Beauty.

Beauty dropped the broom and shrank into the corner.

A low laughter erupted from her Mistress, and at once she had Beauty's long hair twined around her left hand and with her right hand she picked up the broom and thrust its prickly straws into Beauty's sex so that Beauty cried and tried to squeeze her legs together.

"My little slave with a tongue!" she said. And Beauty began to sob. But she couldn't free herself to kiss Mistress Lockley's boots and she didn't dare speak. All she could think of was Tristan telling her it would take a lot of courage to be bad all the time!

Mistress Lockley forced her forward on her hands and knees, and Beauty felt the broom between her legs driving her out of the little bedchamber.

"Get down those stairs!" The Mistress said under her breath, her ferocity scorching Beauty's soul so that she broke into sobs and scurried towards the stairway. She had to stand to descend the stairs, but the broom drove her just as maliciously, plunged into her, tickling and scratching at her tender nether lips as Mistress Lockley came right down behind her.

The Inn was empty, quiet.

"I've sent my bad children off to the Punishment Shop for their morning licking so I could tend to you!" came the Mistress's voice between her tightly clamped jaws. "We're going to have a little session in how to properly use that tongue when it is called upon to be used! Now into the kitchen!"

Beauty fell to her hands and knees again, desperate to obey, the angry commands pushing her to panic. No one had ever flashed upon her with such withering heat before, and to make matters worse, her sex was already brimming with sensation.

Sunlight filled the large immaculate room, pouring

in from the two open doors to the rear yard, striking the fine copper pots and pans that hung from the hooks above, and washing over the iron oven doors in the bricks and the giant rectangular cutting block that stood in the middle of the tile floor, as high and large as the drinking counter outside where Beauty had first been punished.

Mistress Lockley brought her to her feet, and plunging the broom hard between her legs so that its stiff straws lifted her, she forced Beauty back against the cutting block and then lifted her legs so that Beauty quickly scrambled up on the wood that was covered with a light sprinkling of flour.

It was the paddle Beauty expected, and it would be worse than ever before, she knew, with that angry voice driving it. But Mistress Lockley spread Beauty out on her back, drew her hands over her head, and quickly tied them to the edge of the board, telling Beauty to spread her legs or have them spread for her.

Beauty struggled to get her legs wide. The flour on the smooth wood felt silky under her bottom. But her body was being stretched to its full length as her ankles were now tied, and Beauty felt panic again, bouncing helplessly on the smooth unyielding wood as she realized she could not free herself.

In a flurry of soft urgent cries she tried to plead with Mistress Lockley. But the moment she saw Mistress Lockley smiling down at her, Beauty's voice died in her throat and she bit her lip hard, looking up into the clear black eyes that quivered ever so slightly with laughter.

"The soldiers liked those breasts, didn't they?" Mistress Lockley said. And reaching with both hands, she pinched Beauty's nipples between thumb and forefinger. "Answer me!"

"Yes, Mistress," Beauty wailed, her soul quaking with the sense of her vulnerability to those fingers, the flesh around her nipples shriveling as the nipples themselves hardened to knots. A deep pang between her legs caused her to try to close her legs, when that was quite impossible. "Mistress, please, I will never—"

"Shhhh!" Mistress Lockley clamped her hand over Beauty's mouth and Beauty arched her back, sobbing against it. O, it was worse being bound; she could not make herself be still. But she stared at Mistress Lockley with wide eyes and tried to nod, though the hand held her.

"Slaves have no voice," said the Mistress, "until the Master or Mistress asks to hear that voice, and then you answer with the proper respect." She let go of Beauty's mouth.

"Yes, Mistress," Beauty answered.

The firm fingers took hold of her nipples again. "As I was saying," Mistress Lockley went on, "the soldiers liked these breasts."

"Yes, Mistress!" Beauty answered, her voice quavering.

"And this avaricious little mouth." She reached down and pinched shut the pubic lips so that the moisture overflowed and Beauty felt an itch as it trickled.

"Yes, Mistress," she answered breathlessly.

Mistress Lockley lifted a white leather belt and showed it to Beauty, like a tongue extending from her hand. And gathering Beauty's left breast from the top in her left fingers, she bunched the flesh and plumped it as Beauty felt the warmth suffusing her bosom. Beauty couldn't keep quiet. And the moisture between her legs trickled down into the crack of her buttocks. Her spread-eagle body strained in vain to close itself.

The fingers stretched her left nipple and snapped it. And then the white tongue of the leather belt spanked her breast in a series of hard loud slaps. "O!" Beauty gasped aloud, unable to prevent it. The spanking that the Captain's large warm hands had given her bosom was nothing like this. The desire to break free and cover her breasts, both of them, was irresistible and impossible! Yet the breast seethed with feeling as never before and Beauty's body twisted against the wood. The little strap spanked the nipple and the bulging flesh harder and harder.

Beauty was in a frenzy as Mistress Lockley turned her attention to the right breast, plumping it in the same manner, snapping the nipple. Beauty's cries grew louder, her struggling more violent. The nipple was rock hard under the torrent of licks.

Beauty closed her mouth, sealed it shut. She would have screamed at the top of her lungs, "No, I can't bear it." The concentrated blows came faster and faster. Her body became her tortured breasts, her desire fanned by the licks like a torch flame.

Beauty swung her head so violently that the hair streamed over her face. But Mistress Lockley lifted it back and she bent down and looked at Beauty, but Beauty could not look up at her.

"So tumultuous, so exposed!" she said to Beauty, and she kneaded the right breast, pumping it up high again, and then continued to spank it. Beauty gave a high keening scream against her clenched teeth. The fingers tweaked the nipples, massaged the flesh, and the heat roared through Beauty, her hips thrust upwards in a sudden violent convulsion.

"This is how a bad little girl should be punished," the Mistress said.

"Yes, Mistress," Beauty sobbed immediately.

Mercifully the fingers were withdrawn. Beauty's breasts felt huge, heavy, a riot of warm pain and thumping sensation against her. Her low, raw sighs caught in her throat.

And she whimpered when she realized what was coming. She could feel Mistress Lockley's fingers between her legs, pushing the lips apart even as Beauty sought to close herself, the muscles in her legs straining vainly. Her heels thumped the wood, the leather straps pressing into the flesh of her insteps. Again she lost all control, struggling violently in a deluge of tears. But the licking strap was slapping her clitoris. She screamed again at the searing intensity of the mixture of pleasure and pain, her clitoris seeming to harden as never before, the strap snapping up at it over and over as Mistress Lockley swung from beneath the sex with her right hand.

Beauty could feel the lips puffing, the moisture squirting, the slaps sounding wetter and wetter. Her head rolled on the wood; she cried louder and louder, her hips riding up to meet the strap, her whole sex a formless explosion of fire in her.

The strap stopped. It was worse, the heat rising, the tingling like an itch that must somehow find its divine friction. Beauty's breath came in short imploring pants in time with her moans, and through her tears she saw Mistress Lockley looking down at her.

"Are you my impertinent slave?" she asked.

"Your devoted slave," Beauty choked through her tears, "Mistress. Your devoted slave." And she bit her lip, grimacing, praying it was the right answer.

Her breasts and her sex were boiling with the heat, and she heard her hips spanking the wood beneath them, though she had no awareness of moving them. Through the mist of tears she saw the Mistress's pretty black eyes, the black hair with its fancy little braid over the crown of the head, and the breasts swelling so beautifully in the snow-white linen blouse with its thick ruffle. But the Mistress was holding something in her hands. What was it? It was moving.

And Beauty saw it was a big, pretty white cat that stared at her with almond-shaped blue eyes in that wide, inquisitive manner cats have, its pink tongue licking its black nose in a quick gesture.

A wave of absolute shame overcame Beauty. She writhed on the board, a helpless and suffering creature, even more lowly than this proud, disdainful little beast that peered at her from the Mistress's arms with jeweled eyes. But the Mistress had bent down, apparently to reach for something.

And Beauty saw her rise again with a thick dab of yellow cream on her fingers. The fingers smeared the cream to Beauty's throbbing nipples and dabbed it between her legs so that it dripped and slid in dollops into her vagina.

"Just butter, my sweet, fresh butter," said the Mistress. "No perfumed ointments here." And suddenly she dropped the cat on all fours on Beauty's tender belly and chest, and Beauty felt the soft pads of the cat's feet moving up her chest with maddening quickness.

She squirmed, pulled on the straps. The little beast had dipped its head, and the rough, sandy little tongue was eating at her nipple, devouring the butter that covered it. Some deep, deep, hitherto unknown fear made itself known, sending Beauty into wilder and wilder struggles.

But the indifferent little monster with its exquisite white face ate on and on, the nipple exploding under the licks, and Beauty's whole body went tense, lifting itself off the wood and thudding down again.

The creature was lifted, taken to the right breast, and Beauty pulled with all her strength on the straps, the sobs shaking out of her, the little hind feet padding deeply into her belly, the soft stomach hairs of the cat brushing her as the tongue lapped again, cleaning the nipple thoroughly.

Beauty clenched her teeth not to scream the word "No," her eyes squeezing shut again, only to open on the sight of the heart-shaped face dipping down in short quick movements as the tongue lapped, the nipple pushed back and forth by the strength of the sandy lick, the sensation so exquisite, so dreadful, that Beauty screamed louder than she had ever screamed under the paddle.

But the cat was being lifted. Beauty thrashed from side to side, clenching her teeth harder on the "No" that must not come out as she felt those silky ears and that fur between her legs, and the tongue darting at her distended clitoris. "O, but please, no, no," she screamed in the sanctuary of her mind, even as the pleasure jetted through her, mingling with the loathing of the hairy little feline and its horrid mindless feasting. Her hips froze in the air, inches above the wood, the furry nose and mouth pushing deeper and deeper into her. No more tongue on the clitoris, just the maddening brushing of the top of the head against it, and it wasn't enough, it wasn't enough. O, the little monster!

To her utter shame and defeat, Beauty struggled to press her pubis against the creature, to press on the little skull, to make it stroke the clitoris with the slightest pressure. But the tongue had gone down lower, lapping the base of her vagina, lapping the crack of her buttocks, and her sex hungered vainly as the pleasure passed into a high-pitched torment.

Beauty gritted her teeth and shook her head about as the tongue lapped at her pubic hair, as it took what it wanted, oblivious to the desire that racked her.

And when she thought she could stand it no more, that she would go mad, the cat was lifted away. It peered down at her from Mistress Lockley's arms, the Mistress smiling just as sweetly as the cat smiled, it seemed, above her.

"Witch!" Beauty thought, but she did not dare to speak, and she closed her eyes, her sex quivering with all the desire she had ever known collected in it.

Mistress Lockley released the cat. It was gone, out of sight. And Beauty felt the straps on her wrists released, and then the straps on her ankles.

She lay shuddering, resisting with all her will the desire to close her legs, to turn over on the board, hugging her breasts with one hand while with the other she touched her burning sex in an orgy of private pleasure.

There would be no such mercy for her.

"Get down on your hands and knees," said Mistress Lockley. "I think you're finally ready for the paddle."

Beauty climbed to the floor.

And in confusion she turned to hurry after the little

boots that were already far away as they clicked sharply out of the kitchen.

The movement of her legs as she crawled only intensified the craving in her.

And when they reached the counter in the front room of the Inn, she climbed up at once to the snap of Mistress Lockley's fingers.

People were passing back and forth in the square; they chatted at the rim of the well. Two village girls came in with a cheerful hello to Mistress Lockley as they proceeded past her into the kitchen.

Beauty lay shuddering, her little cries like stutters, her chin propped, her buttocks waiting for the paddle.

"You remember I told you I'd cook your buttocks for breakfast!" Mistress Lockley said in that cold, toneless voice.

"Yes, Mistress!" Beauty sobbed.

"No words from you now. Only the nod of that head!"

Beauty nodded, despite her propped head, furiously.

Her sore breasts were pure warmth against the wood, her sex dripping. The tension was unbearable.

"You've been well sauced in your own juices," Mistress Lockley asked, "now, haven't you?"

Beauty gave forth a loud whimpering wail, not knowing how to answer.

Mistress Lockley's hand kneaded her buttocks hard, plumped them as she had done the breasts.

And then they came, the hard punishing spanks, and Beauty bounced and writhed and cried behind her teeth as if she had never known resistance, dignity. Anything to please this dreadful, cold, uncompromising Mistress, anything to make her know Beauty would be good, she wasn't a bad girl, she had been all wrong. And Tristan had warned her. The spanking went on and on, truly chastising her.

"Is that hot enough, is that well done enough?!" the

Mistress demanded, driving the paddle ever faster and faster. She stopped and laid her cool open hand on the blazing skin. "Yes, I think we have a nice well-done little Princess!"

And she flailed again, Beauty's sobs pouring as if they had been purged out of her.

And the thought that she must wait till evening, wait for the Captain before her tormented sex would know its release, brought the sobs out of her in almost luscious abandon.

It was over. The cracks still rang in her ears. She could still feel the paddle as if in a dream. And her sex was like a hollow chamber in which all the pleasures she had known left their loud, reverberating echo. And it would be hours and hours before the Captain came. Hours and hours . . .

"Get up and get down on your knees," Mistress Lockley had just said. Why was she hesitating?

She dropped to the floor and pressed her lips frantically to Mistress Lockley's boots, kissing the sharp little points of the toes, the shapely little ankles showing beneath the fine casing of leather. She felt Mistress Lockley's petticoats on her damp forehead and on the hair, and her kisses became all the more fervent.

"Now you'll work to clean this Inn from top to bottom," Mistress Lockley said, "and you'll keep your legs wide apart as you do it."

Beauty nodded.

Mistress Lockley walked away from her towards the Inn door. "Where are my other lovelies?" she murmured crossly under her breath. "The Punishment Shop takes forever."

Beauty knelt looking at Mistress Lockley's fine little figure against the light of the door, the tiny waist so flattered by the white band and sash of the apron. Beauty sniffled. "Tristan, you were right," she thought. "It's hard to be bad all the time." And she wiped her nose on the back of her hand silently.

(141)

The big white slinky cat came round, padding into view only inches from Beauty. And she shrank back, biting her lip again, and then she covered her head with her arms, because Mistress Lockley was just idly leaning on the Inn door, and the great furry cat was coming closer and closer.

CONVERSA-
TION
WITH
PRINCE
RICHARD

IT WAS late afternoon.
Beauty lay on the cool grass with the other slaves, stirred
only now and then by the prodding stick of one of the
kitchen girls, who forced her legs apart roughly. Yes, she
must not press her legs together, she thought drowsily.

The day's work had exhausted her. She had dropped
a handful of pewter spoons and been chained upside down
to the kitchen wall for an hour. On all fours, she had
carried the heavy laundry baskets on her back to the
clotheslines and knelt still while the village girls, hanging
up the sheets, chatted around her. She had scrubbed and
cleaned and polished, and been paddled at every evidence

of clumsiness or hesitation. And kneeling, she had lapped her dinner from the same big dish as the other slaves, silently thankful for the cool spring water that followed.

Now it was time to sleep, and she had been dozing, more or less, for over an hour.

But very slowly, she realized that no one was about. She was alone with the sleeping slaves, and she saw that the beautiful red-haired Prince was lying opposite her, his cheek against his hand, looking at her.

He was the one she had seen the night before kissing the soldier as he sat on the soldier's lap. He smiled now and with his right fingers blew a little kiss to Beauty.

"What did Mistress Lockley *do* to you this morning?" he whispered.

Beauty flushed.

He reached over and covered her hand with his. "It's all right," he whispered. "We *love* going to the Punishment Shop." He said. And he laughed under his breath.

"How long have you been here?" she asked. He was even more beautiful than Prince Roger. She had seen no slave at the castle who was any more aristocratic. The features of his face were strong like Tristan's features, but he had a smaller build and was more boyish.

"I was sent down from the castle a year ago. My name is Prince Richard. I was at the castle for six months until I was declared incorrigible."

"But why were you so bad?" Beauty asked. "Was it deliberate?"

"Not at all," he said. "I tried to obey, but I would panic and run into the corner. Or I simply could not perform a task for the shame and humiliation I felt. I couldn't command myself. I was passionate as you are passionate. Every paddle and cock and lovely lady's hand that touched me elicited some mortifying display of uncontrollable pleasure. But I couldn't obey. And so I was auctioned off for a full year to be tamed here."

"And now?" Beauty asked.

"I've come very far," he said. "I've been taught. And

I owe it to Mistress Lockley. If it hadn't been for Mistress Lockley I don't know what would have happened to me. Mistress Lockley bound me, punished me, harnessed me, and took me through a dozen forced tasks before she expected anything of my will. Every other night I was paddled on the Public Turntable, made to run the circle of the Maypole. I was fastened in a tent in the Punishment Place and had to take all the cocks that came to me. I was teased and persecuted by the young women. I spent the day usually dangling beneath the sign of the Inn. And I was bound hand and foot for the daily paddling. And only after a good four weeks of that was I unbound and ordered to light the fire and set the table. I tell you I covered her boots with kisses. I lapped the food literally from the palm of her hand."

Slowly Beauty nodded. She was surprised it had taken him so long.

"I worship her," he said. "I shudder to think what would have happened if I had been bought by someone softer."

"Yes," Beauty admitted, and the blood flooded to her face again. She felt it too in her sore buttocks.

"I never thought I could lie still on the bar for the morning paddling," he said. "I never thought I could be sent unbound through the streets to the Place of Punishment or that I would climb the steps and kneel on the Public Turntable without fetters. Or that I could be sent to the nearby Punishment Shop where we went this morning, but now I can do any of those things. Nor did I think I could pleasure the soldiers of the garrison without shrinking or showing panic when they pinioned me. But there is nothing I can't endure completely."

He paused. "You've already learned these things," he said. "I could tell it last night and today. Mistress Lockley loves you."

"She does!" Beauty felt a strong swimming desire in her loins. "O, you must be mistaken."

"No, I'm not. It's difficult for a slave to claim Mistress Lockley's attention. She rarely takes her eyes off you when you're about."

Beauty's heart began to race silently inside her.

"You know, I've something terrible to tell you," said the Prince.

"You don't have to tell me. I know," Beauty whispered. "Now that your year is up, you can't bear the thought of returning to the castle."

"Yes, precisely," he said. "Not because I can't obey and please. I'm quite sure of that. But it's . . . different."

"I know," Beauty said. But her head was teeming. So her cruel Mistress loved her, did she? And why did it give Beauty so much satisfaction? She'd never truly cared that Lady Juliana at the castle adored her. And this mean, proud little Innkeeper and the handsome, remote Captain of the Guard were touching her heart strangely.

"I need hard punishment," Prince Richard said, "I need direct commands, to know my place without hesitation. I don't welcome again those tender groomings and all that flattery. I'd rather be thrown over the Captain's horse and taken out to the camp and tethered to the hitching post there and used that way as I have been."

The image flashed brightly before Beauty. "Has the Captain of the Guard taken you?" she asked shyly.

"O, yes, of course," he said. "But never fear. I saw him last night. And he's quite in love with you, too, and when it comes to Princes, he likes them a little heartier than I, though now and then . . ." He smiled.

"And you have to go back to the castle?" Beauty asked.

"I don't know. Mistress Lockley is in great favor with the Queen because much of the Queen's garrison lodges here. And Mistress Lockley could keep me here, I think, if she paid for me. I earn much for the Inn. And any time I'm sent to the Punishment Shop the customers there pay for my penance. There are always people gathered there, having coffee, talking, women sewing . . . watching the slaves spanked one by one. And though the Master and

Mistress must pay for the service, the customers can add ten pence for another good licking if they desire it. I'm almost always licked three times there, and half that money goes to the shop and half to my Mistress. So I've earned back my price many many times by now and could earn it again if Mistress Lockley wants to keep me."

"O, I must be able to do it too!" Beauty whispered. "Maybe I have proved too obedient too soon!" Her mouth twisted in anguish.

"No, you haven't. What you must do is endear yourself to Mistress Lockley. And you don't do that with disobedience. You do it with a good show of submission. And when you go to the Punishment Shop—and you surely will, as she hasn't the time to paddle us properly every day—you must put up the best show you can, no matter how hard it is. And in some ways its harder than the Public Turntable."

"But why? I saw the turntable and it looked dreadful."

"The Punishment Shop is more intimate and less theatrical," the Prince explained. "The place is crowded, as I told you. Slaves are lined up on a low ramp along the left wall, each waiting as we waited this morning. Then there's the Master with his attendant on the little stage, hardly four feet off the floor, and the tables with the customers are right up against the ramp and the stage, and the customers are laughing and talking amongst themselves, ignoring most of what goes on, only commenting casually.

"But if they like a slave, they'll stop talking and watch. You can see them out of the corner of your eye with their elbows on the edge of the stage, and then the shouts of 'ten pence' and it starts again. The Master is a big rough man. You're thrown right over his knee. He wears a leather apron. He greases you hard before he begins and you're thankful for it. It makes the spanks sting more but it saves your skin, really. And the attendant props your chin and waits to drive you off. And there's a lot of laughing and talking from them both. The Master always squeezes me hard and asks me if I'm being a good little boy, exactly the way he'd talk to a dog, that same voice. He roughs up my hair and teases me mercilessly about my cock and warns me to keep my hips up high so that my cock doesn't disgrace itself on his apron.

"One morning I remember a Prince did come in the Master's lap. And how he was punished. The paddling was merciless and then he was driven round and round through the tavern at a squat, made to touch the tip of his cock to each boot in the place to beg forgiveness while he kept his hands behind his neck. You should have seen him squirming in and out, the patrons sometimes taking pity and tousling his hair, but most of the time ignoring him. And then he was led home at that same painful, disgraceful squat, his cock laced to point straight at the ground in disgrace, and it was hard enough again by that time. In the evening when the customers are drinking wine and the place is ablaze with candles, it can be worse than the Public Turntable. I've never broken down and wailed and whimpered so much for mercy on the Public Turntable."

Beauty was quietly enthralled.

"One night in the shop," the Prince continued, "I remember I was bought three lickings after the one ordered by the Mistress. I thought surely I wouldn't have to take the fourth, it was too much, I was sobbing, and there was a good long line of slaves waiting. But that hand came up with the grease again to rub my welts and scrapes and slap my cock, and I was riding that knee again, putting on an even better show than the ones before it. And the sack of money isn't put into your mouth to bring home as at the Public Turntable. It's shoved good and proper in your anus with the little drawstrings hanging out. And that night I was forced through the whole tavern afterwards, to every table for extra copper coins, and they pushed those into me until I was stuffed as well as a fowl for roasting. Mistress Lockley was delighted with the money I'd earned. But my buttocks were so sore that when she touched them with her fingers I cried frantically. I thought she'd have mercy on me, at least on my cock, but not Mistress Lockley. She gave me to the soldiers that night as always. I had to sit on many a rough lap with those sore buttocks, and my cock was stroked and tormented and slapped I don't know how many times before I was finally allowed to plunge it into a hot little Princess. Even then I was being whipped with a belt to drive me on. And when I came the blows didn't stop, they just went right on. The Mistress said I had very resilient skin, that many slaves couldn't have taken it. After that she saw I got as much as I could take, just as she told me she would."

Beauty was too stunned to say anything. "And I will be sent there," she finally murmured.

"O, surely. At least twice a week we're packed off, all of us. It's only a little ways up the lane, and we're sent on our own, and for some reason, that always seems a terrible part of the punishment. But don't be afraid when the time comes. Just remember, if you come back with that little bag of coins in your buttocks, you'll make the Mistress very happy."

Beauty laid her cheek against the cool grass. "I don't ever want to go back to the castle," she thought. "I don't care how hard it is here, how frightening!" She looked at Prince Richard. "Have you ever thought of running away?" she asked. "I wonder if the Princes don't think of that."

"No," he laughed. "And it was a Princess who ran away last night, by the way. And I'll tell you a secret. They haven't found her. They don't want anyone to know either. Go back to sleep now. The Captain will be in a terrible frame of mind tonight if they haven't captured her by that time. You don't think of running away, do you?"

"No," Beauty shook her head.

He turned to the Inn door. "I think I hear them coming. Go on back to sleep if you can. We have another hour or so."

PUBLIC
TENTS

I N THE early evening, I was
a pony again, safe in my harnesses, thinking almost sar-
donically of my trepidation the night before when the tail
and the bit had seen such unthinkable humiliations. We
reached the manor house before dark, and I was singled
out to be made a footstool for my master for hours beneath the dining table.

The conversation was long. Others were there, rich
merchants and farmers of the town, talking of crops and
weather and the price of the slaves, and the undeniable
fact that the village needed more slaves, not just the fine,
often temperamental little lovelies from the castle, but

solid lesser Tributes who need not ever see the Queen, the sons and daughters of petty nobles under her protection. Such slaves did come from time to time, right to auction in the marketplace. Why couldn't there be more?

My Master was fairly quiet all the time. I started living and breathing for the sound of his voice. But he laughed at this last suggestion and asked dryly, "And who would like to demand that of her Majesty?"

I listened to every word, gleaning, not so much knowledge I did not possess before, but an increased sense of my lowliness. They told little stories about bad slaves, punishments, common events they thought humorous. And it was as if none of the slaves serving the table or those used as footstools like myself had ears or sense, or need be given the slightest consideration.

Finally it was time to go.

With a bursting cock, I took my place to pull the coach back to the town house, wondering if the other ponies had been satisfied as usual in the stable.

And when we reached the village, and the ponies were sent off, my Mistress started to whip me on the short barefoot journey along the dark road to the Place of Public Punishment.

I started crying, weary and desperate from the exertions and the starvation of my loins. The Mistress wielded the strap more vigorously than had the Master. And I was deviled mercilessly by the realization that it was she behind me, in her lovely dress, driving me on with that little hand. The day seemed infinitely longer than the one before it, and whatever I'd felt earlier about welcoming the Public Turntable, I was now in frantic fear of it. My fear was worse than last night. I knew what it was to be whipped there. The Master's affection after seemed like some absurd flight of imagination.

But it wasn't the busy Maypole circle for me, or the brilliantly illuminated turntable.

I was driven through the flowing crowd, into one of the small tents behind the pillories. My Mistress paid ten pence at the entrance and then drew me after her into the shadows.

A naked Princess with long gleaming copper-colored braids squatted on a stool, knees wide, ankles bound together, her hands tethered to the tent pole high above her. She worked her hips desperately when she heard us come in, but her eyes were bound with a red silk blindfold.

When I saw the soft, sweet, moist sex glinting in the torchlight from the square, I thought I could no longer control myself.

I bowed my head, wondering what torment I should know now, but my Mistress said very gently that I was to rise.

"I've paid ten pence for you to have her, Tristan," she said.

I could scarce believe my ears. I turned first to kiss the Mistress's shoes, but she only laughed and told me to stand up and enjoy the girl as I wished.

I started to obey, but I stopped, my head still bowed, the grasping little sex right before my own, realizing that my Mistress stood very near watching. She even stroked my hair. And I understood I was to be looked at, even studied.

I gave a little shudder all over. And when I resigned myself to it, a new ingredient heightened my excitement. My cock darkened all the more and bobbed as if trying to pull me forward.

"Slowly, if you like," said my Mistress. "She's lovely enough to play with."

I nodded. The Princess had an exquisite little mouth, red shuddering lips that gave little gasps now of apprehension and anticipation. It could have been better only if Beauty were kneeling there.

I kissed the Princess violently, my hands greedily clutching her heavy little breasts and bouncing them and massaging them. She went into a paroxysm of longing. Her mouth sucked at mine, her body straining forward, and I lowered my head to suck at her breasts one by one, as she cried, her hips swaying wildly. It was almost too much to wait longer.

But I circled her, running my hands over her gorgeous buttocks, and as I pinched her little welts, very small welts really, she gave a lovely inviting moan and arched her back to show me her tender red sex from the rear as best she could, straining the rope that held her hands above her.

That was how I wanted to take her, her vagina from the rear, stabbing upwards, lifting her, and when I slid in, her tight little sex seemed almost too small and she gave loud gasps as I forced my way into the hot wet depth of her.

Her cries took on a despair. She was being well used, but her little clitoris wasn't being touched by my cock, I knew, and I wasn't going to disappoint her. I reached around her, finding the little core under its hood of wet skin, parting her plump lips a little roughly, and when I pinched the clitoris, she gave a sharp grateful cry, rocking her smooth little buttocks back against me.

My Mistress drew close. Her broad full skirts stroked my leg, and I felt her hand under my chin. It was agony to realize she was looking at me and would see my reddened face at the moment of climax.

But it was my lot. And an exultation swept me up right in the middle of the pleasure. I felt the Mistress's hand on my buttocks. I rammed the little Princess all the harder, feeling my Mistress's gaze, and caressed the wet clit with sharp rhythmic pressure.

My cock burst as I gritted my teeth, my face burning hot, my hips jerking helplessly. A long low groan was torn out of my chest. The Mistress held my head in her hands. And my breath came in loud relieved gasps, the little Princess crying with the same ecstasy.

I leaned forward, embracing the warm little body, and laid my head against the Princess's head, turning to face my Mistress. I felt her soothing fingers on my hair.

And her eyes fixed me steadily. She had a strange expression, thoughtful, almost penetrating. She turned her head a little to the side as if she were weighing some conclusion. And she put her hand on my shoulder to let me know I should stay still, embracing the Princess, and she whipped at my buttocks with the belt as I looked at her. I closed my eyes. But I opened them immediately again, smarting under the strap. And the oddest moment passed between us.

If I was saying something silent it was, "You are my Mistress. You own me. And I will not look away until you tell me to. I will look into what you are and what you do." And she seemed to hear this and to be fascinated.

She stood back and let me remain long enough to collect my strength. I kissed the little Princess's neck.

And then very tentatively I went down on my knees and kissed my Mistress's feet and the end of the strap hanging from her hand.

The little Princess had not been enough for me. My cock was already rising. I could have taken every proffered slave in every tent. And for one desperate moment I was tempted to kiss my Mistress's shoes again and wriggle my hips to tell her this. But the sheer vulgarity of it was beyond me. Besides, she might only have laughed and whipped me. No, I had to wait upon her will. And it seemed to me that in these two days, I had not failed, truly failed, in anything. I would not fail now either.

She sent me out into the square, the strap caressing me in the usual fashion. And her lovely little hand pointed to the bath stalls.

I glanced up at the Public Turntable, half afraid I might give her some idea by doing so, but unable not to look at it. An olive-skinned Princess I did not know was the victim, her black hair mounded on her head, her long, lusciously full body snapping under the cracking paddle without fetters. She looked splendid, her dark eyes narrowed and wet, her mouth open in wild cries. She seemed to be yielding utterly. The crowd danced and whooped, cheering her on. And before we reached the bath stall I saw her showered with coins as I had been.

While I was being bathed, one of the handsomest Princes I had ever beheld, Prince Dmitri from the castle, was taking his turn on the Public Turntable. And my cheeks stung with shame for him when I saw him bound down at the knees and at the neck, hands laced as the crowd scolded him. He sobbed over his leather gag and bridled under the paddling.

But my Mistress had seen me looking at the turntable and with a stab of panic I turned my eyes down.

And I kept them that way as I was driven home at a march along the back road and into the household.

Now I shall sleep in some dim corner somewhere, I thought, bound and perhaps even gagged. It's late and my cock is an iron rod between my legs and my Master is probably sleeping.

But I was being coaxed down the hall. I saw the light under his door. And knocking on the door, my Mistress smiled. "Good-bye, Tristan," she whispered and played with a little lock of my hair before leaving me there.

MISTRESS
LOCKLEY'S
AFFECTIONS

I<small>T</small> WAS almost dark when
Beauty awoke. The sky was still light, though a handful
of tiny stars had appeared. And Mistress Lockley, dressed
for the evening, no doubt, in red with embroidered puffed
sleeves, was sitting on the grass with her skirts in a lovely
circle. The wooden paddle was tethered to her apron sash,
but it was half buried in the white linen. She snapped her
fingers for the awakening slaves to come to her, and as
they gathered around her on their knees, sore buttocks
back on their heels, she gently fed them bits of fresh
peach and apple with her fingers.

"Good girl," she said stroking the chin of a lovely

brown-haired Princess as she put a bit of peeled apple into her eager mouth. And she pinched her nipple gently.

Beauty flushed. But the other slaves were in no way surprised by this sudden affection.

And when Mistress Lockley looked straight at her, Beauty leaned her head forward tentatively for the bit of wet fruit, shivering as the fingers stroked her sore nipples. In a rush of confusing sensation, she remembered every detail of the ordeal in the kitchen. Almost bashfully, she blushed again, glancing shyly at Prince Richard, who was looking at the Mistress eagerly.

Mistress Lockley's face was calm and pretty, her black hair a deep shadow behind her shoulders. She kissed Prince Richard, their open mouths interlocking, her hand stroking his erect penis and reaching down to cradle his balls. His little story had crept into Beauty's dreams as she slept on the grass, and Beauty felt a hot stab of jealousy and excitement. Prince Richard had an almost winsome attitude, his green eyes filled with good humor and his long, almost luscious mouth glistening with the moisture of the bit of peach that was pushed slowly into it.

Beauty did not know exactly why her heart was pounding.

In the same manner Mistress Lockley played with all the slaves. She fondled a little blond-haired Princess between the legs until she writhed like the white kitchen cat, and then made her open her mouth to catch the grapes that were dropped into it. Prince Roger she kissed even more lingeringly than she had Prince Richard, tugging at the dark pubic curls around his cock and examining his balls as he blushed as deeply as Beauty.

Then the Mistress sat as if thinking. It seemed to Beauty the slaves in subtle ways tried to keep her attention. The brown-haired Princess actually bent and kissed the tip of Mistress Lockley's shoe as it peeped from under her ruffled white petticoats.

But one of the kitchen girls was coming with a large flat bowl, which she set on the grass, and with a snap of the fingers, everyone was directed to lap the delicious red wine from it. Beauty had never tasted anything so sweet and good.

A heavy broth followed, with strongly spiced bits of tender meat.

Then the slaves gathered again and Mistress Lockley pointed to Prince Richard and to Beauty and gestured to the Inn door. The others shot them sharp hostile glances. "But what is happening?" Beauty thought. Richard moved on hands and knees as fast as he could, it seemed, but never losing his lithesome manner while doing it. And Beauty followed, feeling awkward in comparison.

Mistress Lockley led the way up the narrow steps behind the chimney and down the corridor past the door of the Captain's room to another bedroom.

As soon as the door closed, and Mistress Lockley lit the candles, Beauty realized it was a woman's chamber. The paneled bed was fitted with embroidered linen and dresses hung on hooks on the wall, and there was a large mirror above the fireplace.

Richard kissed Mistress Lockley's feet and looked up.

"Yes, you may take them off," she said, and as the Prince unlaced her boots, Mistress Lockley unlaced her own bodice and gave it to Beauty with the order to fold it neatly and put it on the table. At the sight of the loosening blouse, and the mark of the bodice lacings still pressed in the wrinkled linen, Beauty felt a tempest inside herself. Her breasts ached as if they were still being spanked on the kitchen cutting block. On her knees, Beauty obeyed the command, her hands trembling as she folded the fabric.

When she turned back Mistress Lockley had removed her ruffled white blouse altogether. The vision of her breasts was stunning. She untied the wooden paddle from her skirts, and then untied the skirts themselves. The Prince took the paddle and drew the skirts off her, and away from her feet. Then the petticoats came down and Beauty took them, her face beating with a strong blush again, as she glanced at the soft black curly pubic hair and the large breasts with their dark, upturned nipples.

Beauty folded the petticoat and laid it down, and timidly turned to look behind her. Mistress Lockley, naked as a slave, and easily as beautiful, her hair a black veil down her back, beckoned for both her slaves to come to her.

She reached for Beauty's head and brought it towards her slowly. Beauty's breath was hoarse and anxious. She was staring at the triangle of hair before her, the dark pink lips barely visible beneath it. She had seen hundreds of naked Princesses in all positions, yet the sight of this naked Mistress dazed her. Her face was moist all over. And of her own will she pressed her mouth to the glistening hair and the peeping lips, shrinking back as if they had been hot coals, her hands to her hot face uncertainly.

Then she put her open mouth on the sex, feeling the tight curls against her mouth, and the soft resilient lips unlike anything, it seemed, she had ever kissed before.

Miss Lockley thrust her hips forward while she lifted Beauty's hands and guided them to her hips so that Beauty suddenly wrapped her arms around Mistress Lockley. Beauty's breasts pumped as if they would burst the nipples, and her own sex convulsed feverishly. She opened her mouth wide and ran her tongue under the thick pooch of red folds, and suddenly forced her tongue between the lips, tasting the musky, salty juices. With a wrenching sigh, she hugged Mistress Lockley tightly. Vaguely she was aware that Richard had risen behind the Mistress and slipped his arms under Mistress Lockley's arms so that he could support her. His hands were on her breasts, pressing on the nipples.

But Beauty lost herself in what was before her. The hot silk of the hair, the plump wet lips, the moisture oozing onto her tongue, all this stirred in her a frenzy.

And the woman's soft sigh above, her helpless sigh, ignited some new spark in Beauty. Madly she licked and stabbed with her tongue as if she were starved for the salty delicious flesh. And hooking the round, tough little clitoris on the tip of her tongue, she sucked on it with all the pressure she could exert, the wet hair covering her own mouth and nose, drenching her in the sweet, musky scent, as she sighed even louder than the Mistress. The very littleness of it drove her on; it was unlike a cock, and yet so like a cock, this little nodule that she knew was the wellspring of her Mistress's rapture, and bent on nothing but that rapture, she licked and sucked and stroked it with her teeth until the Mistress was spreading her legs, tilting her hips, groaning loudly. All the images of the kitchen torture flashed in Beauty's mind—this was the one who had spanked her breasts—and she fed deeper and deeper, until she was almost biting the mound, slurping with her tongue, burrowing into the sex, and rocking her own hips in time with the movement. At last Mistress Lockley cried out, and her hips froze in the air, as her whole body became rigid.

"No! No more!" The Mistress almost screamed. She clutched Beauty's head, tearing it loose gently, and she sank back into the Prince's arms, breathing unevenly.

Beauty fell back on her heels.

She shut her eyes trying not even to hope for satisfaction, trying not to picture the dark, glistening pubis again or to think of the rich taste of it. But her tongue touched the roof of her mouth over and over as if she were still licking Mistress Lockley.

Finally Mistress Lockley stood upright and, turning, wrapped her arms around Richard. She kissed him and churned her hips as she rubbed against him.

It was painful for Beauty to watch, but she couldn't take her eyes off the two towering figures. Richard's red hair fell down over his forehead and his muscular arm squeezed the narrow back of the Mistress against him.

But then Mistress Lockley turned and, gathering

Beauty by the hand, led her to the bed. "Get up on your knees on the bed and face the wall," she said, the color dancing in her cheeks exquisitely. "And spread those gorgeous little legs wide apart," she added. "No one should have to tell you that by now."

Beauty obeyed at once, crawling to the far side against the wall, her back to the room, as she had been told. The passion in her was so furious she couldn't quiet her hips. Again, in a flash she saw the tortures of the kitchen, that smiling face and the little white tongue of the spanking belt coming down on her nipple.

"O, wicked love," she thought, "that has so many unnamed components."

But Mistress Lockley was lying down on the bed beneath Beauty's spread legs and looking up at her.

Her arms wound round Beauty's thighs and pulled them lower, as Beauty straddled her.

Beauty peered down into the Mistress's eyes as her legs stretched wider and wider apart until her sex was just above Mistress Lockley's face, and suddenly she feared the red mouth below her as much as she had feared the mouth of the white cat in the kitchen. The eyes, so large and glassy, were like the eyes of the cat.

"It will devour me," she thought, "it will eat me alive!" But her sex opened in silent ravenous convulsions.

From behind, Richard's hands caught Beauty, caught her sore breasts just as he had caught Mistress Lockley's breasts, and at the same time Beauty felt a jolt to the frame of the bed and saw Mistress Lockley stiffen and shut her eyes.

Richard had entered Mistress Lockley below, standing beside the bed between her spread legs, and Beauty shook with the rapid jamming rhythm.

But immediately the hot delicate tongue had licked up at Beauty. It lapped in long slow strokes at her pubic lips and she gasped at the incredible sweetness of the shrill sensation.

She jumped, afraid of the wet mouth even as she

craved it. But her clitoris had been caught in Mistress Lockley's teeth and Mistress Lockley nibbled at it, sucked at it, licked at it with a fierceness that astonished Beauty. The tongue stabbed into her, filling her, and the teeth gnawed at her, and Richard caught up all of Beauty's weight in his slender, powerful arms, while his thrusts shook the bed in the never-faltering rhythm. "O, she knows how to do it!" Beauty thought. But she lost the thread of her thoughts, her breaths coming long and low, Richard's gentle hands massaging her hurt breasts, the face beneath her pressed into her vagina, the tongue flushing her, the lips clamping onto her whole nether mouth and drawing on it in an orgy of sucking that sent the orgasm searing through her.

It broke in bright waves, causing her almost to collapse, as the strong driving thrusts of the Prince came faster and faster and Mistress Lockley moaned against Beauty and the Prince gave the same deep guttural cry behind her.

Beauty hung exhausted in his arms.

Released, she fell languidly to the side, and for a long time lay with her limbs nestled beside Mistress Lockley. Richard, too, was tumbled in the bed, and Beauty lay in a half-sleep, hearing the dim sounds from below, the voices in the drinking room, the occasional shouts from the square, the sounds of night descending on the village.

When she opened her eyes, Richard was on his knees and just tying the Mistress's apron strings. The Mistress brushed her long dark hair.

She snapped her fingers for Beauty to rise, and Beauty tumbled out of the bed and quickly straightened the coverlet.

She turned and looked up at the Mistress. Richard was already kneeling before the snow-white apron. And Beauty took her place at his side, and the Mistress smiled down at them.

She studied both her slaves. Then she reached down

and clasped Beauty's sex. She kept her warm hand there until Beauty's pubic lips enlarged ever so slightly, and the shrill throb commenced again. With the other hand the Mistress wakened the Prince's cock, pinching the tip, batting gently, playfully at the balls, and whispering, "Come now, young man, no time for resting."

He gave a faint moan, but the cock was obedient. The warm fingers tested the moisture between Beauty's engorging lips. "See, this good little girl is already prepared for service."

She lifted their chins now and smiled down at both of them. Beauty felt dizzy and weak and totally without resistance. She stared up into the lovely dark eyes meekly.

"And in the morning, she will paddle me on the counter," Beauty thought, "as she does the others." And her weakness only increased. Richard's brief story melted over her with lurid vividness: the Punishment Shop, the Public Turntable. The village blazed in her mind and she felt stricken and bedazzled and unable to think whether she was good or bad or should be either.

"Stand up," came the soft low voice, "and march fast. It's already dark and you haven't been bathed yet."

Beauty rose and so did the Prince, and she gave a little cry when she felt the wooden paddle smack her buttocks. "Knees high," came the gentle whisper. "Young man"—another smack—"did you hear me?"

They were paddled fiercely down the steps, Beauty shaken and red-faced and shivering with the passion that was kindled anew, and driven into the yard, there to be bathed in the wooden tubs by the kitchen girls, who went to work with their rough brushes and towels.

SECRETS
IN
THE
INNER
CHAMBER

Tristan:

THE MASTER'S bedroom was immaculate as I entered, just as it had been the night before, the green satin-lined bed gleaming in the candlelight. And when I saw my Master seated at the desk, pen in hand, I went as quietly as I could across the polished oak floor and kissed his boots, not in the old decorous way, but with total affection.

I feared he would stop me as I licked at his ankles and even dared to kiss the smooth leather over his calves, but he did not. He did not even seem to notice me.

My cock was hurting. The little Princess in the Public Tent had been only the first course. And the mere act of entering this room redoubled the hunger. But as before, I didn't dare to beg with any vulgar, pleading movement. I would not have displeased the Master for anything.

I stole a glance upwards at his intent face, his white hair shimmering around it. And he turned, looking down at me, and timidly I looked away, though it took all my control to do it.

"You're well bathed?" he asked.

I nodded and kissed his boots again.

"Get on the bed," he said, "and sit to the foot of the bed in the corner nearest the wall."

I was in ecstasy. I tried to compose myself, the satin coverlet like ice soothing my welts. The two days of constant licking caused even the flinching of a muscle to have endless reverberations.

My Master was getting undressed, I knew, but I didn't dare to look. Then he snuffed all the candles except those by the head of the bed, where an open wine bottle sat beside two jewel-encrusted goblets.

He must be the richest man in the village, I thought, to have so much light. And I felt a slave's pure pride in having a rich Master. Any thought of the Prince I had been in my own land was simply gone from me.

He climbed into bed and sat against the pillows, with one knee up, his left arm resting on it. He reached over and filled the two goblets and then he extended one to me.

I was baffled. Did he mean for me to drink from it as he would? I took it at once and sat back holding it. I was looking unabashedly at him now; he had not commanded me not to. And his lean hard chest with its curling bits of white hair around the nipples and down the center to his belly caught the light of the candle beautifully. His cock was not as hard as mine yet. I wanted to remedy that.

"You may drink the wine as I do," he said, as if he'd read my thoughts. And, quite astonished, I drank as a man for the first time in half a year, feeling a little awkward about it. I gulped too much and had to stop. But it was well-aged burgundy and without equal in my memory.

"Tristan," he said softly.

I looked him straight in the eye and slowly lowered the cup.

"You're to speak to me now," he said, "to answer me."

More amazement. "Yes, Master," I said softly.

"Did you hate me last night when I had you whipped on the turntable?" he asked.

I was shocked.

He took another drink of the wine but without taking his eyes off me. He looked ominous suddenly, though I didn't know why.

"No, Master," I whispered.

"Louder," he said. "I can't hear you."

"No, Master," I answered. I flushed as deeply as I ever had. It wasn't really necessary to recall the turntable. I'd never truly stopped thinking about it.

" 'Sir' will do now and then as well as 'Master,' " he said. "I like both. Did you hate Julia when she stretched your anus with the horsetail phallus?"

"No, Sir," I said, the blush getting hotter.

"Did you hate me when I tethered you with the ponies and made you pull the coach to the manor house? I don't mean today after you had been so well worked and tempered. I mean yesterday when you were staring with such horror at the harnesses."

"No, Sir," I protested.

"Then what did you feel when all those things happened?"

I was too stupefied to answer.

"What did I want from you today when I tethered you behind that pair of ponies, when I plugged your mouth and your anus and made you march in your bare feet?"

"Submission," I said, my mouth dry. My voice sounded unfamiliar to me.

"And . . . in more precise detail?"

"That I . . . I march briskly. And that I be taken through the village in . . . in that fashion. . . ." I was trembling. I tried to steady the goblet with the other hand as if it were a thoughtless gesture.

"In what fashion?" he pressed.

"Harnessed, gagged."

"Yes . . . ?"

"And impaled on a phallus and barefoot." I swallowed, but I didn't look away from him.

"And what do I want from you now?" he said.

I thought for a moment. "I don't know. I . . . That I answer your questions."

"Exactly. So you will answer them, fully," he said politely with a slight lift of his eyebrows, "and with deep descriptive passages, concealing nothing and without so much coaxing. You will give long answers. In fact you will continue your answer until I put another question." He reached for the bottle and filled my goblet.

"And drink your wine whenever you like," he said, "there is plenty of it."

"Thank you, Sir," I murmured, staring at the cup.

"That's a little better!" he said, marking my response. "Now, we'll start again. When you first saw the team of ponies and you realized you were being made to join them, what went through your mind? Let me remind you, you had a stout phallus in your backside with a good horsetail attached to it. But then came the boots and the harness. You are blushing. What did you think?"

"That I couldn't bear it," I said, not daring to pause, my voice quavering. "That I couldn't be made to do it. That I, I would fail somehow. That I couldn't be lashed to a coach and made to pull it like an animal, and the tail, it seemed a dreadful decoration, a stigma." My face was in a fever. I sipped at the wine, but he had not spoken and this meant I had to go on answering him! "I think it was better as the harnesses were tightened and I couldn't get away."

"But you made no move to get away before that. When I strapped you home through the street, I was alone with you. You didn't try to run then, not even when the village toughs whipped you."

"Well, what good would it have done to run?" I asked in consternation. "I'd been taught not to run! I would only have been trussed up somewhere, beaten, maybe my cock whipped—" I stopped, shocked at my own words. "Or maybe I would only have been caught and harnessed anyway, and pulled along truckling by the other ponies. And the mortification would have been greater because all would have known that I was so afraid, out of control, and being so violently forced to it."

I drank from the goblet and shoved my hair out of my eyes. "No, if it was to be done, then it was better to submit; it was inescapable, so it had to be accepted."

I shut my eyes tight for a second. The heat and torrent of my words amazed me.

"But you'd been taught to submit to Lord Stefan, and you did not," he said.

"I tried!" I burst out. "But Lord Stefan . . ."

"Yes . . ."

"It was what the Captain said," I faltered. My voice sounded frail to me now. The words were too rapid. "He had been my lover before, and instead of using that intimacy to his advantage as Master, he allowed it to weaken him."

"What an interesting statement. Did he talk to you as I'm talking to you now?"

"No! No one has ever done that!" I laughed shortly, dryly. "That is, not with me talking back. He ordered me about like any castle Lord. He ordered me stiffly, but he was in a terrible state of agitation. It excited him beyond words to see me erect and bowing to his wishes and yet he couldn't endure it. I think, well, I think sometimes that if our positions had been reversed by fate, I might have showed him how to do it."

My Master laughed, and his laugh was free and slow.

He drank from his cup. His face was animated and a little warmer now. I felt some terrible sense of danger to my soul, looking at him.

"O, that is probably too true," he said. "The best slaves sometimes make the best Masters. But you may never have the opportunity to prove it. I spoke to the Captain about you this afternoon. I made thorough inquiries. When you were free years ago, you bested Lord Stefan in all ways, didn't you? Better rider, swordsman, archer. And he loved you and admired you."

"I tried to shine as his slave," I said. "I journeyed through excruciating humiliations. The Bridle Path, the other games of Festival Night in her Majesty's gardens; I was the Queen's toy now and then; Lord Gregory, the Master of the slaves, incited the most exquisite fear in me. But I never pleased Lord Stefan because he himself did not know how to be pleased! He did not know how to command! I was always distracted by other Lords."

My voice stopped in my throat. Why must I tell these secrets? Why must I lay it all out and amplify my revelation to the Captain? But my Master didn't speak. It was the silence again and I was falling into it.

"I kept thinking of the soldiers' camp," I went on, the silence pulsing in my ears. "And I felt no love for Lord Stefan." I looked into my Master's eyes. The blue was only a glimmer of blue, the dark centers large and almost glittering.

"One has to love the Master or Mistress," I said. "Even the slaves in the village cottages, they can love their gruff and busy Masters or Mistresses, can't they, as I loved . . . the soldiers in the camp who whipped me daily. As I loved for one moment—"

"Yes?" he demanded.

"As I even loved the Whipping Master on the turntable last night. For one moment." That hand lifting my chin, squeezing my cheeks, that smile looming over me. The power in that thick arm . . .

I was trembling as badly as I had then. But still the silence . . .

"Even those toughs, as you called them, who whipped me in the street while you watched," I said, veering away from the image of the turntable. "They had their shabby power."

I had only *thought* I was blushing before. I tried to cool myself with the wine, strengthen my voice, the silence stretching again as I drank.

I put up my left hand to shield my eyes.

"Take down your hand," he said, "and tell me what you felt when you were made to march, after you were properly harnessed."

The word "properly," pierced me.

"It was what I *needed*," I said. I tried not to look at him, but I failed. His eyes were wide, and in the candlelight his face was almost too perfect for a man's face, too fine. I felt a knot in my chest loosening, breaking. "I . . . mean, if I'm to be a slave, it was what I needed. And tonight—when I did it again—I had pride in it."

My shame was too much. My face throbbed.

"I liked it!" I whispered. "That is, this evening when we went out to the manor house, I liked it. I had already been shown by the early barefoot run through the village that one could take pride in being harnessed like that, instead of the other way. And I wanted to please you. I took pleasure in pleasing you."

I drained the cup and I lowered it. There was the wine pouring into it again, and his eyes never letting me go as he put the bottle back on the table.

I felt as if I were falling; I was being opened by my own confessions as surely as the phalluses had opened me.

"But maybe that's not the whole truth," I said, looking at him intently. "Even if I had not been run barefoot through the village, I might have liked the pony harnesses anyway. And maybe, despite all the pain and the misery of it, I liked the barefoot run through the village because you were driving me and you were watching me. I felt sorry for the slaves I saw whom no one seemed to watch."

"In the village someone is always watching," he said. "If I strap you to a wall outside, and I will, there will be those who will notice you. The village toughs will come round to torment you again, grateful for an unattended slave they can torture for nothing. They'd whip you raw in less than half an hour. Someone always sees, comes to punish. And as you said, they have their shabby charm. For a well-tuned slave, the crudest cleaning woman or chimney sweep can have an overwhelming charm if the discipline is engulfing."

"Engulfing." I repeated the word. It was perfect.

My vision blurred. I started to raise my hand again but put it down.

"So you needed it," he said. "You needed to be well harnessed and bitted and shod and driven hard."

I nodded. My throat was so thick I couldn't speak.

"And you wanted to please me," he said. "But why?"

"I don't know!"

"You do know!"

"Because . . . you're my Master. You own me. You are my only hope."

"Hope for what? To be punished all the more?"

"I don't know."

"You do know!"

"My only hope for a deep love, a loss of myself to someone, not merely a loss amid all that strives to break me down and remake me. But a loss to someone who is sublimely cruel, sublimely good at mastering. Someone who might somehow, in the blaze of my suffering, see the depth of submission and love me also." It was too much of an admission. I stopped, crushed, certain I couldn't continue.

But I did go on, slowly.

"I could have loved many Masters or Mistresses perhaps. But you have an eerie beauty that debilitates me and absorbs me. You illuminate the punishments. I don't . . . I don't understand it."

"What did you feel when you realized you were in line for the Public Turntable," he asked, "when you implored me with all those kisses to my boots and the crowd laughed at you?"

The words stung. Again, it was too real for memory. I swallowed hard.

"I felt panic. I cried, to be punished so soon like that, after trying so hard. Not as a spectacle, I thought, for a crowd of common people, and such a crowd, all there to preside over the chastisement. And when you reprimanded me for begging, I was . . . ashamed that I had ever thought I could escape it. I remembered that it wasn't necessary for me to have earned the punishment. I deserved it by being here, and being what I was. I was filled with remorse that I had pleaded with you. I will never do it again, I swear it."

"And then?" he asked. "When you were taken up and mounted without fetters? Did you learn from it?"

"Yes, enormously." I gave another low, harsh laugh. Hardly more than a single syllable. "It was devastating! First there was that fear of losing control when you told the guard, 'No fetters.' "

"But why? What would have happened if you had struggled?"

"I would have been bound down, I knew it. Tonight I saw a slave bound like that. Last night I simply assumed it would happen. I would have resisted with my whole body, bridling the way the Prince was tonight, bucking, the terror crashing against me and washing away from me."

I stopped. Engulfing yes, it had become engulfing.

"But I held still," I said, "and when I realized I wouldn't slip or slide under the blows, all the tension was released. I knew this remarkable exhilaration. I was being offered up to the crowd and I submitted to it. I collected all the crowd's frenzy to myself, and the crowd enlarged my punishment as they enjoyed it, and I belonged to the crowd, to hundreds and hundreds of Masters and Mistresses. I yielded to their lust. I held back nothing, resisted nothing."

I stopped. He nodded slowly, but he didn't speak. The heat pounded silently in my temples. I sipped the wine, thinking of my own words.

"It was the same in a smaller way," I said, "when the Captain thrashed me. He was punishing me for having failed after his training. But he was also testing me to see if I was telling the truth about Stefan, if it was mastering I needed. He was calling my bluff, saying, in effect, 'I'll give it to you and we'll see if yo can endure it.' And I offered myself to his lash, or at least it seemed so. I never thought, not even in the camp when the soldiers punished me, or at the castle when the Lords and Ladies looked on, that I could, in a hot noonday village square, full of passersby, dance for a soldier's thrash like that. The soldiers trained my cock. They trained me. But they never got that from me. And though I'm terrified of what lies ahead, terrified even of the pony harnesses, I feel myself opening to all punishments instead of triumphing over them with sublime form as I did at the castle. I am being turned inside out. I belong to the Captain, and to you, to all who look. I am *becoming* my punishments."

Silently he moved towards me, taking the goblet and setting it aside and then taking me in his arms and kissing me.

My mouth opened wide, eagerly, and then he pulled me onto my knees and went down to put his mouth on my cock and fold his arms around my buttocks. Almost savagely he sucked at the full length of my organ, enveloping me in tight wet hotness as his fingers, spreading my buttocks, pried open my anus. And his head went back and forth, pulling on the full length of my cock, lips tightening and then releasing as his tongue circled the tip; then the rapid, almost mad sucking continued. His fingers stretched my anus wide. My mind went clean. I whispered, "I can't hold back." And when he sucked even harder, with rougher strokes, I steadied his head with both hands and jetted hard into him.

My cries came in short bursting rhythm with the suction that seemed to want to empty me. And when I could stand it no more, and tried gently to release his head, he rose up and pushed me down on the bed on my face, shoving my thighs up and wide and flattening my buttocks to the sheets with the heels of his palms before he lay down and forced his cock into me. I was spread like a frog under him. The muscles in my thighs positively sang with delicious pain. His weight pressed me down all the harder. His teeth opened lightly on the back of my neck. His hands hooked under my crooked knees and forced them up closer to the pillow. And my exhausted cock throbbed and doubled beneath me.

My buttocks bobbed. I groaned from the strain. And his cock, stabbing into my wide-spread buttocks, seemed some inhuman instrument reaming me, coring me, and emptying me.

In a wild series of spurts I came again, unable to remain flat, bucking under him, and he bore down all the more, grinding out his low moan of climax.

I lay panting, not daring to uncramp my bent and flattened legs. Then I felt him pushing my knees down. He was lying beside me. He turned me over to face him, and in that keen high-pitched moment of exhaustion, he started kissing me.

I tried to fight the languor of sleep, my cock begging me for a moment's respite. But he had sent his hook down into my loins again. He was bringing me up, forcing me to my knees, directing my hands to a wooden handle over our heads in the paneled canopy of the bed, and whipping my cock with his hands as he sat with his legs crossed before me.

I watched it engorge with blood under the slaps, the pleasure slower, fuller, excruciating. I moaned aloud and twisted away almost before I could stop myself. But he tugged me forward, wrapping my balls up against my cock with his left hand, and he continued the merciless slapping with the other.

My body was on the rack. My mind was on the rack, and now I realized, as he pinched the tip of my cock, that he meant to tease it out of me. Pinching, stroking with his curled fingers, now licking with his tongue, he had me in a frenzy. He took the cream from the jar he had used last night and greased his right hand and pulled at my cock, squeezing it as if he would destroy it. I was grunting behind my clenched teeth, my hips rocking, and then it shot forth again, the hard spurting and spurting. And I hung from the wooden handle dazed and truly empty.

A light still burned.

I didn't know how much time had passed as I opened my eyes. But it must have been early. Coaches still rolled on the road outside the window.

And I realized my Master was dressed and walking back and forth, his hands clasped behind his back, his hair tousled. He wore the blue velvet doublet unlaced, his linen shirt with its long balloon sleeves open down the front also. Now and then he would pivot sharply, stop, run his fingers through his hair, and then continue pacing.

When I rose on my elbow, afraid of being ordered out, he gestured to the wine goblet and said, "Drink if you wish."

I picked it up at once and sat back against the paneling, watching him.

He paced again, once, back and forth, and then he turned, staring at me.

"I'm in love with you!" he said. He drew close and peered into my eyes. "In love with you! Not merely with punishing you, though that I will do, or with your subservience, which I love and crave, also. I am in love with *you,* your secret soul that is as vulnerable as the reddened flesh under my strap, and all your strength collected under our combined governance!"

I was speechless. All I could do was look at him, lost in the heat of his voice and the look in his eyes. But my soul was soaring.

He drew away from the bed and, glancing sharply back at me, paced and paced again.

"Ever since the Queen commenced the importation of naked pleasure slaves," he said, looking at the carpet beneath his feet, "I have puzzled over what it is that makes a strong, highborn Prince of a slave obey with such complete submission. I have racked my brain to understand it." He paused, then went on, his hands loose at his sides and rising now and then with an easy gesture.

"All those I've questioned in the past have given me timid, guarded answers. You have spoken from your soul, but what is clear is that you accept your slavery as easily as they do. Of course, as the Queen has explained to me, all slaves are examined. And only the likely, as well as the beautiful, are chosen."

He looked at me. I had never realized that there had been an examination. But immediately I recalled the Queen's emissaries whom I had been sent to meet in a chamber of my father's castle. I remembered them ordering me to remove my clothes and how they had touched me and watched me as I stood still for their probing fingers. I had exhibited no sudden passion. But maybe their trained eyes had seen more than I realized. They had kneaded my flesh, asked me questions, studied my face as I blushed and tried to answer.

"Rarely, if ever, does a slave run away," my Master continued. "And most of those who run wish to be caught. It's obvious. Defiance is the motive, boredom the incentive. The few who take the time to steal the Mistress's or Master's clothes succeed in their escape."

"But doesn't the Queen take out her wrath on their Kingdoms?" I asked. "My father himself told me the Queen was all-powerful, fearsome. Her request for slave Tributes couldn't be denied."

"Nonsense," he said. "The Queen isn't going to send her armies into war over one naked slave. All that happens is that the slave reaches his native country somewhat in disgrace. His parents are asked to send him back. If they don't, then the slave earns no great reward. That's all. No bag of gold. Obedient slaves are sent home with a great deal of gold. And of course there's often the parents' shame that their lovely has proved soft and inconstant. Brothers and sisters at home who have served as slaves resent the deserter. But what's all that to a strong young Prince who finds service intolerable?"

He stopped his pacing and stared at me.

"A slave escaped yesterday," he said "It was a Princess, and they have now almost given up the search. She wasn't caught by the loyal peasants or any other village. She's reached the bordering Kingdom of King Lysius, where slaves are always given safe passage."

So what the slave pony Jerard had said was true! I sat, stunned, thinking about this. But I was even more stunned by the fact that the words had so little impact. My mind was in chaos.

He started to pace again, slowly, deep in his thoughts.

"Of course, there are slaves who would never take such a risk," he started up suddenly. "They cannot endure the thought of the search parties, the capture, the public humiliation and even worse punishment. And over and over again their passions are roused, fed, roused again, and fed again so they can no longer tell punishment from pleasure. That is what the Queen wants. And these slaves probably cannot endure the thought of reaching home only to try to convince an ignorant father or mother that service here was unendurable. How to describe what had been done? How to describe that they bore as much of it as they did, or the pleasure that was inevitably incited in them? Nevertheless, why do they accept it so readily? Why do they strain to please? Why are they caught up in the vision of the Queen, the visions of their Masters and Mistresses?"

My head was swimming. And it wasn't the wine that caused it.

"But you've shed much light upon the mind of the slave," he said looking at me again, his face earnest and simple and beautiful in the glow of the candles. "You've shown me that for the true slave, the rigors of the castle and the village become a great adventure. There is something undeniable in the true slave who worships those of unquestioned power. He or she longs for perfection even in the slave state, and perfection for a naked pleasure slave must be yielding to the most extreme punishments. The slave spiritualizes these ordeals, no matter how crude and painful. And all the torments of the village, even more than the more decorous humiliations of the castle, tumble fast one upon the other in an endless current of excitement."

He approached the bed. I think he could see the fear in my face as I looked up.

"And who understands power, worships it, more than those who have had it?" he said. "You who have had power understood it as you knelt at Lord Stefan's foot. Poor Lord Stefan."

I rose and he took me in his arms.

"Tristan," he whispered, "my beautiful Tristan." Our passions had been purged, but we kissed in a fever, our arms tight around each other, the affection overflowing.

"But there is more," I whispered in his ear as he kissed my face almost hungrily. "In this descent, it is the Master who creates the order, the Master who lifts the slave out of the engulfing chaos of abuse, and disciplines the slave, refines him, drives him further in ways that random punishments might never provide. It is the Master, not the punishments, who perfects him."

"Then it is not engulfing," he said, kissing me still. "It is embracing."

"Over and over we are lost," I said, "only to be retrieved by the Master."

"But even without that one all-powerful love," he insisted, "you are enfolded in a womb of relentless attention and pleasure."

"Yes," I agreed. I nodded, kissing his throat, his lips. "But it's glorious," I whispered, "if one adores one's Master, if the mystery is intensified by an irresistible figure at the core of it."

Our embrace was so rough and sweet, it didn't seem that passion could have been any better.

Very slowly, gently, he drew back.

"Get up," he said. "It's only midnight and the spring air is warm outside. I want to walk in the country."

UNDER
THE
STARS

Unfastening HIS breech-
es, he tucked in his shirt, laced it and laced his doublet.
I hastened to lace his boots for him, but he did not ac-
knowledge it. He gestured for me to rise again and follow
him.

Within moments we were outside, and the air was
warm and we were walking silently through the inter-
twining lanes, west, out of the village. I walked at his side
with my hands clasped behind my back, and when we
passed other dark figures, most often lone Masters with
a single marching slave, I dropped my eyes, as seemed
respectful.

Many lights burned in the little windows of the close-peaked-roofed houses. And when we turned into a broad street, I could see far away to the east the lights of the marketplace and hear the dull roar of the crowd in the Place of Public Punishment.

Even the sight of my Master's profile in the dark, the dull luminosity of his hair, excited me. My spent cock was ready to come back to life. A touch, even a command, would have done it. And the concealed state of readiness heightened all of my senses.

We had come to the square of the Inns. There were suddenly bright lights all around us. Torches flared beneath the high painted Sign of the Lion, and the noise of a large crowd swelled through the open doorway.

I followed my Master to the entrance, and he gestured for me to kneel as he went inside, leaving me there. I rested back on my heels and peered into the gloom. Everywhere men laughed, talked, drank from their flagons. My Master was at the counter purchasing a full wineskin, which he already had in his hands as he spoke to the beautiful dark-haired woman with the red skirts whom I had seen that morning punishing Beauty.

And then, high on the wall behind the counter, I saw Beauty. She was bound to the wall, her hands above her head, her beautiful gold hair falling down behind her shoulders, and her legs were straddling the immense keg on which she sat, her eyes closed in pleasant sleep, it seemed, her luscious pink mouth half open. And on either side of her were other such slaves all dozing as if in deep fatigue, their whole attitude one of hopeless contentment.

O, if Beauty and I could only be alone for a moment. If I could only talk to her, tell her what I had learned and the feelings that had been aroused in me.

But my Master had come back, and bidding me to rise, he led the way out of the square. We were soon at the west gates of the village and we walked along the country road that led to the manor house.

He put his arm around me, offered me the wineskin.

It was beautifully quiet now under the high dome of stars. Only one coach passed us on the road and it seemed a moonlight vision.

A team of twelve Princesses brought it smartly along, the lovelies harnessed three across in snow-white leather, and the coach itself was exquisitely gilded. To my amazement, my Mistress Julia rode in the coach beside a tall man, and both waved, as they passed, to my Master.

"That is the Lord Mayor of the village," said my Master softly to me.

We turned before we reached the manor house. But I knew we were already on his land, and we walked over the grass, through the fruit trees, and towards the nearby hills that were densely covered in forest.

I don't know how long we walked. Maybe an hour. And we settled finally on a high slope halfway uphill with the valley spread out before us. The clearing was just large enough for us to make a little fire and to sit back against the side of the hill, the dark trees hovering over us.

My Master tended the fire until it was going well. Then he lay back. I sat up with my leg crossed looking at the towers and peaks of the village. I could see the brilliant glare of the Place of Public Punishment. The wine made me sleepy and my Master stretched out, with his hands beneath his head and his eyes wide open and fixed on the dark blue moonlit sky above and the grand sweep of the constellations.

"I have never loved any slave as I love you," he said calmly.

I tried to restrain myself. To listen only to my heart-beat for a moment in the stillness. But I said all too quickly:

"Will you buy me outright from the Queen and keep me in the village?"

"Do you know what you are asking?" he said. "You've only endured two days here."

"Would it do any good if I begged you on my knees, kissed your boots, prostrated myself?"

"It isn't required," he said. "At the end of the week, I will go to the Queen with my usual accounting of the winter activities of the village. I know as certainly as I know my name that I will offer to purchase you outright and make a strong case for it."

"But Lord Stefan—"

"Leave Lord Stefan to me. I shall make you a prediction about Lord Stefan: Every year on Midsummer Night a strange ritual is enacted. All those in the village who wish to be made into slaves for the following twelve months present themselves to be privately examined. Tents are set up for the purpose and the villagers are stripped and carefully looked over in every particular. And the same takes place among the Lords and Ladies of the castle. No one is entirely sure who has made himself or herself available for the examination.

"But at midnight on Midsummer Night the names are announced both at the castle and on the high platform of the marketplace in the village of all those who have been accepted. It is only a tiny portion, of course, of those who have offered. Only the most beautiful, the most aristocratic in appearance, the strongest. As each name is called, the crowd turns searching for the chosen one— everyone here knows everyone else, quite naturally—and at once he or she is found out, rushed to the platform, and there stripped naked. Of course there is dread, regret, abject fright at the wish being violently fulfilled, the clothing ripped off, the hair let down, and the crowd enjoys it as much as the auction. The regular slave Princes and Princesses, especially those who have been punished by the new villager slave, scream with joy and approbation.

"Then the village victims are sent off to the castle, where for a glorious year they will serve in the lowest capacities, but almost indistinguishable from Princes and Princesses.

"And from the castle we receive those Lords and Ladies who have given themselves over in like manner, having been stripped by their peers in the Castle Pleasure Gardens, sometimes so few that there are only three of them. You cannot imagine the excitement it brings on Midsummer Night when they are brought to be auctioned. Lords and Ladies on the block. The prices are dizzying. The Lord Mayor almost always buys one as he reluctantly gives up last year's prize. Sometimes my sister, Julia, buys another. Once there were as many as five, last year only two, and now and then one. And the Captain of the Guard has told me that this year, all the bets are down that the castle exiles will include Lord Stefan."

I was too amused and surprised to answer.

"From all you've said, Lord Stefan doesn't know how to command and the Queen knows it. If he offers himself he will be chosen."

I laughed softly to myself. "He does not even guess what is in store for him!" I said quietly. I shook my head, and then laughed again under my breath, trying to subdue it.

He turned his head to smile at me. "You'll be mine soon, all mine, mine for three, maybe four, years." And when he rose on his elbow I lay down beside him and embraced him. The passion was rising again, but he bid it be quiet, and I lay still, trying to obey, my head on his chest, his hand on my forehead.

After a long time, I asked: "Master, is a slave ever granted a request?"

"Almost never," he whispered, "because the slave is never allowed to ask. But you may ask. I will permit that much."

"Is it possible for me to discover how it goes with another slave, if she is obedient and resigned or being punished for rebellion?"

"Why?"

"I came down in the cart with the Crown Prince's

slave. Her name is Beauty. She was high-spirited, a sensation at the castle for her hot passions and her inability
to conceal even the most transient emotions. In the cart
she asked me the very same question you asked: Why do
we obey? She's in the Sign of the Lion now. She's the
slave whom the Captain mentioned by name to you today
at the well after he whipped me. Is there any way to
discover if she has found the same acceptance that I've
found? Just to ask, perhaps . . ."

I felt his hand gently tug at my hair, his lips touch
my forehead. He spoke softly. "If you like, I will let you
see her and ask her yourself tomorrow."

"Master!" I was too grateful and amazed to put it
further into words. He let me kiss his lips. Boldly I kissed
his cheeks and even his eyelids. He gave me the faintest
smile. Then he settled me back on his chest.

"You know your day will be hard and very busy
before you see her," he said.

"Yes, Sir," I answered.

"Now, go to sleep," he said. "There's much work
for you to do in the orchards on the farm tomorrow before
we go back to the village. You'll be harnessed to pull a
good-sized basket of fruit back to my town house, and I
want to be done with all that so that by high noon when
the crowd is at its daytime thickest you can be punished
on the Public Turntable."

A little conflagration of panic flared inside me for a
moment. I clung to him a little more tightly. And I felt
his lips brush the top of my head tenderly.

Gently he disengaged himself and turned over on
his stomach to sleep, his face away from me, his left arm
curled under him. "You'll spend the afternoon at the
public stables to be hired out," he said. "You will trot on
the pony track there, harnessed and ready, and I expect
to hear that you showed such spirit you were hired out
immediately."

I looked at his long elegant form in the moonlight,

the gleaming white of his sleeves, the perfect shape of his calves in their sheathing of supple leather. I belonged to him. Completely I belonged to him.

"Yes, Master," I said softly.

I knelt up and, bending over him silently, kissed his right hand, which lay on the grass beside him. "Thank you, Master."

"In the evening," he said, "I'll talk to the Captain about sending Beauty."

An hour must have passed.

The fire was out.

He was sound asleep, I could tell from his breathing. He wore no weapons, not even a dagger concealed on his person. And I knew that I could easily have over-powered him. He hadn't my weight or strength, and six months at the castle had toned my muscles well. I could have taken his clothes from him, left him bound and gagged, and made off to the land of King Lysius. There was even money in his pockets.

And surely he had realized all this before we ever left the village.

He was either putting me to the test or so certain of me that it never crossed his mind. And as I lay awake in the dark, I had to learn for myself what he already knew: Would I or would I not run now that I had the opportunity?

It was no difficult decision. But each time I told myself that of course I would not, I found myself thinking of it. Escape, going home, standing up to my father, telling him to call the Queen's bluff, or going off to some other land in search of adventure. I suppose I would not have been a human being if I didn't at least think of those things.

And I thought too of being caught by the peasants. Being brought back over the saddle of the Captain of the Guard, naked again, to some unspeakable penance for what I'd done, and perhaps losing my Master forever.

I thought of other possibilities. I thought them all through and through, and then I turned over and snuggled close to my Master and slipped my arm gently around his waist, pressing my face into the velvet of his doublet. I had to get to sleep. After all, there was much to be done in the morning. I could almost see the noontime crowd around the turntable.

Sometime before dawn, I awoke.

I thought I heard some sound in the forest. But as I lay listening in the dark, there was only the usual murmur of the creatures of the wood and nothing to break the peace of it. I looked down on the village lying asleep under the heavy, luminous clouds, and it seemed to me something in its appearance had altered. The gates were locked.

But then maybe they were always locked at this hour. It was no concern of mine. And surely they'd be open in the morning.

And turning on my belly, I snuggled close to my Master again.

REVELATIONS
AND
MYSTERIES

As soon as Beauty was bathed, her long hair washed and dried, Mistress Lockley paddled her through the crowded Inn and out under the torchlit Sign of the Lion to stand on the cobblestones.

The square was crowded, young men drifting in and out of the various Inns, most village tradesmen and a very few soldiers. Mistress Lockley straightened Beauty's hair, gave a rough fluff to the curls between her legs, and told Beauty to stand straight with her breasts thrust decently forward.

Almost at once Beauty heard the loud approach of a horse, and looking to the right at the far end of the square, she saw the open gates of the village and the dark shape of the countryside under the paler sky and the black figure of a tall mounted soldier approaching.

The hooves clattered on the stones, echoing up the walls, as the horseman pounded towards the Sign of Lion and reined in his mount sharply.

It was the Captain, as Beauty had hoped and dreamed, his hair a cap of gold in the torchlight.

Mistress Lockley pushed Beauty forward, away from the Inn door, and the Captain walked his horse slowly around Beauty as she stood bathed in the light, looking down at her own shivering breasts, her heart thumping deliciously.

The Captain's huge broadsword flashed in the light, and his velvet cloak fell down behind him to form a deep rose-colored shadow. Beauty's breath halted as she saw the brightly polished boot and the powerful flank of the horse passing again in front of her. Then, as the horse came dangerously close and she almost backed away, she felt the Captain's arm catching her up and lifting her high into the air to bring her down facing him on the horse, her naked legs closing about his waist as she threw her arms around his neck tightly.

The horse reared and raced forward, out of the square and through the village gates, and along the road through the open farmland.

Beauty was jogged up and down, her sex spread wide open against the cold brass of the Captain's belt buckle. And her breasts were pressed against his chest, her head tucked beneath his head against his shoulder.

She saw cottages and fields flying by under the dim crescent moon, the dark outline of an elegant manor house.

The horse turned into the denser darkness of the woods, galloping on as the sky vanished above, the breeze lifting Beauty's hair, the Captain's left hand bracing her.

Finally Beauty saw lights ahead, the flicker of camp-fires. The Captain slowed his pace. And they drew near a little circle of four snow-white tents, and Beauty saw a score of men gathered around the large fire in the center of the circle.

The Captain dismounted, setting Beauty on her knees at his heel, where she crouched, not daring to look up at the other soldiers. The tall trees towered over the camp, delineated in a ghastly flicker of firelight.

Beauty felt a thrill at the lurid flicker, though it struck some deep chord of terror in her.

And then to her shock she saw a rude wooden cross staked in the ground facing the fire, a short stubby phallus sticking up where the two beams were fitted together. The cross was not quite as high as a man, and the cross-piece was nailed to the front of the other beam, the phallus jutting up and forward at a slight angle.

Beauty felt a catch in her throat as she stared at it in the grim unsteady light of the fire. And she looked down at the Captain's boot quickly.

"Well, are the patrols back?" The Captain was asking one of his men. Beauty could see his feet planted before her. "And you've had no luck?"

"All the patrols are back but one, Sir," said the man, "and we have had luck but not what we expected. The Princess is nowhere to be found. She may have made it to the border."

The Captain gave a low disgusted sound.

"But this," said the man, "we flushed from the woods just over the mountain at sundown."

Timidly, Beauty looked up to see a tall, large-boned naked Prince pushed forward into the light of the fire, his body streaked with dirt, his balls laced up tight to his erect penis, with a pair of heavy iron weights dangling from the leather. His long full head of brown hair was snagged with bits of leaf and earth. His legs and massive chest exuded power. He was one of the biggest slaves she'd ever seen. And he looked directly at the Captain with large brown eyes that showed resentful fear and excitement.

"Laurent," the Captain said under his breath. "And no alarm yet even from the castle that he is missing."

"No, Sir. He's been flogged twice; his buttocks are raw, and the men have had a go at him. I thought it was what you would wish, no use keeping him idle. But we waited for your command to mount him."

The Captain nodded. He was eyeing the slave with obvious anger.

"Lady Elvera's personal slave," he said.

The soldier who held the Prince's arms pulled the Prince's head back by the hair; and the light shone full on the Prince's face, his brown eyes flinching, though he still looked at the Captain.

"When did you run away?" the Captain demanded. He took two long strides towards the Prince, and twisted the Prince's head back even more cruelly. Beauty could see them clearly against the light of the fire, the Prince bigger even than the Captain, his body shuddering now as the Captain examined him.

"Forgive me, Sir," the slave said under his breath. "It was late today that I ran away. Forgive me."

"Didn't get very far, did you, my pretty Prince?" the Captain asked. He turned to the officer. "The men have taken their pleasure of him?"

"Two and three times over, Sir. And he's been run and whipped well. He's ready."

The Captain shook his head slowly and took the slave by the arm.

Beauty's soul trembled for him. As she knelt in the dirt, she tried to keep her legs apart and her glances furtive.

"Did you plan this attempt with Princess Lynette?" the Captain asked as he shoved the slave towards the cross.

"No, Sir, I swear it," said the Prince, stumbling as he was thrown forward. "I didn't even know that she'd run away." He kept his hands clasped on his neck, though he almost fell. And Beauty saw his backside for the first time, a perfect mesh of pink stripes and white welts all the way to his ankles.

As he was turned around with his back to the cross, his cock pulsed under the lacings. It was large and red, the tip moist, and the slave's face was coloring darkly.

An excited murmur rose from the company, and Beauty heard men stirring and moving about in the shadows beyond the light of the fire, as if drawing in closer.

The Captain motioned for his men to lift the Prince.

Beauty's throat thickened and went dry. The soldiers lifted the slave, spreading his legs way out on either side of him, and fitted him down on the wooden phallus.

He gave a harsh groan.

A low cheer went up from the soldiers.

But the Prince groaned even louder as his widespread legs were bent all the way back to lie atop the crossbeams. It made Beauty's thighs ache to look at it, the Prince bound flat now to the cross, sore buttocks against the beam under him, the phallus deep inside him.

But it was not finished. As the Prince's arms were laced behind the cross, his head was being bent all the way back flat on top of the upright beam, a long leather belt bound across his open mouth, and buckled to the wood beneath his ears as he stared straight up into the sky helplessly. Beauty saw his glossy tangled hair fall down in back. She saw his throat undulating with his silent swallows.

But the display of his bulging sex seemed the worst, and as the lashings were torn off the cock, it wagged and quavered, pulling at the heavy weight that hung from it. And Beauty felt her own sex again twitching and flinching.

The men had gathered all around as the Captain inspected the work. And the Prince's whole body shuddered and strained on the cross, the iron weight swinging from the swollen penis. Beauty could even see the buttocks rising and contracting on the thick wooden phallus.

The whole figure stood no higher than a short man,

and the Captain stood alongside it now and looked down into the Prince's face and wiped the hair back from his eyes roughly. Beauty could see the eyelids moving, and the Prince's mouth straining to close on the broad leather belt that bound it open.

"Tomorrow," the Captain said, "thus exhibited, you will be mounted on the cart and driven through the village and the countryside. The soldiers will march before and behind, and the drums will beat to rouse the public attention. And I shall send word to the Queen that you have been taken. She may ask to see you. She may not. If she does, you will ride in the same fashion to the castle to be placed there in the garden on display until she decides to make her judgment. If she does not wish to see you, you are sentenced without recourse for the rest of your years here to the village. I shall have you whipped through the streets, then auctioned. Now you will take your whipping from me."

Again the company cheered.

The Captain took the leather strap that was hooked to his waist and stood back to gain the room for the swing of the arm and commenced the whipping. It was not too heavy a strap, nor a wide one, but Beauty winced and secretly covered her face with her fingers, peeping through them to see the flat lash descend upon the inner thighs of the Prince, which brought immediate grunts and groans from him.

The Captain whipped hard, sparing no part of the legs, the strap licking the sides of the calves, the upturned shins, the ankles. Even the soles of the upturned feet, and then he whipped the Prince's naked belly. The rounded flesh quivered and jumped and the Prince moaned against his gag, the tears streaming down the side of his face, his eyes open as they stared above him.

His whole body seemed to vibrate on the cross. The buttocks rose and fell in spasms, revealing the base of the phallus.

And when he was a deep shade of rosy pink from

his pubic hair to his ankles, and chest and stomach were well latticed with swelling ribbons of pink, the Captain drew up to the side of the cross and, taking only the end five or six inches of the strap, lashed the Prince's bouncing cock with it. The Prince strained and pumped on the cross, the iron weight dangling, the cock growing huge and almost purple in color.

The Captain stopped. He looked down into the Prince's eyes and laid his hand on the Prince's forehead again. "Not such a bad whipping, was it, Laurent?" he asked. The Prince's chest heaved. The men throughout the camp laughed softly. "Except that you will receive it again at dawn, and then at noon, and then at twilight."

Another burst of laughter. The Prince sighed deeply and the tears rolled down the side of his face.

"I hope the Queen gives you to me," said the Captain softly.

He snapped his fingers for Beauty to follow him into the tent. And as she crawled on her hands and knees into the warm light beneath the white canvas, an officer walked quickly past her.

"I wish to be alone now," the Captain said to the man.

Beauty settled to the side of the doorway meekly.

"Captain," the officer said, dropping his voice, "I don't know that this can wait. The last patrol came in moments ago while you were whipping the runaway."

"Yes?"

"Well, they didn't find the Princess, Sir. But they swear they saw horsemen in the forest tonight."

The Captain, who had settled on his elbows at a little writing table, looked up. "What?" he asked, incredulously.

"Sir, they swear they saw and heard them. A large party, they said." The soldier drew near to the table.

Through the open door, she saw the Prince's hands twitching under their ropes on the back of the cross and his buttocks riding up and down still, as if he could not settle into his punishment.

"Sir," said the officer, "he is almost sure that they were raiders."

"But they wouldn't dare to come again this soon," the Captain waved it away. "And on a moonlit night. I don't believe it."

"But, Sir, it's only the quarter moon. And it has been two years since their last raid. The sentry says he heard something too, near the camp only moments ago."

"You've doubled the watch!"

"Yes, Sir, I doubled it right away."

The Captain's eyes narrowed. He cocked his head to the side.

"Sir, they were walking their horses through the woods, the soldiers said, without light. And with as little sound as possible. It must be them!"

The Captain considered. "All right, break camp. Get the runaway mounted on the cart and head back to the village. Send a messenger ahead to double the watch on the towers. But I don't want the village alarmed. This is probably nothing." He paused, obviously considering. "It's useless to search the coast tonight," he said.

"Yes, Sir."

"It's almost impossible to search all those coves even by daylight. But we'll go out tomorrow."

He rose angrily as the officer withdrew. He snapped his fingers for Beauty to come to him, and giving her a harsh kiss, he threw her up over his shoulders. "No time for you tonight, pet, not here," he said and squeezed her hip as he carried her.

It was midnight when they returned to the Inn, riding well ahead of the others.

Beauty was thinking of all she had heard and seen, stimulated against her will by Laurent's suffering. And she couldn't wait to tell Prince Roger or Prince Richard what she had heard about the strange riders in the night, and ask what it meant.

But there was no chance for this.

Entering the hot, cheerful din of the drinking room, the Captain gave her over at once to the soldiers at the table nearest the door. And before she knew it she sat spread-legged on the lap of a lovely brawny young man with copper hair, her hips bounced down on a gorgeous thick cock, while a pair of hands from behind massaged her nipples.

As the hours passed, the Captain kept close watch on her. But he was often in fast conversation with his men. And many soldiers came and went in a hurry.

When Beauty grew drowsy he took her from the men and had her mounted high on a cask on the wall, her sex pressed to the rough wood, her hands bound over her head, her vision clouded as she turned her head to sleep, the crowd shimmering beneath her.

She thought again and again of the runaways. Who was the Princess Lynette who had reached the border, the same tall blond Princess who years before had so tormented Beauty's beloved Alexi in her little circus performance for the Court at the castle? And where was she now? Clothed and safe in another Kingdom? Beauty should envy her, she thought, but she couldn't. She couldn't even think of it with any concentration. And her mind returned again and again, without judgment or fear, or even thought, to the stunning image of Prince Laurent mounted on the cross, his massive torso throbbing under the strap, his buttocks riding the wooden phallus.

She slept.

Yet it seemed that sometime before morning she saw Tristan. But that must have been a dream. Beautiful Tristan kneeling at the door of the Inn, looking up at her. His golden hair fell almost to his shoulders, and his large blue-violet eyes gazed up at her with the most complete affection.

She wanted so to talk to him, to tell him how strangely

content she was. But then the vision of Tristan was gone, as surely as it had come. She must have been dreaming.

Through her dreams came Mistress Lockley's voice, in low conversation with the Captain. "Pity that poor Princess," she said, "if they are out there. But so soon, I can scarce believe they'd try it."

"I know," the Captain answered. "But they can come anytime. They can strike the manor houses and the farms and be off before we even know it in the village. That's what they did two years ago. That's why I've doubled the watch, and we'll be patrolling until this is settled."

Beauty opened her eyes. But they had moved away from under the keg and she could no longer hear them.

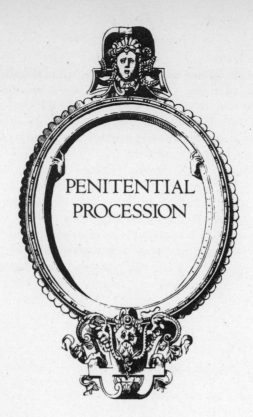

PENITENTIAL
PROCESSION

W<small>HEN BEAUTY</small> awoke, it was
late afternoon and she was alone in the Captain's bed. A
loud roaring came from the square below, with the slow
chilling beat of a deep drum. In spite of the alarm that
the drum sounded in her soul, she thought of the chores
she should have done. She sat up in panic.

But immediately Prince Roger calmed her with a
little gesture. "The Captain said for you to sleep late," he
said. He had the broom in his hands, but he was looking
out of the window.

"What is it?" Beauty asked. She could feel the reverberation of the drum in her belly. And the steady beat filled her with dread. Seeing no one else in the room, she climbed to her feet and came up beside Prince Roger.

"Only the runaway Prince Laurent," he said, putting his arm around Beauty as he pulled her close to the thick little panes. "Being wheeled through the village."

Beauty pressed her forehead to the glass. Below in a great loose crowd of villagers she saw a giant two-wheeled cart being pulled around the well, not by horses, but slaves in bits and harnesses.

The flushed face of Prince Laurent, bound to the cross with his legs straight out, his protuberant sex as hard as ever, stared straight up at Beauty. She saw his eyes wide and seemingly still, the mouth quivering on the thick leather that bound the head flat to the top of the beam, the bound legs shuddering with the cart's uneven movement.

The sight riveted her even more strongly than it had the night before, from this new perspective. She watched the slow progression of the cart and looked at the odd expression on the Prince's face, so devoid of panic. The roaring of the crowd was as bad as it had been at the auction. And as the cart turned round the well and back towards the Sign of the Inn now, Beauty saw the victim fully from the front and she winced at the welts and bands of reddened flesh that covered the insides of his legs, his chest, and his belly. Two whippings more he'd had and a third promised.

But an even more disturbing sight absorbed her as she realized that one of the six slaves harnessed to the cart was Tristan. He was passing directly beneath her again, and it was Tristan without mistake, his thick golden hair shimmering in the sun, his head pulled back by the bit in his mouth, his knees rising sharply. And streaming out from the cleft of his handsomely shaped rump was a sleek black horsetail. No one had to tell her what held it in place. It was the phallus inside him.

Beauty covered her face with her hands, but she felt the familiar secretion between her legs, the first clarion of the day's torments and raptures.

"Don't be so foolish," said Prince Roger. "The runaway Prince deserves it. Besides, his punishment hasn't even begun. The Queen has refused to see him and has sentenced him to four years in the village."

Beauty was thinking of Tristan. She felt his cock inside her. And she felt a mad fascination in seeing him trussed and pulling the cart, and seeing that appalling tail dangling behind him. It confused her and made her feel she had betrayed him.

"Well, maybe that is what the runaway wanted," Beauty sighed, speaking of Laurent. "He was contrite enough last night, however."

"Or maybe it's what he thinks he wanted," said Roger. "He has the turntable now to suffer, then round through the village again, and the turntable again, before he's handed over to the Captain."

The procession circled the well another time, the drum causing Beauty's nerves almost to snap. Again she saw Tristan, marching almost proudly at the head of the team, and the sight of his genitals, and the weights hung on his nipples, and his beautiful face pulled up by the leather bit caused a little torrent of passion inside her.

"Normally the soldiers march fore and aft," Prince Roger said as he picked up his broom again. "I wonder where they are today."

"Looking for mysterious raiders," she thought, but she didn't say it. Now that she had her chance alone with Roger to ask about these things, she was too enthralled by the procession.

"You're to go on down to the yard and rest on the grass," said the Prince.

"Rest again?"

"The Captain won't have you worked today. And tonight, he's hiring you out to Nicolas, the Queen's Chronicler."

"Tristan's Master!" Beauty whispered. "He's asked for me?"

"Paid for you in good coin of the realm," said Roger. He went on with his sweeping. "Go ahead down," he said to her.

And her heart pounding, she watched the procession move slowly into the broad lane that led back to the other end of the village.

TRISTAN
AND
BEAUTY

Sʜᴇ ᴄᴏᴜʟᴅɴ'ᴛ wait until dark.

The hours dragged as she was bathed, combed, and oiled roughly but as thoroughly as she had ever been at the castle. Of course she might not see Tristan tonight. But she was going to the place where Tristan lodged! She could not quiet herself.

Finally darkness descended on the village.

And Prince Richard, "the good little boy," she thought, with a smile, was ordered to take her to Nicolas, the Chronicler.

The Inn was strangely empty, though all else in the

deepening twilight seemed regular. Lights flickered in the pretty little windows along the narrow lanes; the spring air was fragrant and sweet. Prince Richard let her march fairly slowly, only now and then telling her to show a little more spirit, or they both would be whipped. He walked behind her with the strap, only occasionally licking her.

She could see wives and husbands at table through low windows, naked slaves rising from their knees in quick darting motions to set plates or pitchers before them. Slaves bound to the walls moaned and pumped vainly.

"But something *is* different," she said as they came into a broader street, full of fine houses, almost every iron bracket with its manacled slave hanging beside the door, some tightly bound and gagged, others in quiet obedience.

"No soldiers," Richard said under his breath. "And please be quiet. You're not supposed to talk. We'll both finish at the Punishment Shop."

"But where are they?" Beauty asked.

"Do you want a licking?" he threatened. "They're all out searching the coast and the forest for some imagined raiding party. I don't know what it means, but don't breathe a word. It's a secret."

But they had come to Nicolas's door. Richard was leaving her. A maid greeted Beauty and ordered her down on her hands and knees. And in a frenzy of anticipation, Beauty was led right through a fine little house and down a narrow side corridor.

A door was opened for her, and the maid bid her go in and closed the door behind her.

Beauty could scarcely believe her eyes when she looked up and saw Tristan before her. He reached out with both hands and lifted her to her feet. Beside him stood the tall figure of his Master, Nicolas, whom Beauty remembered well enough from the auction.

Her face was crimson when she looked at the man,

because both she and Tristan were standing and embracing each other.

"Calm yourself, Princess," he said in an almost caressing voice. "You may remain as long as you like with my slave, and in this room you are free to be with each other as you please. You will return to your regular servitude when you leave me."

"O, my Lord," Beauty whispered, and dropped to her knees to kiss his boots.

He allowed this courtesy, and then left them both. And Beauty rose and flew into Tristan's arms, Tristan's mouth opening to devour her kisses ravenously.

"Sweet little one, beautiful little one," Tristan said, his lips feeding upon her throat and her face, his organ pushing against her naked belly.

His body seemed almost polished in the dim light of the candles, his golden hair lustrous. She looked up into those beautiful violet-blue eyes and rose on tiptoe to mount him as she had done in the slave cart.

She threw her arms around his neck and forced her dilated sex onto his cock, feeling him seal himself against her. Slowly, he sank back on the green satin coverlet of a little oak-paneled bed. And stretching out on the pillows, he threw back his head as she rode him.

His hands lifted her breasts, pinched her nipples, and held them throbbing as she bucked and reared on his sex, sliding up as high as she could without losing the shaft and plummeting down, her lips dipping to kiss him.

Tristan's face went dark with his groans, and as she felt the cock erupt under her, she came, bucking still, until she was transfixed, her legs outstretched, shimmering with the last shocks of the pleasure.

They lay together arm in arm and slowly he wiped her hair back from her head, whispering, "My darling Beauty," as he kissed her.

"Tristan, why is your Master letting us do this?" she asked. But she was in a sweet drowsy state and she did not really care. Candles burned on the little table beside the bed. She saw the light swell and obliterate the objects of the room except for the golden surface of a large mirror.

"He's a man of mysteries and secrets and strange intensity," Tristan said. "He will do exactly as he pleases. And it pleases him to let me see you, and it will please him tomorrow probably to have me whipped through the village. And very possibly he thinks that the one will enhance the torment of the other."

The remembrance of Tristan, harnessed and horse-tailed, came back to Beauty unbidden. "I saw you," she whispered flushing suddenly. "In the procession."

"Did it seem so terrible?" he whispered comfortingly, kissing her. There was a faint blush on his cheeks that in a face so strong was irresistible.

She was amazed. "You didn't find it terrible?" she asked.

A low laugh came from deep in his chest. She pulled the golden hair that curled up from around his cock to his belly.

"Yes, my darling," he said, "it was deliciously terrible!"

She laughed as she looked into his eyes, and she kissed him again greedily. She snuggled down, kissing and biting at his nipples. "It tantalized me to see it," she confessed, her voice throaty and not her own. "I only prayed you were somehow resigned . . ."

"I am more than resigned, my love," he said, kissing the top of her head as he lay back under her affectionate bites. She mounted his left thigh and pressed her sex against it. He gasped as she bit at his nipple, pinching the other in time with her little bites. And then he tumbled her down on the sheets and opened her mouth again with his tongue.

"But tell me," she insisted, stopping his kiss for a moment, his organ grazing her mound, pressing the tight curling hair against its grain gently. "You must," she dropped her voice to a whisper. "How could you . . . ?

The harnesses and the bit, and that horsetail . . . How have you come to this, this acceptance?" She didn't need him to tell her he was resigned. She could see it and feel it, and she had seen it today in the procession. But she remembered him in the cart when they had come down from the castle, and she had felt the fear in him then that he was too proud to reveal freely.

"I've found my Master," he said, "the one who brings me into harmony with all punishments," Tristan said. "But if you must know," he started kissing her again, his organ opening her nether lips and pushing at her clitoris. "It was, and will always be, utter mortification."

Beauty lifted her hips to receive him. They were at once rocking in unison, Tristan gazing down at her, his arms like pillars supporting his powerful shoulders above her. She lifted her head to suck from his nipples, her hands pinching and parting his buttocks, feeling the hard delicious knots of the welts and measuring them and compressing them as she drew closer to the silky wrinkled lip of his anus. His motions grew swifter, rougher, more agitated as she delved. And suddenly reaching to the table beside her, she pulled one of the thick waxen candles from its silver holder, whipping out the flame and pressing the melted tip with her fingers. And then she plunged it into him, planting it firmly inside. His eyes squeezed shut. Her own sex became a taut sheath against his organ, her clitoris toughening, exploding. And cranking the waxen candle hard she cried out, feeling his hot fluids empty into her.

They lay still, the candle discarded. And she wondered at what she had done, but Tristan only kissed her.

He rose, poured a goblet of wine, and put it to Beauty's lips. Puzzled, she took it, drank it as a Lady might and wondered at the curious sensation.

"But how have you fared, Beauty?" he asked. "Have you been rebellious all the time? Tell me."

She shook her head. "I fell into the hands of a hard and wicked Master and Mistress." She laughed softly.

She described the punishments of Mistress Lockley, the kitchen, the Captain's way with her, and her evenings with the soldiers, lingering on the physical beauty of both her captors.

Tristan listened gravely.

She told about the runaway, Prince Laurent. "I know now that if I run away it will be in order to be found, to be punished like that, to spend all my years in the village," she said. "Tristan, do you think me dreadful to want to do that? I would run away rather than go back to the castle."

"But you might be taken from the Captain and Mistress Lockley," he said, "if you ran away, and sold to someone else for harder use and labor."

"That doesn't matter," she said. "It isn't the Mistress or Master really who puts me in harmony with it, as you said. It's merely the hardness, the coldness, and the relentlessness. I wanted to be cast down, lost among my punishments. I adore the Captain and I adore the Mistress, but there are other harsher Masters and Mistresses probably in the village."

"Ah, you surprise me," he said, offering her the wine again. "I am so totally in love with Nicolas I have no defense against him."

Tristan then explained the things that had happened to him, and how he and Nicolas had made love and talked together, and gone out up onto the hillside.

"The second time on the Public Turntable, today at noon," he said. "I was transported. The fear hadn't left me. It was worse when I was rushed up the steps, because I knew just what would happen. But I saw the whole fairgrounds more clearly under the glare of the sun than I had ever seen it by torchlight. I do not mean I saw literal things. I saw the great scheme of which I was part, and under the grueling punishment, my soul broke open. My whole existence now, be it on the turntable or in the harnesses, or in my Master's arms, is an entreaty to be used like the warmth of a fire is used, to be dissolved in the will of others. My Master's will is the guiding will, and through him I am given to all who witness or desire me."

Beauty was quiet, gazing at him.

"Then you have given over your soul," she said. "You've given it to your Master. That I haven't done, Tristan. My soul is still mine and the only thing a slave can truly possess. And I'm not ready yet to give it. I give my whole body to the Captain, to the soldiers, to Mistress Lockley. But in my soul, I think I belong to no one. I left the castle, not to find the love I had not found there. I left to be tossed and tumbled among harsher and more indifferent Masters."

"And you are indifferent to them?" he asked.

"I am as interested in them as they are in me," she said, reflecting. "No more, no less. But my soul may change in time. Perhaps it's only that I have met no Nicolas, the Chronicler."

She thought of the Crown Prince. She had not loved him. He made her smile. Lady Juliana had affrighted her and disturbed her. The Captain thrilled her, exhausted her, surprised her. Mistress Lockley she secretly liked, for all the dread of her. But that was the extremity of it. She didn't love them. That, and the glory and excitement of belonging to a grand scheme, to use Tristan's word, was the village to her.

"We are two different slaves," she said as she sat up, taking the wine and drinking deeply. "And we are both happy."

"I wish I understood you!" he whispered. "Don't you long to be loved, don't you long to have the pain mingled with tenderness?"

"You don't have to understand me, my love. And there is tenderness." But she paused, imagining the intimacy that existed between Tristan and Nicolas.

"My Master will guide me to greater and greater revelations," Tristan said.

"And my destiny," she answered, "will also have its

momentum. When I saw poor, punished Prince Laurent today, I envied him. And he had no loving Master to guide him."

Tristan sucked in his breath, gazing up at her. "You are a magnificent slave," he said. "Perhaps you know more than I do."

"No, I am a simpler slave in some ways. Your destiny is mingled with greater renunciation of self." She leaned on her elbow and kissed him. His lips were dark red from the wine, and his eyes seemed unusually large and glassy. Gorgeous he was. Mad thoughts came to her, of tethering him in the harnesses herself and . . .

"We must not lose each other. Whatever happens," he said. "Let's take our stolen moments whenever we can to confide in each other. We may not always be allowed . . ."

"With a Master as mad as yours we might have plenty of opportunity," she said.

He smiled. But his gaze was broken suddenly, as if by some distracting thought, and he lay still listening.

"What is it?"

"There is no one on the road outside," he said. "It's absolutely silent. And there are always coaches on the road at this hour."

"All the gates are closed," she said. "And the soldiers are all gone."

"But why?"

"I don't know, much whispering of searching the coast for raiders."

He looked so beautiful to her now, and she wanted to make love again. She drew up on the bed, sitting back on her heels, and looked at his organ, which was already springing to life once more, and then she glanced at her own reflection in the far mirror. She loved the sight of the two of them in the mirror together. But even as she looked she saw another ghostly figure in the mirror. She saw a man with white hair, his arms folded, watching her!

She let out a shriek. Tristan sat up and stared forward. But she had already realized what it was. The mirror was a two-way mirror, one of those ancient tricks of which she'd heard tell as a child. And Tristan's Master had all the while been watching. His dark face was amazingly clear, his white hair almost glowing, his brows knotted seriously.

Tristan half smiled and flushed. And a strange sense of exposure softened Beauty.

But the Master had vanished from the murky glass. The door of the room opened.

He drew near the bed, the elegant man in velvet and balloon sleeves, and he turned Beauty's shoulders towards him. "Repeat this to me, all you've heard about the soldiers and these raiders."

Beauty flushed. "Please don't tell the Captain!" she begged. He nodded, and at once she told what she knew of the story.

For a moment, the Master stood still, thinking.

"Come," he said and drew Beauty up from the bed, "I must take Beauty back to the Inn immediately."

"May I go, please, Master?" Tristan asked.

But Master Nicolas was distracted. He didn't seem to hear the question.

He turned and beckoned for them to follow. They walked quickly down the corridor and out the back door of the house, and Master Nicolas motioned for them to wait as he walked out towards the battlements.

For a long moment he looked from one end of the great wall to the other. The stillness commenced to unnerve Beauty.

"But this is foolish," he whispered as he returned. "They seem to have left the village too little defended."

"The Captain thinks they'll strike the farms outside the walls, the manor houses," Beauty said. "And there's a watch posted, surely."

Master Nicolas shook his head, disapprovingly. He locked the door of his house.

"But, Master," Tristan asked. "Who are these raiders?" His expression had darkened, and there was nothing of a slave in his manner.

"Never mind all of that," Master Nicolas said sternly as he started off ahead of them. "We will take Beauty back to her Mistress. Come quickly."

DISASTER

N~ICOLAS LED~ the way fast through the little tangle of streets, allowing Tristan and Beauty to walk together behind him. Tristan held Beauty tightly in his arms, kissing her and stroking her. And the late-night village seemed peaceful enough, its inhabitants unaware of any danger.

But suddenly as they drew near to the square of the Inns, there came from far off a terrible din of shrieking cries, and the thundering crash of wood against wood, the unmistakable sound of a giant battering ram.

Bells rang from the towers of the village. Everywhere doors opened.

"Run, quick," Nicolas said, turning and reaching out for Beauty and Tristan.

From everywhere people appeared, yelling, shouting. Shutters slammed against windows, men ran to fetch down their manacled slaves. Naked Princes and Princesses darted out from the dimly lit doorway of the Punishment Shop taverns.

Beauty and Tristan raced towards the square only to hear the sound of the great battering ram shatter the wood that resisted it. And just beyond the square Beauty saw the night sky open up as the east gates of the village gave way and the air filled with loud, alien shrieks and ululations.

"Slave raid! Slave raid!" The scream came from all directions.

Tristan took Beauty in his arms, and dashed across the cobblestones towards the Inn, Nicolas beside him. But a great cloud of turbaned riders roared into the square. And Beauty gave a piercing cry as she saw that the doors and windows of all the Inns had already been bolted.

High above her loomed a dark-faced rider in flowing robes, his scimitar gleaming at his side as he bore down on her. Tristan tried to dodge the horse. And a powerful arm swooped down, catching Beauty up and knocking Tristan off his feet as the horse reared and turned, Beauty's body heaved over the saddle.

Beauty screamed and screamed. She struggled under the powerful hand that held her down, lifting her head to see Tristan and Nicolas running towards her. But the dark streak of another rider appeared, and another. And in a flash of white limbs, she saw Tristan suspended between the two horsemen as Nicolas was hurled to the ground, rolling away from the dangerous hooves, his arms around his head for protection. Tristan was being thrown over a horse, one rider assisting the other.

Loud whooping screams filled the air, shrill pulsing cries such as Beauty had never heard before. Beauty's captor reared his horse, and as Beauty sobbed and wailed, a rope was looped about her shoulders, tightening and securing her to the saddle, her legs kicking vainly and furiously. The horse galloped on out of the square back towards the village gates. And everywhere it seemed there were riders shooting past, garments streaming in the wind, naked upturned bottoms bucking helplessly.

Within seconds they were on the open road, the clang of the village bells growing ever more distant.

On and on through the night they rode, over the open fields, crashing through streams and copses, the great gleaming scimitars rising to hack at the overhanging foliage.

How large the party was Beauty could not tell; it seemed to go on forever behind her rider, the soft shouts of some alien tongue filling her ears, along with the sobs and groans of captive Princes and Princesses.

At the same desperate speed the party drove into the hills, up perilous paths and down into wooded valleys. Through a high narrow pass they galloped as if through an endless tunnel.

And finally Beauty could smell the open sea and, lifting her head, she saw before her the dull shimmer of the water in the moonlight.

A great dark ship lay at anchor in the cove, without a single light to mark its sinister presence.

And gasping frantically as the horses rode down the banks and through the shallow waves, Beauty lost consciousness.

EXOTIC MERCHANDISE

BEAUTY WAS lying down when she awoke, and she was so sleepy. She lay still, hardly able to open her eyes, and she could feel the heavy motion of the ship, a feeling she'd known only in her dreams when she was a girl in her father's castle. In terror, she tried to rise, and suddenly a dark, olive-skinned face loomed over her.

She saw a pair of jet-black eyes, exquisitely almond-shaped, looking down at her out of a young flawless countenance. Long black curly hair framed the face, rendering it almost angelic. And she saw a finger bidding her urgently to be absolutely silent. It was a tall young boy who made this gesture, and he stood over her, dressed in a shining tunic of gold silk, girdled in silver at the waist, over long loose trousers of the same fabric.

He sat her up, his dark hands remarkably smooth against her own, and smiling, he nodded vigorously as she obeyed, stroking her hair and making effusive gestures to indicate he found her beautiful.

Beauty opened her mouth, but at once the lovely boy pressed his finger against her lips. His face showed great fear, as his eyebrows knit and he shook his head. Beauty was silent.

He drew a long comb from a pocket of his loose garments and combed her hair. And looking down drowsily, Beauty realized she had been washed and perfumed. Her head felt light. She was scented all over with some sweet spice. She knew the spice. And her skin was gleaming. A dark golden pigment had been oiled into her, and it contained the scent. The scent was cinnamon. How lovely, Beauty, thought. She could feel some coloring on her lips and it tasted like fresh berries. But she was so sleepy! She could hardly keep her eyes open.

And all about her in this dimly lighted room were sleeping Princes and Princesses. She saw Tristan! And with a sluggish surge of excitement she tried to move towards him. Her dark-skinned attendant restrained her with feline grace, his urgent gestures and facial expressions letting her know she must be very quiet and very good. With an exaggerated frown he wagged his finger. He glanced at the sleeping Prince Tristan, and then with the same exquisite tenderness, he stroked Beauty's naked sex and patted it, nodding and smiling.

Beauty was too tired to do more than stare in wonder. All the slaves had been oiled and scented. They looked like golden sculptures on their satin beds.

The boy brushed Beauty's hair with such care she did not feel the slightest pull or tangle. He cradled her face as if she were a very precious thing, and then he stroked her sex again in that same loving fashion, patting it, and this time awakening it as he beamed at Beauty, his thumb softly pressed to her lips again as if to say: "Be good, little one."

But more angels had appeared. A half dozen lean olive-skinned young men who wore the same attentive smiles as they surrounded Beauty and, drawing her arms up over head and pressing her fingers together, lifted her up and stretched her out to carry her. She felt those silky fingers supporting her from her elbows to her feet. And gazing dreamily at the low wooden ceilings, she was carried up a stair and into another room thick with the babble of foreign voices.

She saw brilliant fabric above her, artfully draped, the rich red field covered with tiny intricate bits of gold and glass, and she smelt the strong aroma of incense.

And suddenly she was being set down upon a much bigger, plumper satin pillow, her arms stretched way out to the edge above her head, her fingers beneath it.

She made the tiniest noise only to see her angelic captors evince terror, fingers darting to their lips again, heads shaking in ominous warning.

Then they withdrew, and she was looking up into the faces of a circle of men, their heads wrapped in brilliantly colored silk turbans, their dark eyes flitting over her, heavily jeweled hands gesturing as they talked back and forth, seeming to argue and to haggle.

Her head was raised, her long hair lifted and examined between careful fingers. Her breasts were very softly pinched, and then spanked. Other hands parted her legs, and with the same careful, almost silky manner, fingers pried open her pubic lips, rolled her clitoris as if it were a bauble or a grape, the rapid conversation continuing above her. She tried to be still, gazing up at the bearded chins, quick black eyes. And the hands touching her as if she were of immense value and very very fragile.

But her well-trained vagina tightened, gave forth its juices, fingertips gathering the moisture out of her. Her breasts were spanked again and she moaned, very careful not to open her mouth, and she closed her eyes as even her ears and her naval were probed, her toes and fingers examined.

She let out her breath with a start as her teeth were pried apart, her lips pulled back. She blinked and drowsed again. She was turned over. The voices seemed to grow louder; a half dozen hands pressed her welts and the crisscross of pink stripes that surely covered her buttocks. Her anus must be opened, too, of course, and she squirmed only a little, her eyes closing again as she rested her cheek on the delicious satin. A few sharp slaps roused her only slightly.

And when she was turned on her back again, she could see the nods, and the dark-faced man in the center to her right smiled at her quickly and gave her sex that same approving pat. Then the angelic boys again lifted her.

"I have passed some test," she thought. But she was baffled more than afraid, lulled, and almost unable to remember what she had just been thinking. Pleasure zinged through her like the echo of a plucked lute string.

It was a different room into which she was taken.

And what a strange and marvelous thing! It was filled with six long golden cages. A paddle, delicately enameled and gilded, its long handle twined with silk ribbon, hung from a hook on the end of each cage. And the mattress inside was covered in sky-blue satin. It was full of rose petals, Beauty realized, as she was laid inside one of these cages. She could smell the perfume, and the cage was quite high enough for her to sit up if only she had the stamina. It was better to sleep as her attendants told her to do. And of course, she understood the reason they were fitting the most lovely little golden mesh covering to her vagina, strapping it over her moist clitoris and lips, and clasping the delicate golden chains around her thighs and waist to hold it. She could not touch her private parts. No, she shouldn't. That was never allowed in the castle or the village. The door of the cage closed with a clink and the key turned in the lock, and she closed her eyes again, the most luscious warmth suffusing her.

Sometime later she opened her eyes again, though she could not move, absolutely couldn't move, and she saw Tristan being put into the cage that stretched out at an angle from the foot of her own, those lovely young men—they were men, not boys, just very small and delicate men—patting Tristan's balls and cock with those dark, languid fingers. One of those pretty mesh coverings was being fitted to Tristan, too, and how much larger it was! And she glimpsed for a moment Tristan's face, utterly relaxed in sleep and incomparably beautiful.

ANOTHER
TURN
OF
THE
WHEEL

Tristan:

I SAW BEAUTY stir in her sleep. But she did not awaken.

I was sitting up in the cage, my legs crossed, my eyes fixed on the ceiling of the room with total concentration.

Half an hour ago, we had been flagged by another vessel, I was sure of it. We had dropped anchor, and someone had come aboard, someone who spoke our language.

But I couldn't make out the words themselves, only the familiar tone and inflection. And the longer I listened to the conversation above, the more I was convinced that there was no interpreter. This man had to be from the Queen, and he knew the language of these pirates.

Finally Beauty sat up. She stretched herself like a kitten, and, staring down at the small triangle of metal between her legs, appeared to recall everything. Her eyes were clouded, her gestures uncommonly slow as she moved her long flaxen hair back, blinking at the single lantern that hung from the low ceiling above. Then she saw me.

"Tristan," she whispered. She sat forward, clinging to the bars of the cage.

"Shhhh!" I pointed to the ceiling. And in a hurried whisper told her about the ship coming alongside and the man boarding us.

"I was sure we were sailing far across the sea," she said.

In the cage beneath her, Prince Laurent, the poor runaway, slept on, and Prince Dmitri, a castle slave sent down to the village with us, slept above her.

"But who has come on board?" she whispered.

"Be quiet, Beauty!" I cautioned again. But it was no use. I couldn't make out what was taking place, except that it was continuing vigorously.

Beauty had the most innocent expression on her face, the gold-tinted oil enhancing every detail of her form enticingly. She looked smaller, rounder, more nearly perfected; and crouching in the cage, she appeared some bizarre creature imported from a strange land, to be set in a pleasure garden. We must have all appeared that way.

"We might still be rescued!" she said anxiously.

"I don't know," I answered. Why were there no soldiers? Why was there only that single voice? I couldn't frighten her by telling her we were true captives now, not valuable Tributes under the protection of her Majesty.

Finally Laurent was coming to himself, rising slowly on account of the welts that covered his body, and with the rubbing of gold oil he looked as splendid as Beauty. It was an odd spectacle, in fact, all the welts and stripes so deeply colored with the gold so that they became almost purely ornamental. Maybe all our welts and stripes had always been purely ornamental. His hair, so neglected when he had been on the Punishment Cross, was dressed now and trained into magnificent dark brown curls. He blinked as he looked up at me, clearing the drugged sleep from his eyes rapidly.

Hurriedly I told him what had happened and pointed to the ceiling. We were all listening to the voice, though I don't think either of them heard it any more clearly than I did.

Laurent shook his head and rested back. "What an adventure!" he said slowly, with an almost sleepy indifference.

Beauty smiled in spite of herself at the word and glanced shyly at me. I was too angry to speak. I felt too helpless.

"Wait," I said, kneeling forward and taking hold of the bars. "Someone's coming." I could hear throughout the hold a dull vibration.

The door opened and into the room stepped a pair of the silken dressed boys who had been caring for us. They carried little boat-shaped brass oil lamps. And between them stood a tall elderly gray-haired Lord clothed in familiar doublet and leggings, his sword at his side, his dagger in his thick leather belt, his eyes sweeping the room almost angrily.

The tallest of the two boys gave forth a stream of soft foreign chatter to the Lord, and the man nodded and motioned with an angry expression.

"Tristan, and Beauty," he said, advancing into the room, "and Laurent."

At this, the olive-skinned boys at once seemed disconcerted. They averted their eyes and left the Lord alone with the slaves, closing the door behind them.

"I was afraid of this," he said. "And Elena and Rosalynd and Dmitri. The finest castle slaves. These thieves have such excellent eyes. They freed the others down the coast as soon as they had ferreted out the prizes."

"But what's to happen to us, my Lord?" I demanded. His attitude was too clearly one of exasperation.

"That, my dear Tristan," said the Lord, "is in the hands of your Master, the Sultan."

Beauty gasped.

I felt my face harden, the rage welling up in me, silencing me for the moment as I stared at him. "My Lord," I said, my voice shuddering with anger, "will you not even try to save us?" I saw in my mind's eyes the figure of my Master, Nicolas, thrown down on the stones of the square, as the horse carried me away, my struggles useless. But that was not the half of my anguish. What lay ahead of us?

"What I have done is the best I can do," said the Lord, approaching me. "I have exacted an enormous indemnity for each of you. The Sultan will pay almost anything for plump, soft-skinned, well-trained slaves of the Queen, but he likes his gold as much as the next man. And in two years, he will return you well-fed, in good health with no blemishes, or he will not see his gold again. Believe me, Prince, it has been done a hundred times over. Had I failed to intercept his craft, his emissaries and our emissaries would have met together. He wants no real quarrel with her Majesty. You have never been in any real danger.

"No danger!" I protested. "We are going to a foreign land where . . ."

"Quiet, Tristan," he said sharply. "It is the Sultan who inspired our Queen to her passion for pleasure victims. He sent the Queen her first slaves and explained to her the care with which slaves must be treated. No real harm shall come to you. Though of course . . . of course . . ."

"Of course what!" I demanded.

"You will be more abject," said the Lord, with a

little anxious shrug, as if he couldn't fully explain it. "In the Sultan's palace, you will occupy a much more lowly position. Of course, you will be the playthings of your Masters and Mistresses, very valuable playthings. But you will no longer be treated as beings with high reason. On the contrary, you will be trained as valuable animals are trained, and you must never, heaven help you, try to speak or to evince anything more than the simplest understanding—"

"My Lord," I interrupted.

"As you see," the Lord continued, "the attendants will not even remain in the room here if you are spoken to as if you have wits. They find it too incongruous and unseemly. They retire at the distasteful sight of a slave treated as . . ."

". . . as human," Beauty whispered. Her lower lip was quivering as she tightened her little fists on the bars, but she was not crying.

"Yes, exactly, Princess."

"My Lord." I was furious now. "You must ransom us, we are under her Majesty's protection! This violates all agreements!"

"Out of the question, dear Prince. In the complex exchanges between great powers, some things must be sacrificed. And it violates no agreements. You were sent to serve, and serve you shall, in the Palace of the Sultan. And have no doubt, you will be treasured by your new Masters. Though the Sultan has many slaves from his own land, you captive Princes and Princesses are a special delicacy of sorts, and a great curiosity."

I was too angry and defeated to speak further. It was hopeless. Nothing I said made any difference. I was imprisoned like a creature of the wild, and my mind lapsed into miserable silence.

"I did what I could," said the Lord, his eyes including the others now as he stepped back.

Dmitri was awake and leaning on his elbow as he listened.

"I was ordered to obtain an apology for the raid," the Lord went on, "and a stiff indemnity. I got more gold than I expected." He was going to the door. His hand was on the latch. "Two years, Prince, that's not so long," he said to me. "And when you return, your knowledge and experience will prove of inestimable value at the castle."

"My Master!" I said suddenly. "Nicolas, the Chronicler. Tell me at least, was he harmed in the raid?"

"He's quite alive and, in all probability, fast at work at his written account of the raid for her Majesty. He grieves bitterly for you. But nothing can be done. Now I must leave you. Be brave and be clever, clever at pretending you are not clever, that you are no more than the most abject little bundles of ever-demonstrable passion."

And he left us immediately.

We all remained quiet, hearing the distant shouts of the sailors above. Then we felt the sea surge sluggishly as the other craft pulled away from us.

And the giant ship was moving again, fast, as if at full sail, and I slumped back against the cool gold bars and stared forward.

"Don't be sad, my darling," Beauty said as she peered at me, her long hair veiling her breasts, the light glinting on her polished limbs. "It's only the same whirlwind."

I turned over and stretched out, despite the uncomfortable metal between my legs, and rested my head against my arms, and for a long time I wept in silence.

Finally, when my tears had dried themselves, I heard Beauty's voice again.

"I know you're thinking of your Master," she said gently. "But, Tristan, remember your own words."

I sighed against my arm.

"Remind me, Beauty," I asked quietly.

"That your whole existence is but an entreaty to be dissolved in the will of others. And so it goes on, Tristan, and we move deeper and deeper, all of us, into that dissolution."

"Yes, Beauty," I said softly.

"It's but another turn of the wheel," she said, "and we understand now more keenly what we have always known, since we were made captives."

"Yes," I said, "that we belong to others."

And I turned my head to look up at her. The position of the cages wouldn't allow us to touch more than our fingertips if we tried, and it was better just to see her pretty face and her luscious little arms as she held the bars still.

"It's true," I said. "You're right." And I felt a tightening in my chest and the old familiar awareness of my helplessness, not as a Prince, but as a slave, entirely dependent on the whims of new and unknown Masters.

And gazing at her face, I felt the first stirring of the wonder that was kindled in her eyes. We did not know what torments or rapture lay ahead of us.

Dmitri had turned and gone back into his slumbers. So had Laurent below.

And Beauty stretched again like a cat and lay down on the silken mattress.

The door opened and the young silk-clad attendants came in—six of them, one for each slave, it seemed—and they approached the cages, offering, as they unlocked the doors, a warm, aromatic drink, which surely contained another welcome sleeping potion.

VOLUP-
TUOUS
CAPTIVITY

I<small>T WAS</small> night when Beauty awoke. Turning on her belly she saw stars through a tiny grated window. The great craft creaked and hummed as it rode the waves.

But she was being gathered up, taken from the cage, her dreams not yet dissipated, and laid down upon a giant cushion again, this time atop a long table.

Candles blazed. She could smell the heavy perfume of incense. And from far away came a rich and vibrant music.

The lovely young men surrounded her, rubbing the golden oil into her skin, smiling down at her as they worked, stretching her arms up and back, training her fingers to hold tight again to the edge of the cushion. And she saw a brush dipping down to color her nipples carefully with glittering gold pigment. She was too shocked to make a sound. She lay still as her lips were also painted. Then the soft hairs of the brush skillfully lined her eyes with the gold, stroking it onto her eyelashes. Great jeweled earrings were shown to her and, with a little gasp, she felt her earlobes stabbed, but her silent smiling captors hastened to shush and console her. The earrings dangled from the tiny burning wounds and the pain dissolved as she felt her legs drawn apart and a bowl of brightly colored, glistening fruits was held above her. The little armor of mesh was removed from her sex and tender fingers patted and stroked her until her sex awakened. Then she gazed into the same lovely olive-skinned face of the man who had first greeted her. *Her* attendant, he must be. And she saw that he was taking the fruit from the bowl—dates, pieces of melon and peach, tiny pears, dark red berries—and that he was carefully dipping each piece in a silver cup of honey.

Her legs were stretched wide apart and she realized the honeyed fruit was being placed inside of her. Her well-taught sex tightened irresistibly as the silky fingers forced the quartered melon deep within, and the next piece, and the next, bringing stronger and stronger flushes and sighs from her.

She couldn't keep from moaning, but this her captors seemed to approve. They nodded, their smiles growing ever brighter. She was filled with the fruit. She felt it bulging from her. And now she was shown the glistening bunch of ripe grapes that was laid between her legs. And a lovely sprig of white flowers was dangled over her face, and her mouth was opened and the sprig laid between her teeth, the waxy petals fluttering against her cheeks and chin every so slightly.

She tried not to bite down on the stem, merely to hold it firmly. Her underarms were being painted thickly with honey. And something, a plump date perhaps, was being pressed into her naval. Jeweled bracelets went about her wrists. She was being fitted with heavy anklets. She undulated almost irresistibly on the pillow as the tension mounted in her, the vague infatuation with the smiling faces. And she knew fear, too, as she felt herself slowly transformed into an astonishing ornament.

But she was left alone with the urgent caution to be very still and silent.

And she heard other quick preparations in the room, heard other soft sighs, and she could almost make out the tempo of a heart beating anxiously near her.

Finally her captors appeared again. She was lifted on the great thick cushion, like a treasure. The music grew louder as she was carried up the steps, the walls of her sex clamping against the enormous filling of fruit, the honey and the juices trickling out of her. The gold paint dried on her nipples, tightening the skin. On every inch of her flesh she felt some new stimulation.

Into a large chamber she was brought, the light soft and shimmering. The incense was intoxicating. The air pulsed with the rhythm of tambourines, the strumming of harps, the high metallic notes of other instruments. Over her head the draped cloth of the ceiling came alive with its hundreds of tiny fragments of mirrored glass, glittering beads, intricate gold patterns.

She was set down on the floor again and, turning her head helplessly, saw the musicians far to her left and, directly beside her on her right, her new Masters sitting cross-legged as they banqueted from large dishes of delicious-smelling food, their robes and turbans of ornately embroidered silk, their eyes darting to her now and then as they spoke to one another in rapid muted voices.

She writhed on the pillow, holding the edges tight, keeping her legs well apart as she had been taught so well to do at the village and the castle. And her silent fearful attendants, cautioning her, imploring her, with dire looks and fingers to the lips, again withdrew to the shadows where they stood to watch over her unnoticed by those who feasted.

"Ah, what is this strange world into which I've been reborn?" she thought, the fruit swelling against the stricture of her heated vagina. She felt her hips ride up from the silk, the earrings throb in her ears. The conversation went on in a natural current, now and then one of the dark-turbaned Lords smiling at her before he spoke again to the others.

But another figure had appeared. Something in the corner of her eye, to the left. She saw it was Tristan.

He was being brought in on his hands and knees, by a long gold chain affixed to a jewel-encrusted collar. And he too was polished with gold oil, his nipples gilded. His thick bush of pubic hair was dotted with tiny sparkling jewels and his erect cock glistened under its thin gold burnishing. His ears were pierced not with dangling earrings but with single rubies. And the hair of his head was parted in the middle and had been beautifully brushed with gold dust. Gilt paint lined his eyes, thickened his lashes, defined the startling perfection of his mouth. And his violet-blue eyes burned with an iridescent radiance.

His lips moved in a half-smile as he was led towards her. He didn't seem sad or afraid, rather lost in his desire to do the bidding of the pretty black-haired angel who led him. And as the dark-skinned one guided him to straddle Beauty, pressing his head down to her left underarm until his face touched the honey, he began to lap it.

Beauty sighed, feeling the hard wet pressure of his licking tongue on the rounded curve of her flesh. And her eyes grew wide as he cleaned away the liquid, his hair tickling her face, and then bent to feed upon the right underarm just as greedily.

He seemed an alien god leaning over her, his painted face like something from the very depth of her unavowed dreams, his powerful arms and shoulders polished to a magnificent luster.

With a tug of the fragile gold chain, the lithe, long-fingered guide drew him down now, lowering his gleaming head until, eagerly, he took the honeyed date from her naval.

Beauty's hips and belly rose sharply at the touch of his lips and teeth, the moan breaking from her, the flowers in her mouth shuddering against her cheeks. And as if through a haze, she saw her distant attendants smiling, nodding, coaxing.

Tristan knelt between her legs. And this time the attendant did not have to guide his head. With an almost savage gesture, Tristan gnawed at the dressing of fruit, the soft pressure of his jaws against her pubis maddening her.

He consumed the grapes, and, his mouth pressed to her pubic lips, he grasped with his teeth the thick chunks of melon.

Beauty writhed, clutched at the pillow. Her hips rose uncontrollably. Tristan's mouth ground deeper into her, teeth biting at her clitoris, licking it, as he extracted more of the fruit. And in a fury of rocking, undulating movements, Beauty pushed with all her might to offer it to him.

The conversation in the room had died away. The music was low and rhythmic and almost haunting. And her own moans grew into openmouthed gasps as the distant young men beamed proudly.

Tristan's jaws worked against her, emptying her. And now he lapped the juices from between her legs, his tongue coming up in broad wet strokes to her clitoris again slowly.

She knew her face was blood red. Her nipples were two aching little kernels.

She undulated so violently that her buttocks rose off the pillow.

But with a wrenching moan of disappointment, she saw Tristan's head rise. The little chain was being jerked. She sobbed softly.

Yet it was not over! He was being brought up beside

her and artfully turned around, and positioned over her again, his cock descending to her lips as his mouth opened wide to cover her entire pubis. She raised her head, licking at his cock, trying to catch it in the clamp of her lips, and capturing it suddenly, pulled it lower as she raised her shoulders.

Frantically, she sucked it to the root, the sweet taste of honey and cinnamon mingling with the hot salty smell of Tristan's flesh, her hips riding fast on the cushion as Tristan sucked on the tiny knot between her legs, turning his mouth to close up her thick and pulsing lips with his teeth, his tongue lapping the honey that squeezed out from them.

Groaning, almost crying, Beauty nursed from the cock, her head dangling from it, her mouth contracting in time with the spasms between his legs as she felt him suck with sudden violent strength at her clitoris and the mound above it. And as the fiery shimmering orgasm inundated her, bringing forth her loudest moaning sighs, she felt his come overflow into her.

Locked together they struggled, and around them in the crowded tent, there was only silence. She saw nothing. She had no thoughts. She felt Tristan slip away. She heard the low rumble of voices again. She knew that the cushion had been lifted and she was being carried.

They were moving down the steps, and all around her in the room of the cages there was low excited chatter, the angelic attendants laughing and talking in hushed voices as they set the cushion down on a low table.

Then Beauty was helped to her knees and she saw Tristan kneeling right in front of her. His arms went around her neck, her arms were guided around his waist, and she felt his legs against her legs, his hand pressing her face to his chest as she gazed at the angelic ones who, gathering closer and closer, stroked Beauty and Tristan and kissed them all over.

Beauty saw in the gloom the soft serene faces of the other Princes and Princesses, watching.

But her lovely captors had taken down the painted paddles from her cage and from Tristan's, flashing these exquisite articles in the light so that Beauty saw the intricacy of the ornate curlicues and flowers, and the pale blue ribbons streaming from the handles.

Beauty's head was pulled back gently and the paddle put before her face, touched to her lips so that she kissed it. Above her, Tristan did the same, his lips in that same half-smile as the paddle was withdrawn and he looked down at her.

He clutched her hard as the first stinging slaps came, his strong body obviously trying to contain the little shocks of the spanks as she moaned and twisted under them as Mistress Lockley taught her. All around was the bright airy laughter of the attendants. Tristan kissed her hair, his hands feverishly kneading her flesh as she pressed tighter and tighter to him, her breasts crushed against his chest, her hands spread out on his back, her writhing buttocks flooded with tingling warmth, the old welts little knots under the paddle. Tristan could no longer keep still, the moans coming deep in his chest, his cock rising between her legs, the broad wet tip slipping into her. Her knees left the cushion. Her upturned mouth found Tristan's mouth, as their jubilant captors redoubled the strength of the spanks, eager hands pressing Tristan and Beauty ever tighter together.

Sequel to follow:
In which we learn about
the adventures
of Beauty and Tristan
in the
Palace of the Sultan.